Delta Salvation
Phantom Force Book 1
By
Elle Boon

Cover by Tibbs Designs

Delta Salvation
ISBN: 9781533216083
Delta Salvation, Phantom Force Book 1
Copyright © 2016 Elle Boon
First E-book Publication: March 2016
Cover design by Valerie Tibbs of Tibbs Design
Edited by Janet Rodman Editing

Table of Contents

Dedication

Chapter One

Chapter Two

Chapter Three

Chapter Four

Chapter Five

Chapter Six

Chapter Seven

Chapter Eight

Chapter Nine

Chapter Ten

Chapter Eleven

Chapter Twelve

Chapter Thirteen

Chapter Fourteen

Chapter Fifteen

Biography

Books by Elle Boon

Chapter One Lyric's Accidental Mate

Chapter One Jett's Wild Wolf

Dedication

To the best crit partner and truly the greatest lady I've met in this industry…Caitlyn O'Leary, who pushed me to write about SEALS. This book truly came about because of her.

There are so many people I'd like to thank, beginning with my awesome beta readers Debbie Ramos, Trenda London, and Jenna Underwood. BIG HUGE thank you ladies, you are truly fabulous, and went above and beyond on this book for me. Y'all totally rock and without your input, and help, I'd still be at square one with this book.

Many thanks to my hubby for his unwavering support, my oldest, Jaz for being so damn awesome, and to my Goob who is still my baby even though he's six-foot tall. Without their love and support I'd never be able to do what I love, write.

To the amazingly talented cover artist Valerie Tibbs of Tibbs Design. I love this cover sooo hard, and I know I am still marked down as "that client" with squinty eyes, I Love You.

DELTA SALVATION

PHANTOM FORCE, BOOK 1

Chapter One
Elle Boon

Alexa Gordon picked up her pace, the knowledge she was being followed made her wish she'd taken her coworker up on the offer of a lift home. Stupid is what she was. Not wanting the people she'd worked with to see the shit place she called home, might just cost her her life. If she could just make it another block, there would be row houses instead of industrial buildings that were empty at seven o'clock at night. Figuring she had nothing to lose, she lifted the strap of her purse over her head, and took off at a run, adrenaline racing through her veins.

The beat of her heart echoed in her ears as she ran, the sound of her pursuer's heavier footfalls closing in on her. "Twenty more feet," she wheezed, pumping her arms and wishing she was in better shape. A blow from behind sent her flying forward, on instinct she threw her arms out to block her face from smashing into the uneven sidewalk.

"You thought you could outrun me?" he whispered in her ear.

She stilled beneath the heavy weight of the familiar voiced man. Danny Reed was a psycho of the first order, and one she was sure she'd been free of. It had been over a month with no contact, yet he'd clearly been waiting for her to mess up, and mess up she'd done. "What do you want, Danny?"

His fingers in her hair hurt as he jerked her onto her back, before straddling her body. "You," he grated.

The one word sent warning bells off. He'd tackled her between buildings where no lights illuminated them. She could barely make out his face, but knew without a doubt it was contorted into the mask of fury he'd got when he didn't get his way.

"Why?" They'd only dated a few times before she'd realized he was batshit crazy. After meeting his mama, she understood he came by it naturally. Alexa wanted a family, not some whacked out relations who thought nothing of killing harmless animals, and leaving them on people's steps to find. The image of Mrs. Reed with blood on her hands, a black and white lifeless animal being tossed negligently down, still haunted her.

"Because you're my girlfriend. We belong together, and Mama likes you." Danny's voice became louder as he jerked her arms above her head. "She said I need to teach you a lesson and you'll come to your senses."

Remembering the last time they'd argued, she struggled under him, trying to get away.

He held both her hands in one of his, and then hauled back his fist, shaking it in front of her face. "If you were a good girl I wouldn't have to hurt you. Don't you understand it's your fault?" The first blow knocked her head to the side. Danny scrambled off her, jerking her up by the front of her shirt. "We are meant to be together. Mama said so. Mama is always right."

Alexa spit blood out of her mouth. "Why don't you go fuck your mama?" As soon as the words left her mouth, she regretted them. His arm flew out, an opened handed smack. She raised her arm, intending to protect her face. He grabbed her wrist, twisting until he had her turned around, his front pressing against her back, moving them further into the darkness. Alexa began to scream, hoping someone would hear. The fingers holding her wrist twisted harder, the pain became worse than anything she'd ever felt, and still he twisted until she felt and heard an audible pop. Stars danced before her eyes, air became harder to take in. The cold brick he shoved her against seemed inconsequential to the pain resonating from her arm. As darkness closed in on her, she wished for death, screaming for help with her last breath.

The steady beeping woke her, terror had a scream ripping from her throat.

"Easy. You're safe," a soft voice whispered.

Looking around the room, the beeping machines and curtains next to the bed she was lying in made her heart race. Alexa tried to think back to how she'd landed in the hospital. The heavy weight keeping her left arm down alarmed her, until she noticed the cast. "Where am I? How did I get here?" Her voice didn't sound like her own.

"Would you like a drink of water?" The woman stood up and motioned to the cup with the straw in it.

With a nod, Alexa licked dry lips, accepting the help from the stranger.

"You were brought in last night a little after nine. Luckily for you, a cabbie was driving by and heard you screaming. He stopped, which is unusual in itself. He said he turned his vehicle down the alley between two buildings and saw a man on top of a woman, and honked his horn. Your attacker was pretty focused on you. It took a few honks, and finally the cab driver had to gun his engine, and yelled out the cops were on the way."

She didn't remember anything after her face was slammed against the building. God, she hoped he hadn't raped her.

"Let me push the button and tell the nurse that you're awake. My name is Marley, I'm a woman's advocate. I volunteer here at the hospital, and other places."

Alexa jerked as the curtain was whisked back. "Sorry to startle you. I'm Dr. Johns. How are you feeling this morning?"

She tried not to flinch when he came close, taking her vitals. "I feel like I went ten rounds with Conor McGregor."

Dr. Johns nodded, taking a seat across from Marley. "Do you want me to have Marley leave and a nurse to come in before I go over your injuries?"

Shit! That ass had raped her on a dirty alley's ground. They'd dated for a little over a month, and she hadn't so much as let him get to second base. Now, he'd gone and...she couldn't even think of what happened. Her stomach rolled. "I think I'm going to be sick."

Marley was there with the kidney shaped thing Alexa was sure wouldn't catch the contents of her stomach.

"Miss Gordon, if I may, you weren't violated. What I mean is, you weren't raped, if that is what has you so upset." Dr. Johns looked her in the eyes. "My wife says that is one of the worst things that could happen to a woman. Now, your body took one heck of a beating. Would you like Marley to stay or go?"

Alexa wanted to go. She wanted to rewind time and take a ride home with someone, anyone. Heck, if she could, she would go back and never accept the first date with Danny. "Please stay, Marley."

Nodding, Dr. Johns continued, his soft tone soothing. "Your left arm is broken and the shoulder was dislocated. You have severe trauma to both sides of your face, nothing that time won't heal. A couple of bruised ribs, and six stitches between your breasts. Do you remember how any of this happened? I'm afraid the detectives will be here within the hour, if not sooner."

Stitches between her breasts? She had no clue how that happened, or how her ribs got bruised, which she told the doctor.

After the doctor reassured her she'd be fine with lots of rest, she dozed for what seemed only minutes before a sound had her eyes popping open. Fear had her jerking awake to see two men in uniform entering the room.

When the detectives came, she repeated what she told the doctor and braced for the good cop bad cop, and was stunned they believed her story, and appeared ready to arrest Danny. Anxiety and pain made her hold up her good hand. "What if he gets out on bail and comes after me?"

"Do you have someone you could stay with? A family member or close friend?"

How do you admit you had no one? "I'll figure it out. You just keep him locked up and I'll testify against him. Oh, and his mama is as whacked as him. She'd clearly just killed a small animal, its blood was still on her hands. She tossed it to the side and wanted to shake my hand with the blood still on her, like it was a normal thing."

After she gave as much detail as she could remember, from the first time she'd discovered her boyfriend was not sane, to the horror of the mother, she sighed as the detectives left. She wasn't sure how much good, or what they could do, but hoped like hell they locked him up and threw away the key.

Three months later.

Alexa packed a bag and all the money she'd been saving, looking around the apartment she'd tried to make look cozy. Her landlord understood, after having to repair damage ever since her attack he was probably happy to see her go. Of course, they didn't have proof that Danny had done it, but she knew it was him. She didn't go out at night, and never anywhere alone anymore. Her life had become bleak, with no light save for Marley's help.

"Do you have everything?" Marley asked. The older woman had become one of her closest friends.

Actually, her only friend. She was too scared of what would happen if Danny decided to hurt anyone who was close to her.

She nodded, taking one last look around at the mismatched furniture and other things she couldn't take with her. "You'll make sure someone packs all this up and gives it to another person like me, right?"

Marley nodded. "When you get where you're going, you'll have a setup as nice, if not better than this. Your things will be put in storage, and when someone is in need it will be given to them. That's how the system works." She picked up a discarded picture. "Who is this?"

The couple in the frame was nobody Alexa knew, but everything she wanted. "It's who I want to be someday."

Again Marley nodded. "Let's go before it gets any later."

Yeah, the last thing Alexa wanted was to be out at night. She knew she'd have to at some point, however that point wasn't now.

The little used car sat next to the curb. It was used but had a good motor, and that was what mattered to her when she bought it. "You have the address and my number. I wish you didn't have to go, but until the trial, this is the best thing for you. The safest thing for you." Sorrow entered the usually upbeat tones.

"Hey, it won't be forever. Maybe, I'll come back here for good once Danny's locked up." Alexa doubted she'd ever come back to Chicago, or anywhere near the state where he and his family lived. For the last three months he or someone he knew was stalking her, always leaving little things that seemed innocent. The restraining order worked, but he still found ways to terrorize her. She swore on several occasions someone had been in her bedroom while she slept, but had no proof. The manager had to repair doors painted blood red, with real blood, replace windows that had been broken and had finally told her she had to leave after his pet had come up missing. Alexa prayed the poor thing just wandered off, but feared Danny had taken it.

"Thank you for helping me with everything. I'll stop around ten or so, then finish the drive tomorrow. I should hit Rapid City sometime tomorrow night. I'll call you from there." She hugged

Marley, knowing it would probably be the last time she saw her.

"Take care, Alexa. You need me, I'm just a phone call away." A tear welled in her eye, which Marley was quick to wipe away.

The Following Day...

Alexa ran as if the hounds of hell were after her, looking over her shoulder for the tenth time, she stumbled and fell flat on her face. "Shit! What the hell did I do to deserve this?" She brushed her scraped hands down the front of her torn jeans. Her hands shook as she dug into her back pocket for the cell phone.

The flat tire would've been fine. She knew how to change one of those. If only she would have checked them at her last stop like Marley had warned her, but she'd been tired. The sight of a vehicle coming had her scrambling into the woods, and not a moment too soon as she saw who got out. Some inner self-preservation told her to hide. Damn Danny Reed. If only he wouldn't have followed her. A whimper of fear escaped as a twig snapped to her left, the darkness making it hard for her to see.

She backed away from the sound, finding a large tree with branches low enough for her to grab onto. Alexa quickly stuffed the phone into her pocket and reached for the branch, swinging up onto it and climbing until she was as far as she could go. She heard the sound of heavy footfalls and curses and knew her ex had indeed found her. He was an expert hunter, and she prayed he wouldn't know she'd climbed the tree. Danny's blond head came into view, his red and black plaid shirt almost impossible to see, except the moon came out from behind the clouds just as he stepped below where she hid.

Stuffing her fist into her mouth, she held her breath.

"I know you're here, Alexa. You can't run from me. I won't let you." Danny's voice carried through the woods. He'd used that tone before, just before he'd hit her.

Danny paced back and forth, looking for her tracks she was sure. "Damn it, Lex, I swear if you come back to me, I won't hurt you again. I didn't mean to last time. You just make me so mad."

The moon glinted off something in his hand. She tried to see what it was, but couldn't see clearly until he turned toward the tree. A large hunting knife was held in his fist, the wicked looking blade had to be at least six inches long. Yeah, she just bet he wouldn't hurt her. Alexa had no doubt she wouldn't be walking out of the woods if she spoke up, or if Danny got his hands on her. She wondered if that was the knife he'd used to cut her shirt off, leaving the gash in her chest that required the stitches.

Her ex crouched down at the base of the tree next to hers, his head snapping up as movement sounded all around them. She held on tighter, her legs beginning to shake. Alexa thought her mind was playing tricks on her as wolves seemed to circle the area, and then a woman stepped out. Her head tilted to the side.

Danny lifted his hand. "What the hell? Call your dogs off, woman. I'm looking for my girlfriend. She's lost here somewhere." His voice sounded strained.

The beautiful woman's eyes seemed to glow as she moved forward. "You stink with your lies. You came here hunting, hoping to catch your prey, but instead you are the prey." She licked her lips. "I don't think anyone would miss you. Have fun boys, but drag him away before you...do your thing."

Alexa held still as the woman dressed in military fatigues glided forward to stand below her. In a clear voice she said, "you may come down now. I promise you are safer than you were."

Not sure how to take those words, but knowing she truly had no choice, Alexa began the decent back down. When her feet touched the earth, she gasped as she was pinned to the rough bark of the tree. "I saved your life, now you owe me yours. What will you do in repayment?"

Having given up everything in order to escape a madman, Alexa had nobody who would miss her, save for Marley. She'd been given up for adoption when she was born, and fostered out of the system at eighteen. Yeah, she was a complete loser who wouldn't be missed by anyone. However, she was smart, and had an education. "What do you want?" She asked instead.

The woman smacked her cheek, not a motherly pat. "Good answer. I think you'll do just fine. Come with me. I don't need more men in my ranks, nor do I want any competition with my soldiers." She looked Alexa up and down. "You're not ugly, but you could stand to lose some weight. I could use someone who clearly has nothing to lose. Besides, you owe me. I like that in a soldier. Come on."

"What do I call you?" Alexa asked, running to keep up with the other woman's longer strides.

The blonde stopped and stared, her eyes with their eerie glow held her immobile. "You will call me whatever I tell you. For now, you may call me ma'am."

Alexa nodded, the sounds of the wolves' howls rent the air, making the hair on her arms stand on end. "Do you need to call your *dogs* back? Will they let Danny go, or..."

"Don't ever question me again. You will get that one free pass. I will tell you what to do, when to do it, and how to do it. We clear? As long as you do what you're told, and don't betray me, you will be fine. Trust me, you'll live a lot longer than you would have if you'd stayed up in that tree. Ole Danny boy had no plans to let you live past fucking and gutting you."

She knew he had planned to hurt her, but to hear the other woman say those words, Alexa felt tears well up, choking them back to keep from showing a weakness.

"Good girl. You'll do fine."

"Thank you for saving my life."

Her savior picked up the pace, leading her further through the woods, and toward a clearing. Alexa couldn't believe how close she'd been to salvation before Danny came along, yet wondered if it was truly a sanctuary.

****

Kayan Swift aka Kai, or Kayak to his fellow team members, looked around the newly overtaken military like base. "Anyone find Jase?" Just mentioning the bastard's name made him want to destroy everything in his path. He watched as Oz fingered the automatic rifle in his hands. Yeah, he wasn't the only one feeling twitchy when it came to their former teammate who tried to kill them.

"He's not among the living or dead," Sully Griggs growled.

"Fucking son of a bitch." Kai ran his hand through his short dark hair. Times like these he was glad he didn't have long locks like the men he'd met with Rowan, their former team leader, he'd have been pulling it out in hunks. "We need intel on where the fucker has gone, how he got here, and why he was here. Find me someone who was close to him." Kai spun away from his men. He felt like a failure.

"If you failed, then so did all of us." Kai looked over his shoulder to see Coyle striding up to him. Of all their team members, Coyle was probably one of the quietest, yet deadliest.

Kai grunted. "I'm not even going to dignify that bullshit with an answer."

Coyle squeezed his shoulder. "Right back atcha. Now, let's move on. What we gonna do now?"

"What we do best," he paused, "we go hunting." Now that they knew Jase had escaped the federal prison, there was no place for him to hide.

Commotion near a large building drew their attention. A woman yelling at one of the team leaders, her words making him visibly angry had all of Kai's protective instincts rising. His feet began moving, picking up the pace, eliminating the distance between them.

"Listen you overgrown ape, you can't keep us here. I wasn't here of my own free will, but because some nut job, which I'm hoping she's not coming back, wouldn't allow us to leave."

Kai studied the young woman. Her dark hair was pulled back in a ponytail, but bits of it had fallen free while she angrily stabbed at the soldier with one of her fingers. Her medium sized frame was what you'd call curvy, but her complexion was flawless with its tanned tones. He wondered if she had that coloring all over, then mentally slapped himself for thinking along those lines. She was aligned with the enemy.

"We are processing everyone, before we decide what to do with you. If you'll give us your name, and social, along with all your other pertinent details, we can get the process done quickly. Believe me, we all want to get out of here." The words held a hidden threat that Kai didn't misunderstand, and neither did the woman. Her eyes narrowed.

"I told you my name, but I am not giving you anything else without my lawyer. I know about due process." Her hands were bunched at her sides, knuckles turning white.

"Excuse me soldier. I'll take over. My name is Kai. What is your name?" She turned amethyst eyes on him. He wondered if they were real or contacts.

Her gaze roamed him from head to toe. "Hello, Kai. So, are you the new man in charge?" The woman made it sound like a vile thing instead of something to be proud of. He wanted to laugh at her audacity, but kept his smile in check.

He crossed his arms behind his back, showing her he didn't feel she was any threat to his person. Again, those strange eyes assessed him.

She sighed. "Fine, my name is Alexa."

In a pair of cargo pants that had clearly been meant for a male, Kai wondered if they were her boyfriend's. "Got a last name, Alexa?" He looked to her left hand for any sign of a wedding ring, seeing none. He had to rein himself in before he asked her flat out if she had a boyfriend, and then realized she still hadn't answered him.

Alexa's chest rose swiftly, bringing his attention to her ample breasts. "How about that lawyer I requested?"

"Sweetheart, I hate to break it to you, but you are so far outside the law right now you ain't got no rights except what we give you. Now, what's your last name? I do believe, Kai here has asked you nicely. You don't want me to take over this interrogation." Coyle's deep voice cut in.

Kai held up his hand, stopping Coyle from scaring the woman anymore. "Give her a moment, Coyle, I think she's about to tell us what she knows."

"Alexa Gordon is my name. I'm twenty-seven, haven't been a virgin since I gave it up on prom night to my date, Shawn. I love Italian food, hate seafood, and think my hips are too wide. I also think men with big egos and attitudes are lacking in other areas, clearly having mommy issues, and therefore they feel they need to bully those smaller than them. More than likely they also have small penises, and try to cover that little fact by bulking up." She stared at Coyle and then Kai, eyeing their bodies like slabs of beef.

The sound of their team member Oz's booming laugh had Kai turning to see he was bent over not two feet behind them. "Oz, you have something to say?"

Oz stood up, wheezing, one hand holding his stomach. "I fucking love her. Can I have her?"

With his right hand, Kai flipped him the bird. "Well, Alexa Gordon, I'm gonna need to ask you a few more questions. Like what the hell are you doing in a compound run by shifters, and a man who betrayed his country?" He watched her eyes and body to see how his words would affect her. The slight tremble let him know he'd struck a nerve.

Fear was an emotion he usually used to his benefit in situations such as this, however watching it flow through the woman in front of him, he wanted to wrap his arms around her and promise all was fine. Being a soldier who'd killed more than he liked to remember, he pushed aside his feelings for the small brunette. Finding the traitor was their main mission. For all he knew, she could be his partner, or at the very least know where Jase might have gone.

"Well, Alexa, I can promise you won't be getting any seafood from us, and if you want to know the size of my dick all you gotta do is ask. It's been a while since I've fucked a traitor, however I'll make an exception for you." He let his own eyes travel her body like she'd done his. Her jaw wobbled, tears forming in those odd eyes, and he almost felt bad. Then he remembered the little village he and his team had went in to secure, the sound of children screaming for help. If she was in league with Jase, then she deserved no mercy. Her tears were more than likely something she could turn off and on like a faucet. Kai hardened his heart.

"You are just as bad as the animals here, if not worse. At least they didn't say or do anything like that." Alexa took a deep breath. "What do you want to know? I just want to go home." She used the back of her hand, dashing away tears from her dirt stained cheeks.

****

Alexa swallowed the bile in her throat. The men gathered around her were worse than the ones who'd captured her, holding her against her will, again. That asshat Jase Tyler needed to be strung up and have his nuts put in a vice. Shifters? What the heck were they talking about? She'd heard howls, but hadn't been allowed to leave the building unless escorted by ma'am or the woman's beloved Jase, or one of the other men she trusted, and that was only to go from one building to the next. She thought for sure she would die, without anyone ever knowing what happened to her. Now, she was being accused of being part of their...whatever they were.

She waited for the man named Kai to tell her what he wanted to know, hoping she could give him answers and he'd let her go. God, she wished Marley was here, then was glad the older woman was safe.

"Follow me." Kai spun on his heel, entering the building that had been her prison for the last two weeks.

The space was filled with cots, she'd guess it was what one would imagine a boot camp was like. She'd never signed up, but that didn't matter to ma'am. Every day they made her get up at the ass crack of dawn, going through rigorous training as if she was a soldier. She'd even been learning how to shoot a gun. Not that she'd tell the big oaf in front of her.

"I'd keep moving. You don't want to piss him off."

Jumping at the deep rumble coming from behind her, Alexa hadn't realized the large man named Oz had followed them. Lord, he had to be well over six foot with dark red hair, and muscles upon muscles. How does a man that big move as quiet as a cat? Shit, all this talk about shifters was making her crazy.

He flashed a bright white smile, leaning down to her ear. "I'm not one of the shifters, baby girl."

"Oz, quit flirting with the woman." Kai's voice held a hint of violence.

"Yes, Captain." Oz winked.

"My name is Alexa." She stomped toward his retreating back.

He spun around fast, making her gasp as she ran into him. His arms came up to catch her. "I know your name. What I don't is why you're here." His fingers bit into her biceps for a moment.

"If I tell you my story, you'll let me go? Just like that?" Alexa snapped her fingers.

They walked into the office that had belonged to the woman in charge. The space was filled with electronics that looked straight out of the space station. Damn, she wished she'd have known the woman had all that technology in there.

Kai's black eyes assessed her. "You got someone you want to call?"

Alexa wanted to call Marley, but all her belongings had been taken from her when ma'am and the others had taken her to the compound. Of course, she'd memorized the woman's number, but she'd never drag her into this mess. Having made a real friend, Alexa treasured her, and would never endanger the gentle soul that was Marley.

Sighing, the events of the last few months hitting her, she collapsed into one of the chairs. "I just want my stuff so I can finally leave. My car broke down on the road a couple weeks back. I was running from my ex, and...he was following me." She explained about running into the woods when she realized Danny was following her, then how ma'am had found her, and how the woman's pet *dogs* had dragged her ex away. Kai and Oz listened without interruption as she kept her eyes on the floor between her feet.

"Look at me." Kai's voice whipped like a lash.

Her head jerked up.

"You're telling me you just went off with some woman with glowing eyes while your boyfriend is attacked by wild dogs? Never once thinking about his safety?"

Anger replaced the dejected feeling, standing up in a move faster than either man expected, she pressed both palms into his rock hard abs. "Listen here, buddy, I barely survived his brutal attack just months before. He beat me so bad, would have raped and killed me in a dirty dark alleyway in Chicago without a backwards glance. Luckily for me a cabbie heard my screams, or I wouldn't be standing here in front of an overgrown asshat. So don't think for one minute I have one moment of regret that jackhole is probably puppy kibble. His mama is more than likely torturing another helpless creature, cause yeah, she's as batshit crazy as him. She lifted her shirt to show him the angry red scar that ran between her breasts. "He used his bowie knife to cut my shirt in half, uncaring that he'd sliced into me. The doctor said he'd actually hit bone. Lucky for me I was already passed out from the pain of having my arm twisted behind my back so far that he'd broken my forearm and dislocated my shoulder." She pulled her shirt back down, ashamed when she felt tears tracking down her face.

Oz pulled her into his arms. "It's okay, sweets."

She allowed the big man to comfort her for a second then pulled away. "There you go. That's my story."

"Okay, that's how you got here. Now, I need to know what you saw while you were here. Who you talked to. What you heard. I'm sorry for what you went through, but it's important to our mission that I ask you these questions. As the only other female here, it's imperative." He gestured to the chair. "Please sit back down."

"I don't know how much help I'll be."

"You'd be amazed at what you may have picked up on and had no clue what we can decipher." Kai smiled.

When he smiled like that, she swore the world brightened, then wanted to smack herself upside the head. He was good at interrogations. More than likely it was all part of his plan. First he'd unsettle her with his bad cop, then when that didn't work, he'd charm her. Fine! She would tell them everything she knew, and be on her way. Nothing to hide, except Marley. They would not mess with the older woman if she had anything to say about it.

"Have you or your men found my car or belongings?" She asked after what seemed hours of talking. Her throat was raw from talking. Oz had stood back listening, fetching her bottles of water. Now, her body was telling her she needed the ladies room in the worst way possible, and her stomach reminded her she needed to eat. A loud rumble sounded, but she wasn't embarrassed. It was all their fault for not letting her have any food. Even the woman she was scared shitless of made sure they had three square meals a day, even if they were not the tastiest.

"I think that's enough for now. Let's get you some chow." He nodded, standing and gestured for her to do the same.

Alexa wanted to give him the finger and tell him to go screw himself. "I need to go to the bathroom." Heat crawled up her cheeks at the announcement.

"You'll understand that one of us will need to accompany you there. For your safety. We don't know if there are any triggers that we haven't found yet."

When will this nightmare end?

Chapter Two

Kai found a perverse pleasure in watching the woman Alexa go from dejected to angry in the blink of an eye. He would have Tay check her story out while they fed her, then if what she said was true they'd let her go. Although his body protested, their mission was to find Jase Tyler and bring him in, dead or alive. Preferably dead in his mind, but the higher ups wanted to question him. Although, Kai knew the man wouldn't talk no matter what amount of torture they administered.

"You going to watch me pee, too?"

Her words had him looking down, a grin forming on his lips. "I'll just stand outside. Just remember I have the ears of a hawk."

She rolled her eyes. "Please tell me that's a metaphor, not that you *think* you are one."

He thought of letting her think he might be something other, but then changed his mind. "I'm all human, baby." Holding the door open for her, he let Oz double check the stalls were empty and free of anything that could be holding a weapon or way of escape. Satisfied, they let her in.

With a grimace, she eased past him, making sure not to touch.

"She's a cute little thing," Oz pointed out.

"And that means what exactly? We've faced women ten times prettier, who could kill us without breaking a sweat. What makes you think she's any different?"

Oz shrugged his massive shoulders. "I think she's innocent in all this."

"We'll see what Tay finds out, and save our own personal thoughts until then. You got a problem with my decisions?"

"Nope, Captain. You're the boss." He turned on silent feet and left Kai feeling like a dick.

The sound of the toilet flushing made him aware that he'd not kept his mind on the woman in question. She emerged from the stall, going to the sink to wash her hands, watching him through the mirror. "You know it's weird to have a stranger listen to you go to the bathroom, right? If I didn't have to go so badly, I'd probably have had stage fright. What if I'd needed to go number two?"

Her words made him laugh. "Thankfully you didn't." was all he said and waited for her to dry her hands. She huffed, before making her way out the door, again avoiding touching him.

Tay motioned him back to the office. "Go with Oz and he'll make sure you get something to eat." He hated the thought of her going off with the big guy, but squashed his unreasonable emotions.

Alexa shrugged, walking to where Oz leaned against the wall. Kai left them, hoping his team member had something good to tell him. The brooding look on the usual happy one of Tay didn't bode well.

"Alright. Let's hear it." Kai crossed his arms.

The contents of a purse were laying on the desk. "It didn't take too much digging to find out that woman was terrorized by some fucker by the name of Daniel Reed. He's been reported as missing by his mother Daniella Reed. If I was a guessing man, they are a twisted version of that movie with the mom and son and the shower scene." Tay snapped his fingers. "Anyway, the cops have listed him as a missing person in Chicago, but I don't think they are actively looking for him. However, his truck along with one Alexa Gordon's vehicle is in a large shed at the back of the property here. I haven't found him, yet."

Kai told him Alexa's story, watching Tay's blue eyes narrow. "That matches her hospital records." He turned the computer around, showing Kai the pictures from the medical file.

"I'm guessing we bypassed HIPAA?" Kai joked.

Tay lifted his middle finger, tapping more keys. "She met with a woman who worked with women's advocacy groups. If I was a guessing man, I'd say they were helping her escape the bastard. She doesn't have any family, and no close friends from what I can find. Her last employer was a large firm called CNA, in downtown Chicago. She took the train to and from work, then walked the final few blocks home, in a not so good part of town." Disgust laced Tay's tone.

"She only met Jase a few times. He somehow met the leader of the shifters here, and helped train them. I'm sure they were helping him hide, and possibly helped him escape. Fuck!" Kai punched his hand down on the desk. "Another dead end."

"We gonna let the woman go or what? It's a little tricky letting a human who knows about shifters out in the world. Should we have Kellen and his pack come and take her back to their club?"

Kai leapt over the desk. "I'm in charge of the woman and this entire operation. I'll decide what to do with her, and she sure as shit ain't going anywhere near Kellen Styles, leader of a god damn pack and motorcycle club. I may respect the hell out of him, but not happening while there's breath in my body." For the first time he noticed he had Tay pushed up against the concrete block wall.

Tay had his arms out to his sides. "Man, you need to take a step back. I wasn't questioning your authority here. I am making a suggestion, which is what I do. Fuck!"

"Damn, I'm losing my shit. Sorry, Tay." Kai patted Tay's chest, taking a step back.

"Just don't kiss and make it better."

Leaning against the desk, they stared at one another. "What do you suggest, other than sending her to Kellen?"

"Fix her tire, and let her go about her life. I'm pretty sure she won't say anything, and besides who would believe her?"

"We could put a tag on her and monitor her for a while." Kai agreed.

"I also have a bead on Jase."

"Why the hell didn't you say so?" Kai rounded the desk, looking at the screen. "What did you find?" The pictures of a bruised and beaten Alexa filled the monitor. He hit a few keys, clearing the screen.

Tay, the smallest of the group ambled over, showing him the maps that had been saved. "Looks like he was planning to head back over the border. Feel like heading to Mexico my fearless leader?"

Dread hit his stomach. Jase Tyler was like a rattler, he liked to hide in the grass and wait for someone to come upon him, then he'd strike, hard and fast. Like a poison, he would enter their blood stream and wait for his prey to die.

"We need more intel. Make it so, and let's get ready to move out. I want to get going before his trail gets cold."

"What about the woman?" Tay began putting the purse's contents back inside.

There was no way he could drag her along, yet letting her out of his sight bothered him, which made up his mind. "I want there to be eyes on her. Make sure someone is assigned to follow her, but she is not to know. This is now a military base until further notice. Get the Commander on a secure line for me."

****

"What do you mean I'm free to go? Just like that, you're letting me go?" She was glad they'd found her bags with all her own clothes, but was shocked to find she'd lost a good ten pounds in two weeks. Stress, and working out from sunup till sundown clearly did that to a body. Her black leggings felt good to put on, paired with a V-necked tunic, she was ready to hit the road in her comfy clothes. She wondered if the job Marley had lined up for her was still available, then decided she'd find another if not.

"You know the rules. Tell no one about the compound." Kai focused on her.

She'd agree to just about anything to get away from the hell she'd been forced in, and mean it. Nodding, Alexa held up her right hand. "I promise, but what do I tell the people who were expecting me? I had a job lined up that I missed. An apartment that is probably gone. What am I supposed to do now?" Again, she wished she could face ma'am and hit the woman, then shivered as she remembered what happened when anyone disobeyed her. Nope, Alexa would just dream about it.

"Tay has already taken care of everything for you." Kai handed her a sheet of paper.

It took a few minutes for the words to make sense, but then she frowned. "How do you know I can do this type of work?"

Kai's left eyebrow winged up. "Trust me, we know everything. Now, get going so you will get to your destination before dark. You'll find your apartment is secure, furnished, and the job you are more than suited for. If you have any problems, there is a number on the bottom of that paper, as well as in your apartment where you can reach someone within the organization who can help you. Any questions?"

So many, but she held her tongue. Her little Honda sat out front, looking as it had when she'd purchased it. A large African American man stood behind it, with another dark skinned man with piercing green eyes. They both looked scary, neither smiling.

The darker of the two motioned her over. "I've filled your tank, put new tires on, and checked all your other fluids. You're all ready to go." His deep voice went with his dark looks, but then he smiled. Damn, did all the men in the group come from some GQ issue?

"Hey, I helped." The green eyed one winked, handing her the keys. "I also cleaned out the trash. You really shouldn't eat all that junk food." He eyed her up and down. "Although, it clearly isn't bad for your body.

"Sully, Coyle, quit fucking with her." Kai's hands landed on her shoulders.

"It's like that is it?"

Alexa looked from the dark men to Kai standing too close to her. "Thank you for doing all that for me." She stepped away from the big man who made her feel too much.

"Not a problem. Call me Coyle."

Were they really just going to let her go? "Thank you I think. I mean thank you." Sliding into the seat, she had to adjust the controls to reach the gas and brake. "You didn't give me my phone back." She looked out the open passenger window toward where Kai stood glaring.

"It was broken. I believe Tay replaced it with another." He didn't take his eyes off hers. "He made sure they had the same number in case you had given it to a friend."

Heat crawled up her face. "Thanks." Coyle stood with his body between the door frame, preventing her from closing it. Any minute, she expected one of them to put a bullet in her, but she didn't know why. Inserting the key into the ignition, she started the vehicle, hoping they'd get the hint and move back. "I guess this is goodbye." Her arm stretched out, brushing Coyle's leg.

He banged the top of her car. "Take care, sweets. Don't get in over your head with the baddies." Coyle shut her door.

Ha, she had a feeling they were every bit as bad, if they chose to be.

"Coyle."

She heard the warning in the leaders rumbling voice, and almost felt sorry for Coyle.

"Buckle up for safety."

"For fucks sake, I think the woman knows how to take care of herself."

"You think?" Coyle asked, pointedly looking around the compound grounds.

Alexa had enough, snapping the seatbelt in place, because yes she knew it was smart, then she put the car in gear. An insane urge to look in her rearview mirror drew her gaze, but she found herself disappointed to find all three men had disappeared back inside the building. "What did you expect them to do? Wave until the dust settled like you were a loved one leaving?" She snorted, then turned the radio up, glad her CD was still inside and seemed to work. Hearing the familiar sound of Metallica blaring through the speakers made her feel almost normal.

The past couple of weeks came back as she pulled into the town of Rapid City, only a half hour had passed. The address of her new apartment was typed on the top of the paper they'd given her, along with her new job information. "It won't hurt to drive by and take a look at the place." Then she'd give Marley a call and see if the other place was still available. Her mind made up, she was surprised to find the expensive looking building. She double checked the address, then pulled under the canopy. A uniformed man came out, startling her so much she almost ran over him. Geez, get it together.

"I'm sorry. I don't know if I'm in the right place." She showed him the paper with the address on top.

"Good evening, Ms. Gordon. We were told to expect you. Do you need help with your luggage?" He stood straight, peering into the back window.

"Um, no. I think I'll just take stock and see what I need to get at the store." It was a half-truth.

He inclined his head, then made to open her door. "If you'll allow me I will park your car for you."

Panic made her grip the steering wheel. "I'm not sure how long I'll be inside. I'll just leave it on the street."

"That's no problem. I'll just leave it over there." He indicated a small alcove where other vehicles were.

Releasing her death grip on the wheel, she grabbed her purse, stuffing the papers inside along with the cell phone. Once she was out, she reached into the back and grabbed her bag. "Thank you."

Again, he tilted his head, waiting for something. Alexa didn't have any cash and felt inferior. "I'm sorry, I don't have any money for a tip," she blurted.

A smile split his somber face. "It's not necessary, miss. I just need you to give me the keys."

She slapped her forehead. Her first instinct had been to keep all her belongings on her person. Digging the keys back out of her bag, she handed them over. "Sorry."

"Not a problem. The front desk will need to clear you before you can get inside. It's protocol."

She liked the level of security, but with Danny more than likely no longer on this earth, she didn't think she needed it. However, she wasn't about to tell him that.

"I won't be long." She figured it would be easier to change her mind and park her car, than to ask them to fetch it.

Inside was every bit as nice as the outside. Surely she had fallen and was now in a coma. She stared around the gleaming foyer with the leather furniture placed for guests to wait or whatever the rich did. A coffee station she'd only seen in restaurants sat in one corner, along with a multitude of snacks. What the hell? Did they feed the wealthy who came to visit or what? She had no clue if that was normal, but the huge stone fireplace drew her eyes. She always wanted one, especially growing up in Chicago and its cold winters.

"You must be Alexa." A tall gorgeous man sauntered over, his voice like smooth velvet.

Alexa held her breath. No way did she fit into this world. His suit alone looked like it cost more than her five thousand dollar used car. "That's me," she said over brightly.

"My name is JoJo. I'm the manager of the Peltier Building. Let me show you to your apartment. How was your trip? I bet you are exhausted after such a long drive. Chicago," he sighed. "The Windy City. I've never been there, but my fiancé has. He's a dancer and singer and travels everywhere." He winked at her. "Now, don't get upset. I know I'm dashing, but alas, we just celebrated our two year anniversary."

Instantly, she knew she would like JoJo. He was one of the most handsome men she'd ever seen, built like a god, and he had zero interest in women. Yes, he was perfect. "Dang, my seduction plans are foiled again." She smiled for the first time in what seemed forever.

****

"See, I told you. She is going to be fine. Now, can we get our heads out of our asses?" Sully crossed his arms over his chest.

Kai kicked Sully's feet off the desk. "The only head up anyone's ass is gonna be yours, up your own if you don't shut it." He narrowed his eyes as he watched Alexa smile up at the operative Joe. He wondered what the Casanova had said that made her smile.

Oz snickered. "Dude, you got it for the little brunette or what?"

"She's not a brunette. Her hair is like dark silk, almost black." He wished he could call the words back, but he realized too late his friends wouldn't let him.

"So it's like that?" Coyle asked.

Tay cleared his throat. "Don't matter. She's safe. We got eyes and ears on her. Now, we have to move out, boys. I've got a lock on Tyler. Or at least where he was two days ago. Seems he had a heads up that something was about to go down, and scatted before the shit hit the fan here." Video feed showed a man resembling their old friend crossing the border.

"What identification did he use to cross over?" Kai used the mouse, enlarging the screen.

Kai wasn't convinced Jase Tyler had actually left the country. Something didn't feel right.

"Your gut telling you it's not him?" Sully spoke up.

"Doesn't seem right. Why would he purposefully go where he knows the government has eyes? Where he knows software has face recognition?"

"Maybe he got stupid, or bit by one of the wild wolves here?" Oz didn't sound convinced.

"Let's load it up, boys. I see our future will be in a little Cantina not far from the border." Kai leaned down, taking one last look at the image on the screen.

Tay waited, and then he packed up the computer. They'd leave a contingent of men behind, cleaning up and clearing out any signs of what was here.

He walked out and found Rowan Shade leaning on the side of his pickup. "How's it going?"

"Can't complain." His former team leader grinned.

"I'm assuming you're not here for a social visit, nor are you wanting to come back to the team, as much as I'd like the former."

"You always were a straight shooter. This place is not government property my friend. I own it and all the acreage around it." He held his hand up.

Kai whistled through his teeth. "How'd you manage this or do I want to know?"

Rowan's deep chuckle was his answer.

"Not sure if the higher ups are gonna like this."

Broad shoulders encased in a black ripped tank shrugged. "Trust and believe, brother, they don't want to fuck with what's mine. Kellen Styles has more than enough to make sure none of them want to come sniffing around him and his. Besides, the Commander owes me. I've already called in a few markers. You know I don't just leave things to fall into place."

Shit! When Rowan got that freaky look on his face, Kai knew it was time to accept it was a done deal. "So, is everyone to move out and leave you and your boys to take over or what?"

"I'd appreciate you taking out the trash when you move out." He indicated all the military vehicles. "You know this was a covert ops, so nobody truly knew you were here. It's a matter of loading up and moving out. I've handled everything else. The people that were here you've cleared as *other*, they're mine. Kellen, Xan and I will handle them accordingly."

"There was a man who came up missing. His truck is in the back shed. Can one of you tell me where he's located?" Kai tapped his nose.

Rowan laughed. "You want me to be your hound dog?"

"Something like that. I need to know that the woman he's beaten and terrorized is safe."

Blue eyes blazed. "Show me where it's at."

Just like that, Rowan became the soldier Kai knew. Of course, he may be following Kai, but Rowan Shade would always be the leader, even when he was no longer in charge. He proved it by sidestepping Kai, and heading straight to the back of the building. "Which vehicle?" His voice had gone deeper.

They both moved toward the truck he indicated. His old friend walked around, opening the door and then shutting it back after a minute. "Give me a half hour or so. I'll let you know. Watch my truck."

Staring at Rowan's retreating form, Kai looked into the truck wondering what Rowan was able to find they didn't.

"He's still Phantom Force even if he's retired. Once a SEAL, always a SEAL," Sully said.

Kai hadn't heard him come in, but wasn't surprised. They were more than that, even though technically the government used them on missions most teams weren't sent on. They were ghosts. Phantom Force was sent in when shit needed to be done, no questions asked, and lines crossed the big dogs didn't want to know about.

"What's Shade doing?" Sully nodded at the retreating form.

"He's going to snoop around and see if the owner of this rig is still among the living."

Being a smart man, Sully didn't say a word.

"He also informed me we are on his property. Has all the official paperwork to prove it and everything." They exited the building, the sunset almost looking majestic.

"Yeah, Tay said he has some email correspondence. I guess that means we ain't got no reason to stick around."

"Nope. None whatsoever," he agreed. The need to follow Alexa and make sure she settled in burned in his gut.

"You know all you gotta do is make a phone call to find out how the girl is doing." Sully's unblinking green eyes unnerved him.

"Let's focus on the job at hand, brother."

"We following the lead into Mexico?" Coyle stood with his hands behind his back.

Kai rubbed the back of his neck, an itch he couldn't shake as if he was missing a vital piece of information. "As soon as Rowan comes back, we'll head down for a little recon."

Oz stepped up next to Coyle. "I'll buy the first round of tequila, and no, we are not chasing it with cotton candy. That shit will kill you." He glared at Tay who walked out of the barrack.

53

"Hey, that's the only way to drink that rot gut shit." Tay lifted his middle finger.

Holding up his hand, they all turned as one, watching Rowan stride out of the woods dressed in a pair of jeans with his shirt held in his hands. "You can rest at ease. That boy won't be bothering anyone, let alone your girl ever again." He lifted a piece of torn fabric. "This was what's left of his shirt. I can lead you to where I found it, but you won't find much else."

That was what he'd figured, having it confirmed eased a knot around his stomach. One less thing for him to worry about. "I appreciate you coming out and doing your thing, Rowan."

"Hey, we'll always be brothers." Rowan held his hand out, pulling Kai in for a hug.

Kai grunted, realizing his buddy was a whole hell of a lot stronger than ever. "You keep eating those Wheaties, and you'll be flipping trucks."

Rowan grunted. "I need to get back to Lyric. You need me, or any of the Iron Wolves, you give me a holler." With that, Rowan strolled away.

They waited till his taillights disappeared, then turned as one to Kai. "Let's roll out. I want to be in a dirty town by morning." It was the last place he wanted to be, but a necessary evil.

A chorus of Hoorahs echoed in the still night, making Kai grin.

"Whose idea was it to come here again," Oz asked.

"I think we were following some asshole, and one of you, not pointing any fingers, thought it was a good idea to have a drink. If my memory serves me correctly, someone said something about tequila and women." Kai leaned back in his chair, keeping his eyes and ears open. They'd been in the little tavern for over an hour, pretending to drink and joke around. The waitress and bartender kept looking at them as if they were bombs ready to blow, which wasn't too far off the mark. His neck tingled, an inner warning Kai never ignored.

When the waitress circled back, he reached out, pulling her onto his lap. "Hey sweet thing, is there anywhere around here we could party. We're on leave, and could use a little relief." He let his eyes wander over her curves, his hands never strayed past her hips, but he squeezed, making her think he wanted more than the liquor she was serving.

She licked her lips. "Si, senor." In broken English she told them to meet her an hour after closing. The bartender watched them with narrowed eyes until she returned to him. A knowing glint entered his gaze as Kai stared at the two heads bent together.

Without letting them know he was aware of their conversation, Kai picked up the deck of cards, and began dealing. As he lay down each card, the rest of the team got the message he needed them to have. It was a strategy they'd used many times before, and luckily, they always carried a marked deck.

Coyle stood, tossing his hand into the pile. "That's it. I'm out."

"Pussy." Tay laughed

Oz lay his cards on the table with relish. "Read em and weep boys."

"Motherfucker," Kai groused.

Laughing, Tay wagged his finger. "Sorry, but my hand beats yours."

"Damn, you cheating again?" Oz growled.

Tay stood up, knocking his chair over. "Fuck you. I don't never cheat."

"Bullshit. You're nothing but a lying cheating bastard. I saw you with Linda last week. Who is not your girl, but Coyle's. What do you think he'll have to say about that?" Oz pointed his finger toward the bathroom.

Kai jumped between his two men. "Listen you two, now isn't the place for this shit."

Oz knocked Kai out of the way, and all hell broke loose.

"Fuck, Sully, grab one of them." Kai reached for Oz.

Sully pointed at Coyle. "I am not sure which one."

"You screwing my old lady?" Coyle's voice was deadly.

Tay looked between Oz and Coyle. "Man, it was nothing. She came onto me. What was I supposed to do? You should thank me. Besides, she was a shitty fuck."

A roar that would've done Rowan proud flew from Coyle, and then the man leapt over the table, tackling Tay.

Kai watched the bartender reach under the dirty counter, more than likely for a weapon. Sully grabbed the man from behind, quickly stopping him. The little waitress appeared to be trying to sneak out the back, exactly as Kai had expected. He followed, keeping to the shadows. A few times she looked back as if sensing his presence. The small house she entered a couple blocks down had all the windows boarded up, but Kai was faster than she was. He easily kept the door from locking into place, and she was too intent on getting inside, thinking she'd made a quick escape.

Making sure the door was locked as he entered, Kai looked around the empty space.

"Are you sure you weren't followed?"

"Yes, they think I'm a dumb waitress." Her voice no longer held the broken English from before.

A deep chuckle could be heard. "You realize those are not some ordinary military boys, don't you, Milly?"

"I don't give a shit who they are. I'm paid to tell you when there are suspicious men in town, and you keep me safe. That is our deal. Now, I gotta go. Jose will notice I left, but he'll think I got scared and ran home," Milly said.

"You know I could get you out of here and set up real nice...for a price."

Milly laughed. "Yeah, no thanks, Burns. Gotta go."

"Don't you want to know who those guys are?" Burns asked.

"Nope. Questions get you dead real quick."

Kai heard light footsteps coming back toward him, and flattened himself against the wall, waiting until she walked out the door. He and Burns were gonna have a chat, and if he could do something for young Milly he would, but first he'd find out if she'd had her hand in any missions that got people killed. She didn't seem to mind she may have been sentencing the five of his team to death.

The sound of the other man's boots pacing came closer to where Kai stood.

"Houston, we got a problem." His voice faded.

Kai waited, listening to the other man's conversation.

"Yeah, well you didn't cover your tracks good enough, nor did you kill the fuckers like you were supposed to."

Burns laughed, a nervous sound that made Kai's lips twitch. "I'm pretty sure my days, if not hours, are numbered. Just thought I'd give you a heads up. Not sure why, except to ask you to look out for Milly for me. She's a decent girl who was in the wrong place at the wrong time, with the wrong guy."

In that moment Kai understood Burns knew he was there. He waited for the operative to hang up, then said, "put your arms above your head and walk this way, Burns."

"Did you come in when Milly did or after she left?"

"Does it matter? Do what I said. My team are all around this place." He was more than a hundred percent positive they'd already figured out all the ins and outs of the location, and if there were any traps, and disabled them.

"I guess not. You know I won't tell you anything, no matter what you do to me. My life was over the moment you stepped through that door." Burns voice sounded resigned.

"You tell me what I need to know, and you can have a new life." Kai could give him that. Not one he'd like, but a new one just the same.

The man named Burns laughed. "It was good chatting with you. When you catch Tyler, tell him the Devil always collects his dues." Kai rushed around the corner, knowing it was too late.

A sound Kai was familiar with, almost like a whoosh of air sounded, and then a heavy thud. Burns ended his own life before Kai could extract information from him. Seconds later, his team entered from the sides and front. Oz and Tay shook their heads, while Sully studied the body and the room.

"We need to scat real quick like. I have a feeling this place is a set up, too." Coyle stared at the equipment on the desks.

"What did he say?" Tay asked.

Kai reached under the dead man for his phone. "Think you can trace the last call he made?"

Nodding, Tay pocketed the phone. "I can hack anything."

"You need anything else from here?" Kai indicated all the computers.

"More than likely he has it encrypted so that it will infect whatever I load it to. Besides, we don't have time. This," he tapped his pocket. "Will give me a more accurate location than the computer, and knowing Jase, he isn't a computer freak. I'd say he's relying on others to do that."

He hated to agree, but their old team member was lazy in that respect. His specialty was tracking. "Let's head back to base. How long before you can get a lock?"

Tay rolled his eyes. "I'm gonna need a computer that I trust. So a few hours, boss."

Shit! He hated that Jase had led them on a wild goose chase. They took the time to cover their tracks, making sure nothing could lead back to them.

Once they were safely away, Kai twisted his head back and forth. "Did you at least get to hit each other before following me?" He asked as they neared a corner.

Coyle rubbed his knuckles. "Hoorah that was fun."

"For who, exactly? I had Oz and you on my ass," Tay grumbled.

Kai held up his fist, and his team went silent, becoming the ghosts they were known for. He lifted two fingers, and made a circular motion.

They heard movement in the alley, which wasn't unusual, but they weren't taking any chances. As the men passed, completely unaware of the danger, the Phantom team slipped down the alley. "We need to get the girl. Her name is Milly. I don't know what she can or can't tell us, but she knew Burns."

"I'll get her," Oz offered.

"We stick together. I don't trust her. She's willing to trade our lives for her own." Kai indicated they follow him. Nobody said another word as they made their way back to the bar.

The bartender looked up. "You come to tear up my bar again?"

Kai looked at the dirty establishment. "Where's the little waitress. She was gonna meet me after she got off work."

"She left early. Said all that violence upset her."

"I should apologize. Where does she live, and I'll do so in person." Kai smiled.

The big bastard crossed his arms. "I ain't telling you shit. You boys need to go back over the border and leave good girls like Millicent alone."

A laugh bubbled up. "We can do this the hard way or the easy way, my friend. Trust me though, your Millicent is far from a good girl."

An hour later, they stood outside another house on the outskirts of the little town. With hand motions, they moved in. Kai and his team had seen enough to know she lived alone and was already in bed. Her pitiful attempts at security would keep out most amorous men. Not his team. Hopefully, by morning, they'd have more information to go on.

Chapter Three

Not dreaming was a mantra she kept having to remind herself. If the apartment wasn't so down to earth, and something she'd have chosen if she'd had the money, Alexa swore she'd have left. A file on the counter had her name on the front. Inside was everything they'd promised. A checking account with enough cash to get her started, along with what looked like a promising job.

"How do they know I can even do this type of work?" She tapped the folder. "Stupid question. They're some super military that has the ability to know everything."

The refrigerator had been filled with the basic necessities, and she was too tired to do more than pour herself a glass of milk and sit on the large sofa. She wondered if they used the apartment for one of the guys she'd met, then dismissed it from her mind. None of them looked like they'd want to stay at a place that wasn't their own. After she drained the glass, her first thought was to kick off her shoes and take a nap. However, she didn't know the first thing about the town, or where the job she was supposed to be working was. Alexa wanted to have an exit plan just in case things went to shit, and she needed to run.

"No time like the present to acquaint yourself with your new town." Taking the glass to the sink, she rinsed it, then grabbed the folder before heading out the door.

"Hello, gorgeous. Already leaving us?" JoJo asked.

Alexa nearly jumped out of her skin at the sound of the concierge's voice coming from behind her. "Jesus you scared the crap out of me."

Shrewd brown eyes assessed her. "Where you heading? Aren't you tired from your long trip?"

"I thought I'd drive around and get an idea of where everything is."

He nodded. "I have your keys behind the desk."

For one crazy moment she thought he was going to try and stop her from leaving, fear a friend she had become so accustomed to having, she hated it. The training ma'am had made her do gave Alexa newfound confidence. Straightening her spine, she held her hand out taking the keys and smiled, before walking out. The same guy stood out front, but he didn't give her any notice as she went to her used car parked next to an expensive one. She wasn't even sure of the name on the emblem gracing the hood, only that she was way out of her element.

Rapid City was a good sized city, with a lot of things to explore and see for tourists. She made mental notes of things she wanted to do while she drove around, keeping her eyes out for anyone who might be tailing her. One thing Danny taught her, was not to think you were safe, just because you thought you were.

She'd driven hundreds of miles, and he'd clearly been waiting for the right opportunity. Or as she'd realized too late, he'd done something to either her car or the road to make her have a flat tire, waiting for the inevitable to happen. She shivered at the last image of her ex being dragged away by the pack of wild dogs. In the time she'd been held, the only sign of the animals had been the howls. Ma'am had informed her she'd handled the situation and not to question her if she wanted to see another day. Mrs. Reed was probably worried sick, but Alexa couldn't work up any sad feelings for either of them.

Her fingers cramped from the tight grip on the steering wheel, making them unclench took a little effort. Pulling into a small coffee shop, the wifi sign meant she could pull up a map and find the directions to the office building. If she'd been thinking clearly, instead of needing to make sure she could leave the apartments, she'd have asked JoJo. "Oh, well. No sense crying over spilled milk." The lot was surprisingly full, making it difficult to find a spot close to the door. She drove around the lot, and then back around. "Woohoo," she cheered as a car was backing out near the front.

Once inside, she ordered a Chai Tea Latte, not needing any caffeine so late in the evening. "Can you tell me where The Steinem Building is?"

The little brunette stared at Alexa like she'd grown two heads. "I have no clue." Shrugging her shoulders, she looked to the next customer.

Alexa went to the end of the counter and waited.

"The Steinem Building is two blocks north of here." An older woman smiled, and then proceeded to give exact directions on a piece of paper.

"Thank you. I'm new to town, and was trying to figure my way around before reporting in for my first day. Don't want to show up late." Alexa laughed.

"I work in the building as well. Lots of offices there. Maybe I'll see you. There's a decent café there, but I usually bring my lunch, however, there is also a coffee shop in the lobby. I swear they make the best lattes, or I just need the extra boost at eight a.m. My name is Debra by the way." She held out her hand.

"Alexa. Thank you for the directions." Hearing her name being called pulled her away from the conversation. Although she didn't want to think about why she was nervous, making friends didn't come easily, nor trusting them.

Waving her hand in farewell, Alexa got back in her car and drove to the office building in downtown Rapid City. She liked that it wasn't in some secluded area where she would feel closed off, nor did the buildings next to it look deserted. She made note of all the alleyways, and streets, driving around each one a couple times until she felt certain she could navigate them without getting lost.

Her stomach growled as she passed a fast food chain. The thought of going back and cooking held no appeal, neither did a greasy burger, but her body needed substance. Three square meals had become a highlight. Sad what her life had turned into, but she swore she wasn't going to be that woman anymore. First she'd get a decent meal, and then tomorrow she'd grocery shop. Make friends, and get a life. So why did all seem doable, except the last. She swiped at a tear that fell down her cheek. She wanted someone to come and carry her home, and tell her it was all a bad dream. Only her life had never been anything but one bad dream after another.

"Buck up girl. You can get through this like you've always done." What she needed to do was get a cat or a dog and quit talking to herself, she laughed at the image of herself surrounded by animals. That would top it off as the last on her loser status. A single woman with no friends, save for her pets.

A bar and grill drew her attention, its neon sign with the brightly colored fruit had her turning the wheel sharply, making a vehicle behind her honk.

Her new motto was to quit apologizing, so instead of raising her hand in apology, she kept driving into the lot and pulled into the first available space. She wasn't going to drink, but she was going to get something that wasn't premade.

The only seat available was at the bar. Again, a new resolution meant not cowering. Thanking the young lady, she took the barstool, ordered a water and asked for a menu. After she ordered she sat watching the others gathered around, cheering on their favorite team on the big screen above the bar. Alexa didn't follow sports, but their energy was infectious. She found herself enthralled in the excitement.

Her five cheese pasta arrived, the yummy noodles drenched in creamy goodness had her salivating on her first bite.

****

"What the fuck do you mean you lost her in traffic? Did you put a tracker on her vehicle?" JoJo cursed.

"Not enough time. I thought you were gonna keep her inside longer." Blake answered.

JoJo shook his head, knowing his partner was kicking his own ass. "Shit, I thought she'd crash, too. Damn, Kai is gonna kick our asses. Back track and find her. She has to come back here some time if all else fails. However, we won't know if she makes contact with Tyler or not. I'm gonna step up security here."

"Sorry man. She literally shot through a stop light and turned without signaling, almost causing an accident."

"Go back where you lost her and do a perimeter search. Who do you have with you?"

"Mad and Dex." Blake named two of the SEAL team members.

Groaning, JoJo pounded his head on the counter of the front desk. Kai was so gonna beat his ass. The two men with the worst reputations with women were with his partner, and now he was relying on them to search and find her, probably seduce her. Fuck, his life was just a ball of cotton candy. Not!

"Tell them Kai said to watch, protect, and report. Not, and I repeat, not fuck her."

Blake's deep chuckle came over the line. "They said it's been a long dry spell and aren't making any promises. Something about a petite woman was just what their doctor ordered."

"Yeah, well tell them the doctor will be ordering bone scans and splints if they disobey the captain."

He hung up before he heard anymore, knowing the two with his boyfriend would do as they damn well pleased, Kai be damned. He'd noticed Alexa had taken her bag with her, and the surveillance footage showed she'd not unpacked a damn thing. If the rest of the mission continued, he was going to need to take up a hobby, or he and Blake were going to get into all kinds of trouble.

The vibrating of his cell had him jerking back to the desk. Seeing no caller id had him tensing. "Yes?"

"We got a problem. Where's the woman?"

JoJo's throat tightened at the deep timbre of Kayan Swift's question. "She's out scouting the area.

Something about wanting to familiarize herself with her new town."

"What aren't you telling me?"

Damn! "Nothing. Blake, Mad and Dex are trailing her." Truth. Kai would hear a lie even thousands of miles away.

"Seems Jase had his eyes on her, and maybe even now has her in his sights. Tell the three stooges not to let her out of theirs or they'll answer to me." The threat wasn't an idle one.

"Got it." JoJo took a deep breath.

"We'll be back on U.S. soil in less than eight hours. Have a detailed report for me, and JoJo...don't lose the woman."

As the line went dead, JoJo was sure his heart stopped beating. "And JoJo, don't lose the woman. Like I'm some sort of keeper or some shit." Punching his security code into the keypad, he let himself into the office behind him. Pulling up the video feed on the monitors of the cameras outside of the apartment building was like taking candy from a baby, and from there he spent the next few minutes following Alexa as she drove around town. He zoomed in on her face and grimaced at the tears streaking down her cheeks, watching as she dashed them away. A few more turns and he saw when she ditched the team, pulling into a restaurant.

"Damn, girl, you hungry or what?" JoJo grabbed his cell and dialed Blake. "Have you found our girl?"

Blake growled. "No, damn it."

With a laugh, he told him where Alexa had gone, then waited to hear they'd found her car before telling them about Kai's call.

"Dude, you should've opened with that one."

"Sure, then the three of you would've headed to the hills. PS. He'll be here in less than eight hours, so don't fucking lose her again." JoJo hung up, then leaned back in the chair. "This job is going to give me a damn heart attack."

****

The back of Kai's neck itched, which meant the SEALs back at home were hiding something from him, or something else was going on. He didn't like the unknown, and having an ex-team member like Jase Tyler one step ahead of him made his teeth ache. He unclenched his jaws, figuring at this rate he'd be needing replacement molars in no time.

"What did they do to put that look on your face, boss." Oz's red brow quirked.

"I think they lost Alexa, and more than likely, Jase Tyler has her in his sights as we speak." Kai hated the fact he couldn't reach her right that second. A ridiculous notion. He was a man with no ties except to his team. No liabilities was a motto they all lived by.

"Dayum, that is just so fucked, man. He's not that damn good. You're giving him too much credit. Yeah, he's got a head start on us, but give us some credit, too. We are not without some skills. You want us just to step out and put a target on our chest, and shout we're right here?" Coyle crossed his arms over his chest.

He knew his team was better than Jase was, but the other man had been with a group of unknowns for some time, and Kai wasn't sure what he'd become, wasn't sure what he'd do to survive. No, he knew what his ex-team member would do. He'd kill each and every one of them if he could. However, he was a coward and would use someone else to do his dirty work, just like he did on their last mission, along with this latest trip into Mexico.

"I know each and every one of you are worth ten of that asshat. But," he raised his hand. "He has the element of surprise, not to mention we don't know his agenda. I feel like we are chasing our tails, while he's playing with his balls."

Tay laughed. "I'd rather chase some tails, than play with my balls any day, boss."

A round of laughter followed Tay's comment. "I'm sure y'all have had some fun watching others play with balls on that farm out in middle America, but I can honestly say the only licking I do is on the female variety." Sully waggled his tongue.

Kai left the team to work on finding Jase. Pulling out his phone, he searched through the encrypted info for anything that looked suspicious. He glanced at Tay, waiting for more info to filter through. The technical guru of the team was working away on the phone they'd taken off the dead man, his fingers flying across the laptop. Every once in a while Tay's blond head would bob or he'd run his hand over his jaw. A sure sign he wasn't having much luck.

A few more hours and they'd be on home soil. Kai pictured the woman named Alexa. His worry for how she was settling in had him rethinking his plans to be the one in charge of befriending her. Many times they'd portrayed themselves as single and willing, but it didn't sit well with him to try that angle with the damaged woman. All her protests aside, she had been hurt more than she'd let on. Her hospital records showed the near death experience she'd suffered at the hands of an ex-lover, yet an air of innocence surrounded her. Kai couldn't find any remorse in knowing the man who'd tried to kill her was no longer breathing.

He pulled up the records he'd requested on the Reed family, finding Mrs. Reed had perished in a house fire. Reading on, he was shocked to see they'd found several barrels with what appeared to be human remains in them. Kai shook his head, nausea roiled in his gut at what could have happened if Alexa hadn't escaped when she had. "Crazy fucking family."

"What's that, Cap?" Tay looked up from his computer.

Unable to explain why he was captivated by a woman he shouldn't be, Kai pointed at the screen in front of his team member. "You get anything yet?"

Tay narrowed his blue eyes. "Actually, I just did. Check it out. Our boy has been talking to some old friends, and when I say old, I mean as in our old buddy, Rowan."

"Bullshit. Was it a one-way call? Can you tell if it lasted more than a couple seconds? Where was the call placed from?" Shit! Kai couldn't let himself believe they had two traitors in their midst. Especially not Rowan. It would take a hell of a lot more than he and his team to take out what Rowan was into now with the Iron Wolves MC. Besides, the man had been the one to call them in to help destroy the compound where Jase had been hiding out. It didn't make sense. Kai wouldn't believe a red herring again, but he also wouldn't allow evidence to be pushed under a rug either.

"Looks like it was a call made several months back, one-way and lasted no more than a few seconds. So, either he didn't reach Rowan, or Rowan told him to go fuck himself." Tay's fingers began tapping on the keyboard again. "Now this is

79

interesting, though. You know our boy, Dex, right?" When Kai nodded, Tay continued. "Dex has a second phone, one he says is just for his hookups. There's not been any reason to tap it, but I've always kept the number in my files. I just cross referenced all our numbers in the database with every number that has been called from Jase's phone, or has called Jase. Guess who calls on a weekly basis?"

"Fucking Dex," Kai growled.

Oz and Coyle stopped talking, while Sully cracked his knuckles.

"Do you think JoJo and Blake are compromised as well?" Kai looked at his team, the men he trusted with his life.

Sully shook his head, then stopped. "We can't take the chance they aren't. Fuck, this shit just keeps getting better and better. What the hell are they getting out of fucking over their country?"

Oz looked down at his hands. "A one-way ticket to hell is my guess, or maybe my answer, cause when I get my hands on either of them..."

Kai understood and agreed, but he couldn't say it. "We land in a few hours. I suggest we all get a couple hours rest. It may be the last we get for another long stretch."

He leaned his head back and closed his eyes. They'd all learned to take what snatches of sleep they could, where they could.

As the altitude changed his body became alert almost instantly, along with the rest of his team. Tay had his computer held against his chest, rubbing his eyes with one hand, while Coyle stretched his legs out in front of him with a grunt. Oz's eyes stared straight ahead, the anger still burning in the blue depths.

"Want to jump out of a perfectly good plane again, Oz?" Sully asked.

Oz lifted his middle finger, but a ghost of a smile appeared on his face.

"When we land, we are going to get two rigs and head straight to the apartment building where Ms. Gordon is staying. I'm assuming Tyler has a reason for having Dex on her ass. I'm also assuming she's still alive since we haven't heard from anyone otherwise. Tay, when we get a signal, I want Rowan on the line. Oz, Coyle and Sully, you take one vehicle and head to the office where the woman is working. I want you in the office, and I want you to find out what, who and where she's gone today. Tay, you and I will go have a talk with JoJo. It'll be great fun to see our old pal again." Kai smiled, watching his team smile in turn, knowing they all wanted a piece of the action and would soon get to kick some ass was always a win.

"What about Dex?" Tay asked.

"Leave Dex to me."

"You realize he's gonna run, or worse, try to kill us right?" Tay looked around the group.

Oz laughed. "Yeehaw, that'll be great. Can I play with him first, before I rip his arms off and beat him with them?

"Such a barbarian, Oz." Kai winked. "That's why you're on my team. However, I think we have to let him live. Beat him senseless, but he will have to live to see another day, my friend."

Coyle raised his hand. "May I point out we haven't given him a fair trial. I mean they may have been discussing Jase turning himself in, or returning some dishes or shit. Whatever it was, we might want to find out what Dex was talking to the bastard about, before the beatdown."

"Damn, when did Coyle become the sane one of us?" Sully punched Coyle in the arm, then flinched when Coyle punched him back.

"I've always been the level headed one, y'all were just too screwed in the head to realize it," Coyle joked.

The pilot indicated they needed to fasten their seatbelts. Kai sent a prayer up to the heavens as they made their final descent into Ellsworth Air Force Base.

"We got a meeting at the U.S. Defense Department with Commander Lee in forty-eight hours. I want to have something good to report, boys."

"Do we all gotta go, or just you? That man scares the crap out of me."

Coming from Coyle, the statement should've made Kai laugh, but Commander Lee was a man not to cross. "For right now it's all of us. I'll see what I can do to get you pussies out of it." He looked at the members of his team, all SEALs, yet they'd each been plucked out of their original teams and brought together. "We train for war and fight to win, we get knocked down and get right back up stronger. Yet you're scared of an old man behind a desk?" Kai shook his head. "I'll let you hide behind me."

"Thanks, dad." Sully put his hand over his heart, while the other guys flipped him the bird.

Kai waited for the plane to touch down, then dialed Rowan's number. Hearing the phone ring on the other end, he worried the other man wasn't going to answer.

"Yo, what's up, Kai?" Rowan answered a bit breathlessly.

"Did I interrupt you doing something important?"

Feminine laughter sounded through the phone. "You could say that. Whatcha need?"

"We tracked Jase to Mexico."

Kai let his words fall into silence.

"He's not stupid enough to go down there, man. Y'all didn't go chasing shadows did you? Just a second, darlin."

The sound of fabric shuffling let Kai know Rowan was still in bed. "When's the last time you talked to Jase?"

"Are you accusing me of something, Kayan?" Rowan's voice went deeper.

"I'm not accusing you, brother, I'm asking. Your number was found in his. I'm asking as a courtesy if he's made contact or tried to make contact at all since he escaped Leavenworth."

Rowan's growl would've scared a lesser man. "I don't even know what the fuckhead's number is. My answer is no, I have not spoken to, nor has he left a message for me. I can check my cell, but I've missed a shit-ton of calls in the past few months. Hell, I miss calls all the damn time. If you don't leave me a message, then you don't want to talk to me badly enough is my motto. You want to come down here, and ask me face to face if I'm a traitor like that bastard? Then come on down, boy, but you best believe I will kick your ass once you realize I ain't no traitor."

A sigh escaped Kai as the plane finally came to a stop. "I don't need to, Rowan. I know you're not. I also am not stupid enough to come down there and get my ass handed to me by you. Fuck, I hate having that bastard out there, or actually here on U.S. soil, more than likely right under our noses."

"My mate says you're a dumbass, but that I need to calm down cause you're just trying to save a bunch of lives or some shit. What I can tell you is that Jase's scent was faint back at the compound, meaning he'd been gone for some time before we came in. I can also tell you he is nothing like me, if that helps you at all." Rowan's voice trailed off and he could hear Lyric in the background.

"Hiya, Kai," Lyric said.

Kai looked up to the heavens thinking he didn't want a woman if he became a sap like Rowan. "Hello, Ms. Carmichael."

"I'm going to give you some free advice. One...don't ever doubt Rowan again, or I'll hunt you down and take a bite out of your ass you won't get back. Two...if you need our help, we are only a call away, but only if you don't piss me off," Lyric growled.

Yeah, Kai didn't think he'd be calling on Rowan and his new family anytime soon.

"I will keep that in mind, Lyric. Can you let Rowan know I'll be in touch?"

"Sure thing, sugar."

After he hung up he felt like he'd just went a round with a heavy weight champion.

"You look a little green around the gills. I'm assuming from your side of the convo, that Rowan most def didn't talk to Tyler, and his little lady is now gunning for your balls." Oz threw his arm around Kai's shoulder.

"That pretty much sums up the conversation. I think the woman he fell for might already be planning my funeral."

Tay passed them. "Big difference is, she probably already has the coffin picked out."

"Nah, they burn their dead," Coyle laughed.

Fuck, he really wanted to smack them all upside their heads, but he was going to need his entire team to have their wits about them.

"It'll take us less than twenty minutes to get to Rapid City, give or take a few more to get to our locations. I want us to rendezvous at the apartment building in two hours. That should give you three time to get info, and be back to hear what JoJo had to say. I plan to make that boy sweat." Kai truly did like the younger SEAL. He and his partner had always seemed solid. If they found out either man was in league with Jase, Kai wouldn't think twice about turning them over to Commander Lee.

"Don't underestimate either man. They are both top notch in the field, along with Mad and Dex. What's the name of their other team member?" Sully asked.

Raising his eyebrows, Kai stepped onto the tarmac. "Hailey Ashley," Kai said.

"There's a saying about not trusting someone with two first names."

Oz looked around the group. "Can someone please throat punch Coyle?"

"Why? What did I say?" Coyle side stepped Sully's fist.

Chapter Four

Alexa finished her dinner, looking around the crowded bar at the mix of people, and realized she could fit in there. Heck, if she tried really hard, she could fit in anywhere. She'd never allowed herself to relax her guard enough to make real relationships, always expecting them to leave her. Starting now, all that was in the past.

She motioned for her check, wanting to head home. A good night's rest would go a long way to starting tomorrow out on the right foot.

"You ready for a drink? I have three gentlemen ready to buy you one."

A moment passed before she unglued her tongue from the roof of her mouth. "Oh, um, I would love to, but I have to work tomorrow and I'm driving. Please tell them thank you." Alexa smiled, a real one that felt good. This whole fitting in thing was going to be easier than she'd thought.

After paying her bill, she stood with more confidence. The feeling of being watched didn't bother her, assuming it was one or all of the men who'd wanted to buy her a drink. At the door, she remembered her life wasn't all sunshine and roses, and stopped before she exited. There was still crazy people out there. She'd never again take life for granted, and that meant safety first.

Fishing her keys out, eyes alert for danger, Alexa began walking paying attention to her surroundings. The well-lit parking lot was filled to maximum capacity with cars parked all around her little Honda. A big truck was too close for comfort on the driver's side, but on the passenger side there was a smaller compact that had a clear view inside. On instinct, she went around to that side and climbed over the console. "I may look like an idiot shimmying over the bucket seats, but I feel much better." Again, she realized she was talking to herself and hit the automatic locks as she started the car.

The food and events of the past few weeks began to catch up with her as she drove, yawning she missed her turn, but shrugged, glad she'd mapped out alternate ways home earlier. It took an extra ten minutes, and she was actually glad to pull up and have the valet guy there. She wondered how many hours he worked in one shift, then figured he was probably ready to clock out.

"Would you like me to help you unload your things onto a cart before I take this down to the garage?"

Alexa looked at his name tag before answering. "I don't have a lot, but I'd really appreciate that, Blake, thanks."

His smile seemed forced, but again she figured it was due to him ready to end his shift. She opened the glove box and pushed the button for the trunk while Blake went to get the roll cart. Damn, he had a mighty fine ass. Alexa pocketed her keys and walked to the back of the car, intent on helping him.

"I got this," Blake said.

His rude tone made her ire rise. "Listen, buddy. I can get my own shit, if you just stand back, then I'll hand you my keys and you can park the fucking car, or I can do that, too."

91

"Whoa, chill. I didn't mean to upset you." Blake held up his hands.

She reached in for one of the used suitcases she'd packed before leaving Chicago. "You didn't upset me, I'm just done putting up with jackholes is all."

Blake chuckled. "I think we'll get along just fine. I'm truly sorry. I sorta got my ass chewed out earlier, and I took it out on you. My sincere apology. Now, let me get these for you." He took the last two bags and set them on the cart.

Alexa stared at his palm as he held it out, finally realizing he was waiting for her keys. "It's fine. We all have bad days. Just try not to take it out on the innocent next time."

A strange look passed over his face and then was gone. "Will do. I'll push this in and JoJo can help you up with them while I park your car."

"I got it. No need for you to..." she trailed off as Blake ignored her, pushing the lock button on her car and walked into the building with her things. Too tired to complain, she followed after him.

"Yo, JoJo, our girls back and has her stuff. You need to take it up for her. She looks ready to fall flat on her beautiful face." Blake winked over his shoulder.

Throwing up her hands in defeat, she watched JoJo stroll out of an office, his short hair looking perfectly styled and grabbed the cart from Blake. "Welcome back. I hope you found what you needed, Alexa."

"Oh, yeah. All is good. I can make it to work tomorrow with no problems."

JoJo nodded, but he looked as strained as Blake had. Again, she figured they were both ready to get off of work.

The usually chatty guy, or at least she thought he was usually chatty was quiet on the way up. A pensive expression on his too handsome face. When he didn't seem inclined to talk she stayed quiet until they reached her door. "Thanks, JoJo. Have a good night."

"I'll help you unload and then take the cart back down with me."

She unlocked the door, holding it while he pushed her luggage inside, gazing around the space. "Do you need anything else?" He asked.

"I'm going to shower then hit the hay."

"Sounds like a solid plan. Have a good night."

She stared at his back, the stiffness in his shoulders very expressive.

"Be sure and lock your doors. Although this is a secure building, we still tell our tenants it's better to be safe than sorry." He gave a brief smile and wave, standing out in the hallway.

Alexa hurried to the door, wanting to smack her forehead, and did as he said. She assured herself she'd have locked all the locks, and for good measure she pulled one of the chairs from the dining room in front of the door, and lodged it under the handle. If someone was intent on getting in, they'd have a hard time getting past all that.

Inside her bedroom she unpacked her bathroom bag and opened her suitcase, pulling out an outfit that didn't need ironing. A quick shower later, and then she was climbing between the cool sheets. She prayed her sleep would be uninterrupted. Since her attack, it was a toss-up if she'd sleep a full night, let alone if she'd be plagued with nightmares. One of the great things about ma'am and her training was she felt marginally better about taking care of an attacker. Not much, but a little bit. At least now she knew where to strike for maximum damage.

Rolling over, she punched her pillow, an image of the tall dark man who'd captivated her appeared in her vision. Kai Swift. He was every woman's dream come to life, or at least hers. He reminded her of Jason Momoa and the Rock mixed together, and holy shit didn't that just make her all tingly inside. Rolling back over she tried to erase the image of him. A man like that wouldn't want a damaged woman like her.

What seemed like hours later, she finally fell into a dream filled sleep.

****

Kai entered the apartment building, knowing Alexa lived just a few stories up did nothing to calm him. Since finding Dex's number in Jase's phone, Tay had been working nonstop, digging into the other man's life. What they found didn't set off any of their radars, yet something wasn't right. He wouldn't do anything until he met with the other team, and assess them for himself. Jase could have fabricated the entire thing. A sort of red herring just to throw them off, or to fuck with their minds. One thing the man was clearly good at was mind fucking them.

"How's it going, JoJo?" Kai eyed the shorter man.

JoJo met his stare. "I'm level, man. You?"

His respect for the other man went up a notch. "Good to hear. Where's your partner?" He'd expected to see Blake out front acting as a doorman. That was his cover for the op, and was a little displeased when the other man was nowhere to be seen.

"He wasn't outside?" JoJo stepped around the counter.

Instantly Kai's stance changed to battle ready.

"Dude, I ain't stupid." JoJo raised his hands. "Blake was outside just ten minutes ago. Check the feed if you don't believe me."

Tay looked to Kai for permission before stepping around them. "Why weren't you watching his back?"

Kai waited for him to answer Tay's question, watching both men's expressions.

"I got a call from Mad. He said Dex was sick, so it was just he and Hailey today trailing after Ms. Gordon. I said that was fine. She was at the Steinem building and figured she'd be safe there. If she left they were to call me. I had just hung up when you walked in. Less than ten minutes had passed since the last time I talked to Blake. Now, have you found anything on the fucking feed, man, or do I need to look?" JoJo's voice had taken on a shaky quality.

Recognition hit Kai. JoJo and Blake were more than just partners on a team. "Find anything, Tay?"

"You ain't gonna like it, Cap, but we got a problem." Tay turned the monitor around for Kai to see. A figure dressed in black walked up behind Blake. The man was a couple inches taller than their operative, and with a needle in hand shoved it into his neck. Within seconds, Blake dropped onto the concrete, his head smashing without a care.

JoJo whimpered. "Shit, I need to find Blake."

Kai didn't wait to see anymore, he strode out the door, the pooling blood still warm. "Fuck it all."

Tay stood over him guarding his six, while JoJo squatted next to him. "From the video he was lifted and taken back around the corner, then thrown into a van. So fucking cliché, man."

Anxiety laced the other SEAL's words. However, Kai wasn't sure if he trusted them or not. He reached over and squeezed his shoulder. "We'll get him back. Tay, pull up the cameras surrounding the building." Standing, he dialed Commander Lee, walking a few paces away conscious there could be a sniper in any of the buildings surrounding them. "Sir, we have a problem." In as few words as possible, he outlined the situation. With a promise of backup, Commander Lee hung up.

Dialing Oz, Kai waited for the other man to answer, then quickly called Coyle.

"Hey, Cap. Don't have time to talk right now." Coyle's deep baritone voice sounded strained.

"What's going on?" Kai went back inside. "Lock it down, boys." He motioned to JoJo, watching his expression at being ordered around.

"I'm afraid we got some issues on the inside here. Oz is down, but Sully has him. Gotta go."

The sound of tires squealing and gunshots could be heard.

To give him credit, JoJo nodded, quickly pressing buttons. The snick of locks going into place were reassuring.

Tay looked up from his laptop. "I got the van. They dumped it about two blocks from here. Two figures got out. I'm guessing they left Blake inside. Let's go."

"You're coming with us. Any stupid moves, kid, and I'll kill you without blinking an eye. Feel me?" Kai didn't raise his voice, letting the threat show in his eyes. He'd killed many in the name of his country and if he had to kill a fellow officer, he'd hate to do it, but he'd do it.

"Trust me, I'll kill for Blake. We're on the same side, Captain." JoJo shrugged out of the suit jacket he wore as a concierge, leaving him in the fitted black shirt and slacks.

Kai and Tay had on their fatigues, looking much more suited for the operation, but knew JoJo was every bit as much up for the task as them. He nodded and waved him forward. "You got a rig?"

"Oh, yeah."

They followed out the side and into the garage, looking each way before entering. All three slid out silent as wraiths. The midnight Hummer wasn't exactly going to blend, but Kai approved none the less. The blacked out windows would keep any from seeing who was inside, but he paused as did Tay.

JoJo sighed. "Fuck, you are some untrusting ones."

"You've no clue. Open the doors, and make it quick. Times a ticking." Kai waited, his gun in hand, with Tay at his back.

"Keys." Kai held his hand out.

"Dammit. Why can't I drive?" JoJo groused but handed them over.

"Let's go. I have the coordinates. What's going on with our team?" Tay climbed into the back, his phone in hand.

"Oz is hurt, but Sully has him. Coyle is in pursuit of the shooter. Get a lock on him while you're at it." Kai swore under his breath. This was supposed to be an easy in and out mission. Check up on the girl and find the bad guy. What was so important about Alexa Gordon?

He followed Tay's directions, finding the van in the alley he'd seen on the footage was easy. Kai scanned the perimeter before getting out. "Tay, I want you on my six. JoJo, I need you to stay here until we know what we're facing."

"Fuck that. He's my partner."

"Which is why you will stay here and guard our backs. Don't argue, JoJo." Kai pushed open the door at the same time as Tay, their guns were out as they approached the vehicle. As Kai looked around, Tay ran a bomb detector along the entire van. "It's clear," Tay announced.

Finding the back doors locked didn't surprise them, what did was the lack of tinting. He could see the downed Blake lying inside, his chest moving up and down, but the amount of blood pouring from his head worried him. "Call for a bus," Kai yelled over his shoulder.

He and Tay made eye contact, then with efficiency, he got the door open. Tay stayed outside, back to the vehicle while Kai climbed in. He felt a pulse, thready but there. A glance around Blake's body and he found no other wounds, but they weren't sure what had been injected into him. "He's alive, but we need to get him out of here."

The inside of the vehicle had been hollowed out except for the two bucket seats in the front, making Kai wonder why they'd abandoned it.

Sirens getting louder had Kai hopping down. "Damn it. We don't have time to waste. JoJo, I need you to stay with Blake."

JoJo nodded. "Yes, sir."

The operative did as told without argument, meaning he cared more for his downed team member, or it was a testament to the fact he was dirty. Either way, Kai figured they'd find out sooner rather than later.

"I'll return your rig when we can."

Again, JoJo nodded.

Kai and Tay climbed into the Hummer, making tracks to the building where his own team was. "You realize this has become a shitfest, right?"

Kai turned the corner, passing an ambulance in route.

"Yep. Think that was a set up?" Tay tilted his head backward.

"Well, if it was, they fucked their own guy in the process, and JoJo was a supreme actor. Like Oscar material. I tagged both men, so we can keep tabs on them."

"What about Lee, can we trust him?"

The Commander was the highest ranking officer, but for Jase Tyler to have escaped from a federal prison, he had to have had help. At the very least, Kai needed to think anyone could have been in on it. He and his teams lives depended on him being prepared for all situations.

"We will trust him until we can't. For now it's us five, and keeping Lee abreast of the situation as well." Using the voice command on his phone, he had Commander Lee's secretary on the line moments before they pulled into the underground car park across from the Steinem Building.

"What the hell is going on? I got a call from A1 Apartments informing me you locked it down, and that one of the other team members is down, and enroute to the hospital. This was supposed to be a covert op, not a mission our entire nation is gonna hear about."

He pinched the bridge of his nose. "Commander, this was not what I wanted either. I'm calling to apprise you of the situation. I'll give you an update when I have one, sir."

"Status?"

The barked order made Kai want to tell the man to go fuck himself, but self-preservation won out. In as few words as possible, leaving out his emotions, he explained what happened, and what they knew.

"Is the woman in league with Tyler?"

Kai met Tay's eyes before answering. "That is what we plan to find out, sir. I'll keep you abreast of what we find. You need to send backup to the hospital. This was a professional hit on Blake. We need to know what the hell we're facing. Tyler may have his hands a lot deeper than we'd initially thought." Kai wished he could see the Commander's face when he dropped that bombshell.

"I've already figured that out, soldier."

To be called soldier, was taking him down a couple notches. Or, he was reminding Kai he was in charge. Either way, Kai didn't give the man the satisfaction of a response. Silence tended to unnerve most people.

"Keep me updated, and for fucksake, don't blow up anything we can't blame on a natural god damn disaster." Commander Lee hung up.

Tay laughed as he slapped his thigh. "I hate that asshole."

Grunting, Kai pulled the rig into the underground garage, using the access badge they'd secured the day before.

"Can you locate our girl's car under all this concrete?"

Tay gave him a droll look as his finger was already moving over his computer. "Childs play, Captain."

He listened to the directions his friend gave him, locating Alexa's little Honda amongst the expensive vehicles. Kai gazed around the packed lot, finding a larger space near the elevator, and backed into the spot with the rear end as close to the concrete wall as possible. He made sure he and Tay had enough room on both sides to get in and out easily. They were always prepared for any situation.

"Let's try to get in and out without anyone seeing us."

Tay looked at both their attires, then raised his blond brows. "Kai, we're in fatigues. Pretty sure everyone in there is in suits."

"Shit, you know what I mean."

Raising both his hands, Tay smiled. "Hey, Oz and Coyle are the ones who like to shoot first. I always make friends."

Kai grunted as he opened the door, scanning the parking area.

"I won't remind you of that one time in Belize."

"Now, that is just rude. I don't bring up all the times you've..." They both went quiet as the elevator pinged.

He and Tay slid along the side, becoming as silent as mice, watching two women get off and walk down the rows of cars, disappearing out of sight. They waited until they couldn't hear or see either before moving toward the elevator. Using the access card, they stepped inside and pushed the button for Alexa's floor.

Nerves jumped in his stomach, but he assured himself it was from anticipating the thrill of the mission, and nothing to do with seeing the woman again.

Each man stood on one side of the elevator, using the small bit of the opening as protection. Kai was the first to step out once he felt sure there was no imminent danger to him or his teammate. The young woman at the front desk didn't spare them a glance, and Kai took note of her name and appearance. Tay's unobtrusive picture taking went completely unnoticed as well, making Kai shake his head. How the hell this was supposed to be a secure building he had no clue.

Tay shrugged, strolling after Kai. "That was too fucking easy, man."

"Yeah. My neck is itching."

Never a good sign.

"Think the girl is in on it. Our girl, not just the girl at the desk?" Tay tilted his head to the side.

Kai's gut said no, but he hadn't made it to thirty-one years of age by not thinking of all possibilities. "There are no metal detectors. No security guards. And the chick at the desk didn't even look up. I mean her conversation was about her boyfriend, but still..."

The offices they passed had glass walls with the doors open. Most were occupied, and the occupants paid no mind to them as they passed.

"She's in the large open area at the end. Sounds like it's full of civilians. Feel like doing a remake of the movie where you sweep her off her feet and whisk her off into the sunset?" Tay whispered.

"I'm not in the right outfit." Kai stopped at the front of the area, scanning over the partitions, looking for one dark haired beauty with amethyst eyes. The cubicles were chest high, but from his vantage he could see most everyone. After a few seconds, he found the one he was searching for, and began to move in her direction. Whispers started, but he and Tay ignored them.

****

Alexa stared at her screen. She wasn't sure how she could stretch out the work to last a full eight hours without going crazy. Her boss had said she could bring a book in to read surreptitiously, and for that she was grateful. Tonight she'd head to the library and check out a few. She loved to read, but hadn't had time or money to do so in a long time.

She smiled as she thought of the ones she hoped would be available. An increase in noise had her looking up, but the three walls around her kept her from seeing anything. The others had decorated their little spaces with family photos, making her ache for things she didn't have. Alexa pushed aside old hurts and concentrated on what she'd do to make her cubicle more cheerful.

Realizing people were getting more excited, she rolled her chair to the entrance and looked out, nearly falling over backward when she saw the last man she'd ever thought to see again, striding toward her. His long legs eating up the space like he owned it.

God, he was gorgeous with a capital G. Alexa licked her lips, and realized he was coming right to where she sat ogling him. It took her a minute to bring her eyes up to his face. Damn it she had to stop drooling. His own dark eyes were fierce as they took her in.

Why the hell was he angry? "Hello, guys. What can I do for you?" Alexa was proud she didn't stutter once.

Kai blinked. "We need to speak with you in private, Ms. Gordon."

She sat frozen as he stopped a couple inches from where she sat. With his legs braced apart, his arms held loosely at his side, he made quite the intimidating picture. "Um, I don't know."

"That wasn't a question, but a statement, Alexa," Kai said.

Hell, she wasn't sure what to do or say. Her first thought was *Yes, sir. May I have another?* But that seemed totally inappropriate, especially when he looked ready to do serious harm to her person. "There's a break room around the corner."

Alexa waited until he took a step back, then stood up. She straightened her pencil skirt, grabbed her purse from under the desk and then led the way, feeling both men's eyes on her the entire way.

Once inside, she placed a table between them. "Okay, what's going on? Did Danny contact you? Is he back? Oh, god, did he do something to Marley?" Her knees got weak thinking of the only woman who'd ever helped her.

"No on all accounts," Kai answered.

"Thank you, Jesus. Then why are you here?" She placed her palm over her heart, feeling like it was about to pound out of her chest.

"What do you know about Jase Tyler?" Kai fired the question at her.

That was the last thing she'd expected him to ask her. "I've already told you everything I know about him the last time you questioned me. What has he done now? Who is he? I mean I thought he was Ma'am's number one thug?" She shrugged. "He was nice enough, but always watchful. I don't think he actually liked the leader, but they worked together. I tried to stay out of both of their way, and do as I was told. I wasn't there long enough to know more than that."

"Did you ever talk to him?" Kai placed his hands on the table, bringing his face closer to hers.

Alexa reared back. "Listen, I don't know what you think happened there, but I was not in the know on anything. I was lucky to survive with my life." She hated that her voice quivered. Hated that they were bringing back memories she was trying to bury.

Kai turned away. "That man is a traitor to our country."

She swiped a tear away. "Seriously? He seemed nice. I mean..." She stopped at the fury blazing from both Kai and Tay's faces. "Hey, I don't know his history. All I have to go on is the fact he stepped in and saved me when Ma'am almost beat me for not keeping up in an exercise training the second day. Do I have Stockholm syndrome? Hell, I don't think so, but who the hell knows. I'm pretty sure I need a therapist, but you are not one, so leave me alone please." She collapsed in a chair, glad one was behind her.

"Kai, let's look at it from her side here. She has been through a lot in a short time." The other man said.

"Leave her alone? Her life, our lives may depend on something she may not even know she is aware of. I'm sorry, Ms. Gordon, but you're going to have to come with us."

She looked up to see Kai had walked around the table and now stood right in front of her. She had to stop taking her eyes off the big man. Shaking herself out of the stupor she regained her feet. "Listen, I'm a U.S. citizen, and as such, I have rights. You can't just waltz in here and take me away without my consent." There, that made her feel better. She wasn't out in the middle of nowhere on some property where no one would hear her screams for help.

The blond shut the door and she recognized the danger she was in. Two larger than life men in military fatigues had walked right past the security of the car park, past the front desk lady, who admittedly wasn't very attentive, and up to her little cubicle. She'd not only voluntarily took her purse and walked away with the two men, they looked very official and intimidating. Alexa couldn't imagine anyone stopping to question them if they took the new girl out, even if she was protesting loudly. What was the saying? Out of the frying pan and into the fire?

She had to keep her senses about her, and try to get out of this situation alive. Having survived two terrible attacks, surely she hadn't made it out of them, only to be killed now.

"We aren't here to kill you damn it," Kai growled.

Did she say that out loud? "How the heck am I supposed to believe that? You come in like two beasts, drag me back here demanding answers to things I don't know, and then tell me I'm to go with you. Like that should make me have the feel goods." She sniffed, wiping her arm across her nose and hating that she was too scared to reach into her purse for a napkin.

"I'm truly sorry for scaring you, and for what it's worth, you're safer with us, than left here. If what you're saying is true, then you could be a target. Jase Tyler used to be one of our team members, and for some reason you are on his radar. Now, we could leave you here, and hope we're wrong, but in my experience, I haven't been wrong often." Kai folded his massive arms over his chest. In his cargo pants and tan T-shirt with the huge knife strapped to his thigh along with the black belt holding a multitude of weapons around his waist, he made a very intimidating picture.

Tay grunted, making her eyes jerk to his. She saw an odd expression flash in his blue orbs, then it was gone in an instant. Both men wore matching outfits, but Kai was darker, more, in her mind. She thought it was because he was the leader.

"So, are you coming willingly, or do I need to knock you out and carry you like a sack of potatoes? Trust me, I've carried men out of war-torn countries on my shoulders for miles, and never broke a sweat. I won't have a problem doing it to you through a busy office. Besides, Tay says your co-workers might find it romantic if they think I'm a suitor."

Alexa was sure her jaw was hanging open. "Are you saying I'm fat?"

Kai unfolded his arms. "Where the hell did you get that idea?"

Tay shrugged his shoulders. "You've got me, captain. You dug that hole, I'll let you get yourself out of it."

"You just said carrying a man for miles was no problem, so carrying me for a short distance wouldn't be. Hence, I must be fat." She poked him in the chest, feeling the rock hard pecs beneath her finger. "That is rude, buddy."

"I didn't mean it that way, I was just pointing out I could and would do it without a problem. You are so far from...what I mean to say is, I think your form is perfect." He grabbed her finger, holding it between his own.

She could feel the warmth of his body in that one touch. "Well next time think before you talk."

He nodded. "Yes, ma'am."

The way Kai's lips kicked up at the corners let her know he was fighting a smile, and she swore he was the most handsome man she'd ever seen. Hands down, he was gorgeous from his dark hair and eyes, to his ripped body. She wondered if she could wrap both hands around one of his biceps, and knew she couldn't.

"I need to tell my supervisor I'm leaving. I don't want to lose my job on my first day. Oh god, what if I get fired? I can't get fired." Standing so close she inhaled Kai's scent, panic setting in.

"You won't get fired. I'll make sure your boss is taken care of," Kai swore.

"We need to move," Tay said looking at his phone.

Alexa had forgotten about the other man as she was almost on top of Kai. Her hand was still clasped in Kai's and felt heat crawl up her cheeks. "Sorry," she muttered taking a step back. The chair behind her made her stumble, but Kai's quick reflexes kept her on her feet.

"Easy. When we walk out of here, I want you between Tay and I. I'll lead, with Tay taking up the rear. I don't want you to look around. Keep your eyes on my back, and don't speak to anyone. Try to look relaxed, and normal. Can you do that? When we reach the garage, I want you to stay with Tay while I look around to make sure it's safe to come out. Follow all my orders without question. Got it?" He tipped her chin up to his face.

"What if someone talks to me?" Alexa bit her lip.

"Do you know anyone yet?"

She thought about it and shook her head.

Kai nodded. "Then nobody should stop to chat. If they do, then smile and say you are heading out for lunch. I'll do the rest of the talking. Just smile and agree with what I say."

She sucked in a breath and prayed she could do as they told her. "Okay, let's do this."

Tay patted her shoulder. "Don't worry. We've done this before."

"You've kidnapped a woman from her office?"

"Yep," Tay said.

Alexa wasn't sure if he was serious and was too nervous to ask.

"I just sent an email to her boss. He is in a meeting, but his secretary has replied with an okay." Tay opened the door, looking both ways before holding it for Kai.

It was surreal and a little like she was in a movie. She wasn't sure if it was a horror flick, but she was sure she wasn't cut out to be a heroine.

"Come on, we got you." Kai reached for her hand.

His reassuring touch did funny things to her.

Chapter Five

Kai looked around for signs of his team, wondering where Coyle was. He knew Oz had been shot and that Sully had gone with him. The other team was an unknown. Dex, Hailey and Mad were somewhere, and he didn't trust any of them. He and Tay had purposely made it sound and look as though they were alone as they'd come into the building. Whoever had shot Oz would think they only had two men left to take out. Big mistake. Coyle was just like his name, coiled and ready to strike at any given moment. Kai could feel his teammate watching, waiting, ready to pounce when needed.

They made it to the reception desk, the young woman was on the phone again, her conversation animated. Kai's ears picked up her side of the conversation, but he didn't take for granted it was one hundred percent real. His life depended on being cynical. He watched her eyes dart to the side, looking at them without turning her head. Using his right hand, he signaled to Tay, letting him know she was communicating with someone.

He pressed the button to the elevator, then decided to take the stairs. Having his back to the open area, and not knowing who could be coming out of one of the three enclosures made them sitting ducks.

"Damn, I could use some exercise. How about you?" Kai strode toward the stairs, not waiting for his companions to agree, keeping Alexa's hand in his.

Inside the stairwell, he turned to Tay. "This is a clusterfuck of epic proportions. They'll be expecting us to go down. Do you have the layouts of the building?"

"There's a rooftop with a place for employees to get some fresh air and shit. We could easily get down from there if she's not scared of heights, however, I don't think it would go unnoticed as this building is all glass." Tay pointed out.

Mind made up, Kai started down. "Stay right behind me. I need both hands free, but if you need to hold onto my shirt go ahead. If we encounter anyone, just hug the wall."

"I'm scared."

Alexa's whisper hit him in his solar plexus. He'd been in the military for too long he'd forgotten what it felt like to be scared. Seen countless faces of men, women, and children with fear etched on their dirt streaked expressions. Yet, hearing true worry on the woman he was forcing into a situation that could very well end her life, made him stop in his tracks. "On my honor, I'll protect you with my life."

She swallowed audibly. "I'll try not to scream."

They reached the bottom level, and his internal radar was perking up.

"Stay here with Tay. I'm going to scope out the situation. If I'm not back in five, you take her back out the front, make all kinds of noise and get attention. You feel me?" Kai met Tay's eyes.

"I've got your six, Cap."

Kai slipped out the door, knowing there were probably eyes on them. He'd seen cameras in the stairwell as they'd come down. The over fifteen minutes of wasted time it had taken to get Alexa to agree to go with them, gave their enemies a heads up, but Kai had faith in himself and Tay. Once he was sure their vehicle hadn't been tampered with, he motioned for Tay and Alexa to come out. They'd taken a couple steps, when the sound of feet shifting off to his right had him throwing Alexa onto the concrete floor. He rolled so he took the brunt of the fall. A bullet whizzed past his shoulder by mere inches. He gave the woman in his arms credit when she didn't scream, her body going with his, allowing him to maneuver them further into the protection of another vehicle.

"How many shooters, Tay?" Kai was sure he'd only heard the echo from one, but several shots had been fired at him and Alexa as he'd rolled, one had hit his thigh, but he didn't let it slow him.

"Just the one I think. I'm going to lay out a line of fire. Get Alexa to the rig. I'm right behind you."

More gunshots rang out. If Kai didn't think the authorities were aware something was going on, they would be soon. He heard a grunt, and hoped like hell it wasn't Tay who'd been hit. "I need you to stay low, and follow me. See that black Hummer?" At her nod, he continued. "That's our car. I'm going to need you to get in and do it quick. Feel me?"

Big scared eyes blinked up at him. "Yeah. I can do that."

"Good girl. Let's go. Stay low." He tucked her hand into the back of his pants. He had a feeling she needed something to hang onto.

Reaching the driver's side, Kai opened the back door and lifted Alexa into the back, then got into the front. He fired the engine, exhaling when Tay jumped into the passenger seat. "Yeehaw. I think I got the fucker, but I'm sure it was just a surface wound."

More shots rang out, pinging off their rig as he roared out of the garage. "At least we won't owe JoJo for windows. Smart man getting a bullet proof vehicle. Make contact with Oz. I need to know how he's doing and where he's at."

"I'm assuming we aren't going back to the apartment building?"

Kai looked at Tay, his eyes narrowed. "This is much larger than we'd thought."

"Sweets, can you hand me my laptop?" Tay turned in his seat.

"I want to go home now please." Her voice broke.

"You're doing great, Alexa." Kai looked at her in the rearview mirror. "Just a little longer and we'll have you somewhere safe."

Fuck, he didn't know how to tell her he had no idea where that somewhere was at the moment. An image of Rowan's hunting cabin popped into his head. Their former team member could be counted on, and Kai was sure he wasn't using the place. He was also sure Jase Tyler wouldn't know about the cabin. They needed to dump the vehicle they were in and get one that wasn't potentially tagged by the traitor.

"Contact Rowan. I think he and his new family can help us out."

Tay dialed Rowan, putting the phone on speaker. "This is Shade, and this had better be an emergency. I'm busy making babies."

"Oh my gawd, you can't answer the phone like that." A woman's high pitched voice interrupted Rowan.

"The hell I can't. We were busy. What's up, boys?" Rowan's deep voice asked.

Kai laughed. "It's good to know you haven't lost your sense of humor. Tell Lyric I said hello."

"She can hear you. What did I tell you about flirting with my wife?" Rowan laughed at something Lyric must've done.

"We got a problem," Kai said then explained in a few short sentences what they needed. He waited for Rowan to ask questions, not surprised when none came.

"I'll have a vehicle waiting for you at the gas station outside of town with the keys to my cabin inside. You'll need to stop and get some groceries and shit. Other amenities are all stocked up."

"I'm going to leave this rig there. Can you have someone look it over and tell me if there's a tracker on it?"

Rowan's deep chuckle had Kai missing him on their team. "Y'all don't even know what I have available here. Kellen and Xan have a garage that tricks out custom cars and shit. You should see their Knight XV Urban Assault vehicles. I want one."

Kai was sure he heard Rowan whimper. "Now that you're a civilian get yourself one. Thanks for doing this. I'll repay you."

"Of course you will. Alright, I got to get off here. If you need me to get you square, holler."

The line went dead before he could find out anything more. "He'll hook us up."

"You need a medic?" Tay indicated the blood on Kai's leg.

Looking down, Kai dismissed the injury. "I'll deal with it when we stop."

A gasp from the backseat pulled his attention to the woman they'd commandeered, or kidnapped from the Steinem building. She'd been a trooper, but he could see the glassy look in her eyes, and was sure she was in a state of shock. The petite young woman had been through a lot in her young life. He'd read her file. At twenty-seven years of age she'd been beaten to near death, then held for weeks in a compound with a crazy woman after being chased down by the same bastard who'd nearly killed her. Now, she was being targeted again, and he didn't know why. Was she in Jase's sights because of her time at the compound, or something else?

Whatever the reason, Kai couldn't let her out of protection, or guard, until they figured out what was going on.

"Hey, it's nothing. I've had worse when I've shaved on the field." He tried to put her at ease.

"I'm so tired of blood and gore. Just damn tired." She closed her eyes.

He could see exhaustion lining her features, wanted to wrap her up in his arms and tell her it would be over tomorrow, but didn't want to lie.

"Close your eyes. You're safe, luv." Tay stared at him as he murmured the endearment, but he ignored his teammate.

Even before he finished talking she'd leaned her head back and closed her eyes. He kept his focus on the road in front of him, and the traffic behind him.

"Coyle and Oz are safe. I've sent them a message about what went down. They'll rendezvous when the heat cools. They're keeping their eyes on the others." Tay's words were barely above a whisper.

The short trip down was made in silence, save for the tapping of Tay's fingers on the keyboard of the computer. Pulling into the small gas station, he scanned the area for anything that looked out of place. Rowan leaned on the side of a large pickup dressed in a pair of cargo pants and a ribbed tank top, leaving his huge arms bare. At six foot three, the man was an impressive figure to be sure. The tiny woman standing next to him was a surprise that Kai didn't think he'd ever see. A SEAL, especially Rowan, bringing a female on a mission was a shock. He had to remind himself that the other man was no longer part of the team officially.

As they rolled to a stop, he saw both stand straighter, their heads lift and look around. Kai trusted Rowan, but still drove around, making sure he didn't get any bad feelings. If his neck started to itch, friend or no, he was making tracks.

Alexa jerked up when he came to a stop, her gaze scanning the station. Fear clear in her entire body language. He wanted to reach over and reassure her, but Rowan and his woman were waiting.

"Stay inside until I give the all clear," he said a little more gruffly than he liked.

Rounding the vehicle, he clasped hands with Rowan, then hugged Lyric, knowing it would make the other man growl.

"Stop feeling up my mate." Rowan's growl wasn't filled with true warning, but Kai released Lyric just the same.

He looked at the big truck and whistled. "You letting me have your baby, huh?"

A very animalistic growl came out of his old team member's throat. "No, I'm letting you borrow my rig. You fuck it up and you buy me a new one."

Kai nodded toward the Hummer. "Not sure if that's tagged, or what, but you can drive it while I hole up in your cabin."

Rowan nodded. "Kellen and his guys will make sure it's clean. Besides, I can guarantee nothing will get past the Iron Wolves."

Lyric patted his arm. "Let's get this show on the road. I don't like standing out here in the open like this."

Both Rowan and Lyric lifted their heads, and Kai got the distinct impression they were doing more than looking around. He waved for Alexa and Tay to move, watching Lyric's eyes flash for a moment. Yeah, they needed to move out.

"Load up. Tay, you take shotgun, Alexa in the middle."

He could see his orders made her pause in her confident strides, but she continued to the big pickup. Before Tay could help her into the front, Kai was there, giving her the boost into the tall cab. Again, he ignored the arch of one of Tay's blond brows.

"I packed a couple changes of clothes for your lady friend. I figured if y'all were anything like

Rowan, you didn't think about small things, like a girl's need for clean panties. Oh, and they are new. As big guy here, doesn't think I have a reason to wear them, even though I buy them all the damn time." Lyric's face lit up with obvious love for her mate.

****

Alexa swore her face was redder than a ripe tomato. "Thank you. I didn't even think about that."

"My name is Lyric, and trust me, us girls need to stick together."

She wasn't sure about that. Didn't have much luck in making or keeping friends, but the expression on the beautiful woman's face staring at her through the open door, made her think she could depend on Lyric. "Thank you for lending me your clothes. I'll make sure they get back to you."

Lyric waved her hand. "No need. Those are just some I don't wear anymore, except for the underwear, which I'm clearly not going to be wearing anytime soon."

Rowan grabbed Lyric and pulled her back to his chest. "I don't hear any complaints from you, darlin."

A shiver stole down her spine at the deep drawl from the large man. She could see the love the couple didn't try to hide zinging between them, and felt a stab of jealousy. All her life she wanted to be loved. Alexa gave a mental slap before reminding herself she was lucky to be alive.

"I do appreciate all you've done for me. All of you." Her eyes watered.

"Let's roll." Kai jumped into the driver's seat, making further conversation impossible.

Sandwiched between the two men with the heat of their bodies warming her, she felt as if all the air in the vehicle was being sucked out of her lungs. "Please roll the windows down," she gasped.

Kai's head turned toward her. "What's the matter?"

She pressed her hand to her throat, the tightness made it almost impossible to suck oxygen in.

"Shit, she's having a panic attack." Tay's voice sounded far off.

A hand on the back of her neck, and then pressure pushing her head between her legs was the last thing she expected.

"Breathe, baby. Everything's gonna be alright. I've got you."

His soothing voice and reassuring words almost made her laugh. Having her head between her knees while sitting between two gorgeous men, would be comical if she could get a deep enough breath in. Kai's big palm began massaging her back. She knew it was his, but didn't know how. Slowly, the ability to take air in and out became easier. God, she hated to show any weakness.

"Now I'm singing Bob Marley's song in my head." A giggle escaped her.

"I love that song. Of course, I promised the team we'd all vacation on a beach in Jamaica one day."

Tay snorted. "He improvised and had us all drinking pina coladas with umbrellas in a destination we can't tell you."

"Oh, really. I can't see you big bad SEALs drinking fru fru drinks like that." Alexa realized she was talking while still leaning over, and tried to sit up. Kai's hand pressed, then was gone. The thought he hated moving away from touching her was erased, when she looked at the stony visage of the man driving them.

"How far until we get to your friends place?" The side road they'd turned onto led them away from the city, deeper into what looked like the Black Hills.

"It'll be a bit. Why don't you rest your head on the back of the seat and get some sleep." Kai didn't take his eyes off the road.

She shook her head. "I couldn't even if I tried. Besides, this is gorgeous. I will probably never get a chance to road trip through this part of the country again." Hell, she wasn't sure if she'd live long enough to drive out of the location they were driving into. Yes, Kai and his team swore to protect her, but they were up against a man who seemed to be two steps ahead of them.

"Aw, luv, you'll get a chance to do anything you want. When this is over, I will make sure you can." Kai patted her thigh.

Alexa knew she shouldn't, but she needed to feel a connection. Her hand landed on top of his, holding him to her. Even with the other man in the vehicle, sitting right next to her, she entwined her fingers with his. To give Tay credit, he never looked up from the laptop he seemed to have connected to him.

If she could build a dream man, Kai Swift would be pretty damn near what she'd have chosen. He was gorgeous. Well built. But what she really loved about him was he didn't seem to realize he kept reassuring her in little ways, making sure she was comfortable. Seeing to her safety was part of his job, but he went above and beyond that. He didn't have to allow her to hold his hand, or rub her back when she was freaking out. She'd seen military shows and the detachment they were taught to display.

Kai was doing none of those things. Oh, she could tell he wasn't sure about what he was doing, but when he turned his hand around on her thigh, her heart nearly stopped.

The cabin they pulled up to was an amazing structure. The large A-frame home was two stories with floor to ceiling windows. A deck wrapped around three sides, but what amazed her was the fact it looked as though the front was pointed outward like a boat's bow, only all glass. She wondered how safe the home was, and if Kai was freaking out as well.

"Stay here with Tay while I make sure it's secure." Kai pulled his hand out from hers and exited before she could utter a response.

"He's usually a man of few words." Tay's fingers stilled.

"Um, okay." Staring at the front of the home, the anticipation for what she wasn't sure raced through her.

"You don't understand the significance of what I'm telling you, but you will."

Lights flared from the dark home.

"Knowing Rowan, this place is a fortress. I'd say we are gonna be as safe here as anywhere." Tay tucked the laptop away in a backpack.

"Rowan used to be a member of your squad? Was he hurt and left?"

"He was a member of our Team," he corrected her.

She waited for him to say more, thinking he'd explain, but as the silence stretched, it became clear he wasn't going to elaborate and she gave up. "Should you go check on him?" Waving toward the front of the vehicle, she screamed when the door next to her opened.

"Damn, you got a set of lungs on you." Kai's dark eyes twinkled.

Realizing she was plastered against Tay's side, she moved away from the blond man. "Why the heck didn't you knock on the window? Jesus, where did you come from?" She'd been watching out the front and hadn't seen him.

"Why didn't you lock the door when I left?" He quirked a brow.

Honestly, she hadn't thought of it. Going forward, Alexa promised herself she would lock, and double lock every door.

"Come on. Looks like Ro made sure everything is top notch." He held his hand out, making it clear he expected Alexa to go out his side.

Both men reached into the back and pulled out a few bags, but when she offered to help they gave her a droll stare. Being big bad SEALs meant they did all the heavy lifting. She'd have to show them her appreciation with some cooking.

"There are four bedrooms. Two on the main floor and two on the upper level. Alexa and I will take the two upstairs, while Tay will take one of the ones downstairs."

Tay nodded. "Sounds solid. I'm assuming Rowan left instructions in regards to his security, but I'm going to get into the mainframe and restructure it to meet my specs. I'll let him know when we leave. I can guarantee it'll be better than when we got here."

Alexa ignored the men and stared at the splendor of her surroundings. They'd entered through the front door, where she received her first sight of the grandest home. Staring at the fifty plus foot ceiling with a stone fireplace on one side, with an open floor plan that let her see all the way into the kitchen area, had her mouth hanging open.

"Damn, this place is a retreat, not his home?" She ran her hand over the butter soft leather furniture, stared at the other gorgeous pieces Alexa knew cost more than she'd make in ten years of working.

Kai shrugged. "In our line of work you learn to invest well. Come on, I'll show you to your room, and then we'll whip up some chow."

Breathe in and out and don't touch anything you might break, she mumbled to herself, following Kai up the stairs made of the same wood as the home. Almost too stunned at the prospect of staying there,

Alexa peered into the room he indicated. God, did they not make anything that wasn't overly large and expensive out here?

"Do I have time for a quick shower?" She waited for Kai to hand her the bag of stuff Lyric had given her, then walk away. While they stood there, time seemed to stand still.

He took a deep breath, bringing their chests closer. "Make it fast." He stepped past her, his confidant stride made her own legs wish for one iota of the same.

"Will do," she said staying by the door.

Kai placed the bag on the bed. "I'll see you downstairs."

She sucked in her tummy as he went out the door. It took her a few seconds to realize she was ogling his fine ass. At the top of the stairs, he glanced over his shoulder and winked. Alexa hustled into the room, slamming the door on his smirking face. Her only saving grace was he couldn't see how red her face surely was.

She tossed off her clothes on the way to the bathroom, expecting to find more wood like the rest of the house. What she encountered was straight out of Better Homes and Gardens. Remembering her promise to hurry, she opted for the shower when all she wanted was to hop in the tub made for three or four.

Chapter Six

Alexa dressed in her borrowed clothes, happy they fit, and grateful for the new underwear. The sound of men's voices could be heard from below, their banter made her smile. Again, she wished she'd had real friends. With resolve, she shook her hands out like a prize fighter entering the ring and skipped down the stairs. Scents of something heavenly hit her as soon as she entered the first floor.

"Sorry, I took too long. I planned to make you both dinner."

"Tay is a great cook. Besides, he lost at rock, paper, scissors." Kai leaned against the counter with a bottle of water in his hand.

"Wow, I'd have liked to have seen that. This smells great." She watched Tay flip burgers on the stove. "Can I make a salad or anything?"

Both men looked at her like she'd grown two heads. "My apologies ma'am, but we don't have the fixings for that. You can whip up some instant mashed potatoes if you'd like."

Her mouth threatened to drop open, but she controlled it. "I can do that."

After dinner she insisted on loading the dishwasher, while Tay did what they called a 'perimeter check'. She understood the need for such actions, but hated both men were willing to put their lives on the line for her.

"What's put that look on your face?" Kai's deep voice made her jump.

She chewed on her lip. "You guys do this sort of thing all the time, right?"

Kai nodded. "Although not in such nice accommodations. Or with such a gorgeous woman to protect."

Damn, did he have to say things like that to make her resemble a tomato? "How does this work? Can I go outside or am I stuck inside? I mean I don't want to be a bother, and I'm fine doing what you tell me."

The big man coughed, making her grab a bottle of water out of the fridge. "Here. Are you okay?"

Taking the bottle from her, Kai downed the drink before he responded. "Yeah, I swallowed down the wrong pipe."

His big brown eyes sparkled.

"This place is as secure as we can hope on short notice. There's even a panic room, which I didn't know about until you were in the shower. Rowan's given me the code. Follow me." He indicated the hallway near the room Tay was sleeping in.

She did her best not to stare at his ass, following him down the corridor, running her hands over the polished wood a sense of wonder fell over her. What would it be like to own a home of her own like the one she was being led through, flittered across her mind.

"I've reset the code to one only you, me and Tay know. That means, if something happens you lock yourself in here, and don't let anyone in. Period. Got me?" His military gear made him look totally in control, and ready to kick ass.

Shit, she needed to get her mind off his ass.

"Alright. Like I said, I'll do whatever you say." She swallowed, her throat all of a sudden seemed dry and she licked her lips for a second time, noticing the way he tracked her movements.

****

Kai felt his control snap. Watching her eat had been a test of his control, knowing she'd been naked just moments before had already set his body on fire. Now he wanted to trace her lips with his own tongue, wanted to see if she was as sweet as she looked. "Woman, you are testing my limits."

Alexa sucked her bottom lip into her mouth, making him growl.

"I don't mean to do..."

He pressed Alexa's back against the wall, bent his head and captured her lips with his. Hearing her moan had him reaching down with one arm and lifting her, letting her feel the hard press of his desire against her abdomen.

Pulling back he rested his forehead against hers. "You make me lose my head, luv."

"Pretty sure if we keep going I'll lose my borrowed panties." She nuzzled into his neck.

"That is no way to rein me in." He bit her earlobe.

She sighed. "You're the one tempting me."

He was sure it was both of them. There was something about Alexa that drew him to her like a moth to a flame. Without second guessing himself, he bent and took her lips in another kiss. Delving inside with his tongue, tasting the burger they'd had for dinner mixed with the glass of wine she'd had.

Her hands gripped his shirt pulling him closer, kneading his chest like a little kitten. Both his hands found her ass, lifting her up, and without words she wrapped her legs around his hips.

A noise alerted him to the fact they were no longer alone, and it took him longer than he liked to separate from the woman he held. He rubbed the moisture from their kiss into her mouth, wishing like hell Tay hadn't chose that moment to return. However, fucking their charge against the wall would be bad he told himself.

"I'm going to go stall Tay while you take a moment. I'm sorry for stepping over the line."

He turned away quickly, hating the hurt he saw in her strange colored eyes.

"Hey, it takes two to tango." She ducked her head.

Kai took great pleasure in seeing the rosy hue covering her face, and wanted to check for himself if it covered more of her body. "Baby, I want to do the horizontal tango with you." He turned before he could make good on his words. Her gasp wasn't one of outrage, and the telltale sign of her pebble hard nipples were a sure sign she was as turned on as he.

There was no way Tay wouldn't notice the signs as he rounded the room into the kitchen area, but the other man kept his back to Kai, rooting in the fridge for more water.

"Did you get her all sorted out with the safe room?"

Kai wanted to laugh, but suppressed it. "Yep, she's good to go. How did the perimeter look?"

"Rowan has cameras set up along with enough lights to light up a football field. There's early warning alarms set to go off if anything larger than a hundred pounds steps within 25 yards of the house, so unless someone is aware of the triggers, we should be good." Tay turned with a smile on his tan face.

Raising his middle finger, Kai flipped him the bird. "I'll take first watch, while you get some rest."

Tay shook his head. "I got first watch. I want to run some programs and do some upgrades on Rowan's security. I won't rest until I do, so you get some shut eye." He raised his bottle toward the entryway.

"Alright. You got first watch. I'm going to go up and shower then get a few hours' sleep. Ms. Gordon, what are your plans?" Kai asked without turning around.

"I think I'll turn in as well. I'm exhausted."

Kai finally turned to look at Alexa. His dick, which he'd finally gotten under control swelled at the sight of her swollen lips. He imagined those same lips traveling all over his body, and knew he needed to get away quickly. "I'm going to take a quick check around outside before I turn in. Goodnight, Alexa."

He strode past her without another word. Fuck!

Outside he took deep breaths, the scents of pine and fresh outdoor smells hit him. The cool breeze helped him gain some much needed restraint. Being around the petite woman was shredding everything he'd known about himself, and he wasn't sure he liked it.

Fifteen minutes later he walked up the back steps, entered the code and waited. When the red light flashed instead of green he panicked. He tried again and the flashing red had him taking a step back. The sound of the tumbler locks disengaging made him squint in the dark, his hand went to the gun at his side as he stepped next to the edge.

"At ease, Kai. I told you I was changing the codes so only you and I would know them. Although I trust Rowan, I don't trust anyone who may have had access to this place, or his computers." Tay's voice carried out the door.

"Damn it, Tay. You could've shot me a text or something. My first instinct was to shoot first and ask questions last." Kai stared at Tay, looking at the man still dressed in his fatigues.

Tay shrugged. "I didn't want to disturb you while you did a perimeter check. I figured you'd come back in the front."

He didn't like the way Tay had a knowing smirk on his tan face. His surfer boy good looks was enough to set Kai's nerves on edge, but he ignored the urge to punch him. "I'm going to get a few hours rest, and then I'll take over watch. Anything I need to know about?" He nodded toward the laptop open on the granite counter.

"Our guys are good. Should be here in the morning, early afternoon. No hits on Alexa, so either it was a fishing expo, or Tyler has cut his losses, or..."

Yeah, the last or was bothersome. They didn't have time to have her scanned for a tag, but she could very well have been like they'd done others. He voiced his concern, watching Tay's eyes widen.

"Shit, dude, what the hell we gonna do if that's the case?" Tay began to pace.

"We do what we do best. What's our code?" He waited a beat. "Failure is not an option."

Both he and Tay yelled "Hoorah" at the same time. He pulled Tay in for a back slap, then turned away. "Don't go outside while I'm sleeping. The windows are bulletproof. The only thing getting through the doors are major fire power, a big rig, or someone who knows the code. The first two I'll hear, the last, we are in a shit ton of trouble if it happens."

"Yes, dad." Tay saluted smartly, his middle finger tapping his forehead.

"No respect, asshole."

His actions were light, but Kai was secure in the knowledge Tay was guarding his and their... he wasn't sure what Alexa was to them, only that they were her protection detail. The fact Tyler had his sights on her made her their number one priority. He wasn't fooling himself that they were using her as a sort of bait, knowing their old team mate would follow where they took her. They only needed to find out why, and keep her safe in the process. He'd do his best to keep the fact she was being used by them as such, but the security of their country, his team was at stake. Besides, he reassured himself, they would make sure she was alive to live a long, healthy, happy life. Unlike what Tyler had plans to do. The bastard only cared for himself and what he could get out of things.

Up the stairs he paused outside the door to Alexa's room, then went across to his own. His duffel sat on the end of the bed with clean clothes. More of the same as what he was wearing. Grabbing out a clean pair of boxer briefs, he entered the ensuite and took a quick shower, leaning into the water he thought of Alexa across the hall. His body responded, and he looked down knowing he'd not get any rest with a hard on to rival a steel pole. "Good god, the woman is a menace," he growled, taking himself in hand. He made quick work of bringing himself off, images of Alexa's tiny hand doing the work, her gorgeous eyes looking at him so trustingly had him coming before he'd realized it.

Using the soap on the ledge, he washed up and got out, drying off Kai had just slipped on the briefs when he was sure he'd heard a woman's whimper. He grabbed his glock and was slipping out the door silent as a ghost.

Tay stood at the bottom of the steps, gun in hand.

Kai gave him a motion with his hands, easing inside the unlocked door. Lying on the big bed he could see Alexa thrashing with the moonlight spilling over the bed, highlighting her form. She cried out again, the sound had him hurrying to the side of the bed.

He flicked on the bedside lamp. "Alexa, wake up." Touching her bare shoulder, he felt her jerk.

Alexa's eyes popped open. "Oh, god." She scurried to the head of the bed.

The blanket lay at her knees, leaving her in a tank top and small pair of boy short panties. "It was just a dream. You okay now?" He began backing away.

"Don't go. Please stay." Her hand reached out.

He was not equipped, or more aptly he was completely equipped for this. "What do you need? I can get you a drink or something." He looked toward the open door.

"Could you sit with me for a little while?" Her voice quivered.

What the hell was he supposed to do? "Sure. Scoot over." Now, if his dick would just listen to his mind and stay down, he'd be fine.

Alexa breathed a sigh. "Thank you."

With his back against the headboard, Kai sat with Alexa and thought he was definitely getting brownie points for sainthood. Her shiver had him reaching down for the blanket she'd kicked off. When his palm brushed her smooth thigh, he pictured her naked in the shower using a razor and wanted to kick his overactive imagination. He tucked the blanket around them both, using it to hide his growing bulge and her cold form.

"Lay down and get some rest." The wood poles on the headboard dug into his back, but he ignored the pain.

"I don't think I can go back to sleep." She shivered. "How about we talk?"

Torture. That was what he was being put through. Hell, he'd been tortured, and still he thought he'd come out of it a lot easier than lying next to a half dressed Alexa. "What do you want to talk about?" He'd dated plenty, was actually good at drivel and shit.

"Where are you from originally?" She asked.

"My family originated from New Zealand, but I was born in Hawaii. I'm Polynesian if you hadn't guessed."

She turned to look at him. "Can you do the haka dance?"

He raised his eyebrows, shocked she knew what it was. "You a Rugby fan?"

Nodding, she licked her lips. "I love to watch the All Blacks."

Her actions made his cock jump, but her words made him smile. "The haka is the ancestral war cry, dance or challenge of the Maori people of New Zealand. The All Blacks are my favorite team as well. I love to watch them perform it before each game. Many New Zealand teams do it and other teams all over have begun doing it as well."

"Can you do it? The haka dance like them?" Her eyes sparkled.

Kai laughed. "It would be a matter of dishonor had I not learned it. My family is very big on tradition."

"I bet it was hard to learn," Alexa said looking away.

He knew she had no family traditions and cursed her family for leaving her. "Tomorrow I could teach you."

She brought her hands up to her chest, making his eyes zero in on the hardened tips. "That would be fantastic."

"You should get some rest," he murmured, preparing to get out of the bed. His control was barely on its tether.

Her hand grabbed his arm. "Could you stay with me? Just until I fall asleep."

The pleading in her trembling voice had him staying where he was. "Scoot down and get comfortable."

Saint Kai was definitely going on his uniform.

"Thank you," she said around a yawn.

Kai nodded and pulled a pillow behind him.

"You should lay down beside me. We can both rest in this bed. I mean we're adults, right?" Her clear eyed gaze showed him she had no clue he was hard as a rock beneath the blanket.

"Baby, you have no clue what you do to me." He warned her.

Her indrawn breath and quick look down at his lap showed the cover wasn't truly hiding his condition.

"It's kinda hard to hide something like that, but it's biological. We're adults and can ignore pesky things we can't control." She snuggled down and turned her back to him.

Pesky things his ass. Speaking of ass, hers was pointed right at him, and he swore it was the sweetest thing he'd seen. When he'd gripped it in his palms, she'd had more than a handful, and he'd loved it. He didn't want a skinny woman, and Alexa Gordon was definitely a curvy in all the right places.

"Fine, I'll ignore him if you can." Kai moved down to lay flat on the bed, sure he wouldn't get a wink of sleep.

Hours later, he woke with his hand gripping one firm breast and his hips cradling Alexa's. His dick he'd promised to ignore had wedged itself between her thighs, and he'd somehow been thrusting in his sleep. Hearing Alexa's moan, he quickly realized she wasn't unaffected by their sleep play.

Kai reluctantly lifted his hand away from her breast, but her hand grabbed his and put it back.

****

"Don't stop," she moaned.

"Woman, if I don't, I will be balls deep inside you in five minutes or less."

Alexa used the grip on his hand and pushed until he reached her mound. She was so turned on, she was sure it would take less than thirty seconds for her to come, let alone five minutes. "I don't care. I want you."

Kai groaned, his finger dipped beneath the fabric. "Damn you're wet."

Lifting her leg, she gave him room for his big hand. "What do you expect when I woke with a gorgeous man snuggled to my back, his hand playing with me, and his manly part rubbing against me?"

"Manly part? Luv, that is my dick, and he has wanted inside you since we first saw you." His hips moved the cloth covered appendage against her.

She closed her eyes and held the gasp inside as his fingers moved through her folds. "Do you always talk like he is a second person?" Alexa turned her head to look at Kai over her shoulder.

It was still dark out, but she knew the sun would be coming up anytime, the colors coming in through the windows proclaimed it as the time just before dawn, one of her favorite times of the day. She had always wanted to make love just before the sun rose, and figured if she had a target on her back, then Kai was just the man to do it with.

Reaching around her hip, she gripped his erection, moving her hand up and down his length. "I want you, Kai."

Indecision was written all over his face, but she wasn't willing to let him turn her down. She worked his briefs with one hand, freeing him from the fabric. Fluid leaked from the tip, and she spread it over the top, and continued to massage him. "Please don't make me beg. I could be killed today, or tomorrow. Heck, I should have died a few times already." Then a thought occurred to her that had her releasing him. "Oh, do you have a girlfriend? I'm so sorry." She flipped to her back, stopping when his big hand pressed on her stomach.

"No, I don't have a girlfriend. My hand wouldn't have been down your panties, playing with your pussy if I did. It's just..." He ran his hand across his jaw. "You're in an extreme situation. You just got out of two other situations. I don't want to take advantage of you." He blew out his breath.

Alexa laughed. "I am the one who was practically begging you, Kai. If you don't want me, just say so.

You don't have to make up excuses or whatever. I know I'm not supermodel perfect like your other women," she gasped as he loomed over her.

"You are beyond gorgeous. I love the way you fill my hands." His hands plumped her breasts. "Your ass was made to be held from behind while I pound into you. Or hell, while I held you against the wall and fucked you hard and deep. And your eyes are the most gorgeous I've ever seen. I was sure they were contacts, but they're real. I've never seen eyes that looked almost amethyst in color. I want to pull your briefs off and see if you're a natural brunette, or if that dark hair comes from a bottle. So don't tell me you're not the most gorgeous thing I've ever seen, because I can't remember ever thinking about any other woman I've met, let alone wanted to fuck as much as I've thought about you."

She was stunned speechless by his outpouring of words. "Really?"

Kai bent his head. "Yes, really." He licked her lips, then sealed his mouth over hers. There was no gentle exploration, but a marauder taking what he wanted, and she let him.

The sound of heavy footsteps interrupted them. Kai rolled off her, his hand grabbing the gun and pulling her onto the floor.

"Yo, Kai. Just thought I'd give you a heads up that the team will be here in less than ten minutes." Tay's voice floated through the open door.

Alexa giggled against Kai.

"Shit!" He helped her back onto the bed, but didn't join her.

"Um, do you think he heard us?" She looked up at him.

A blank stare was her answer.

"Kai, I'm sorry if I embarrassed you in front of your teammate." Without him next to her, she felt bereft.

"Hey, you didn't do shit. I let my guard down and I could have gotten you and I both killed. That's never happened. It can't happen on a mission." He tipped her face up to his.

She could see he was still hard, but was determined to ignore it, then she noticed the bandage peeking out from the bottom of his boxer briefs. "How's your leg?"

"Nothing more than a scratch. In a couple days I won't even know it was there." The gun was pointed toward the floor, the stark white bandage a reminder they were in danger.

Her throat was parched, but she didn't want him to think she was following him around. "I guess it's your turn to be up." It was a statement.

"Yeah. I'm going to go get dressed. If you need anything holler, otherwise try to get some more sleep. You aren't used to going on a few hours like we are. The rest of my team will be here soon and we'll have extra protection. When you feel up to it, come down and I'll introduce you."

Feeling like an idiot she nodded and watched him walk out the door. She counted to a thousand before she got up and went into her bathroom and got herself a drink from the sink. She kept the lights off just in case anyone was doing a perimeter check. The fact she even knew those words made her feel slightly nauseous. A bath sounded divine, but again didn't want to alert the others to her being awake.

Being super spy SEALs, they probably knew she was awake. Alexa looked at the huge bath, and then at the large windows over it with the view of the yard.

"Why do they always put them there for anyone to see in or out?" With the sun finally coming up she didn't really need the lights on in order to take a bath. The filling only took moments, long enough for her to grab a quick change of clothing, and then she was sinking into the warm water.

Her body still ached for Kai, which was unusual in itself. She wasn't a virgin, but she'd not had many lovers. In fact her two previous ones had been so long ago, she was practically a born again virgin. The first time was in high school. Senior year and she was tired of being the only one who seemed to be not doing it. A guy she thought liked her had finally asked her out, and while she'd been leery at first, he'd won her over. Ten years later she still cursed the jackhole, but her naiveté was really her undoing. She waited another three years, and again, thought that guy was the one. "Pfft, there is no one. You just settle for someone, or learn to take care of things yourself."

Alexa was tired of getting herself off, and with nothing but the memory of Kai's hand on her, she didn't feel the urge any longer. Washing in record time, hating that she couldn't even enjoy the luxurious tub, she climbed out. A glance out the floor to ceiling window overlooking the large yard, she wondered who was out doing the perimeter check.

The clothing fit her as if they were her own, but were much nicer than any in her own closet. The other woman clearly had great taste and money. Alexa shook her hair out, the dark mass was always a pain in the ass, but she couldn't bring herself to cut it off. As the sun rose higher she realized she was wasting time, and at some point she'd have to go down and face the music.

Taking a deep breath, Alexa walked out the door. The smell of bacon had her hurrying the final steps.

The men ringing the counter were all big and gorgeous. Each stood as she walked in, even though she hadn't made a sound.

"Alexa, it's good to see you're unharmed. How was your night?"

She wracked her brain for the correct name. The red haired man had actually been nice to her, while the big black man scared the crap out of her. Oz, his name came to her in a flash.

"It was uneventful, thank you for asking. How are you?" Alexa looked at the man for signs of his injury, knowing he'd been shot.

Oz waved his hand. "I've had worse," he grimaced.

She didn't want to know what could be worse than getting shot. Since her association with the SEAL team she'd been shot at, and seen one of the men get hit with a bullet and act like it was nothing. Now, facing the red haired man who was as sweet as can be say the same thing, she was sure she wanted to go home. Or she had been dropped in a rabbit hole a few weeks back and was ready to get out. Either way, Alexa was out of her element and wanted to fast forward, or rewind to a time where nobody was trying to kill her or those around her.

"Hey, don't look like that. We're too tough to kill. Are you hungry?" Oz asked indicating the pile of bacon on a plate near the stove.

Her stomach rumbled, but the thought of putting anything in it made her feel nauseous. "I think I'll just get some fresh air and then see if my tummy feels up to eating."

"No can do," Coyle's deep voice stopped her in her tracks.

She'd forgotten about the other man for a few seconds. "I can't go outside?"

Coyle shook his head. "It's too dangerous. If someone with a sniper rifle wanted to take your head off from a distance, then all the security in the world couldn't protect it. Your only safe bet is inside this house. You don't want to eat, then go take a walk around the house, but stay inside."

She'd had enough of his attitude, and wasn't sure why he was angry at her. "What the heck did I do to piss you off?"

He stared at her without saying a word.

Poking her finger into his sternum, she wouldn't let him get away with silence. "Listen, buddy. You have a problem with me, then be a big boy and say it. Otherwise shut your mouth. What's that saying?" She tapped her lip. "Grow a pair? Or, something about staying on the porch with the pups cause you can't run with the big dogs? I don't know, and I don't care. All I know is I didn't steal your best girl, nor did I piss in your cereal. Stop being a dick unless you want to tell me why you're being that way. I've had a rough few weeks, No, scratch that. My life has been a big ole ball of one rough patch after another. But do you see me stomping around acting like a jackhole? No. Either shut up and be nice, or just shut up." Her finger began to hurt from stabbing into his rock hard abs, but she felt better having gotten to speak her mind.

The sound of clapping made her turn to see Oz doing a slow clap with a cheesy grin on his face.

Thinking she had better get out of the kitchen before Coyle retaliated, Alexa spun on her bare feet, and went in search of something to do other than eat. Her stomach that was rumbling loudly in protest, was also doing a fairly good show of flips as well. At the rate she was going she'd be dropping another dress size and wasn't sure to be happy or sad.

Bumping into a solid body had her gasping, but before she could fall flat on her rear, Kai's strong arms pulled her into his body. "What's wrong?"

His big brown eyes could almost make a woman think he cared. "Nothing. I'm going back up to my room for a little while." Her stomach decided to voice a loud protest.

"You haven't eaten yet and neither have I. Come on, you and I should do so before those two eat everything in sight." Kai grabbed her hand, towing her back toward where she'd just fled.

"Kai, I don't want to eat," she protested.

He looked her up and down. "Too bad. We have things to discuss and I'm hungry, and you need to eat. I can hear your stomach growling."

"Wow, that's quite a feat all the way up there and all." Knowing she was being bitchy didn't stop her from trying again. "Seriously, I'd rather not."

"Tell me what happened." His abrupt stop had her bumping into him.

"Why are you always stopping and making me run into you like that. You realize you are not all soft and cushiony right?"

The heated look he gave her had thoughts of what they'd been doing until Tay interrupted them, had heat crawling up her face.

"Believe me, I know exactly what I am, and what you are under our clothes."

She licked her lips, and he groaned.

"If you keep tempting me like that, I will carry you up those steps and make good on my words from earlier, and my team be damned." Real promise was shining through in his gaze.

Alexa wanted to do just that.

The grip on her arm tightened. "Big mistake there, luv."

With a nod, she moved around him, pulling him with her. Sure, having a hot interlude with Kai would be a definite highlight, but she had no doubt he'd leave her heartbroken at the end. No thank you.

Coyle stood when they entered. "I'm sorry for being an asshole. You didn't deserve my words, and I promise to be a gentleman if you'll sit and eat." He indicated the plate of bacon still filled.

Oz's blue eyes pleaded with her. "Come on, I need to eat before I take my pain meds."

If they were manipulating her it was working.

"You want some eggs? I can whip up some scrambled, or some scrambled." Coyle moved to the fridge.

"Scrambled sounds great." She smiled and sat on the last barstool, leaving two between her and Coyle. The man may have apologized, but she still didn't like him, didn't trust him not to turn on her.

"How you feeling, Oz?" Kai grabbed the eggs from Oz.

"Dude, I had a vest on. No worries," he said rubbing his chest."

Yeah, she didn't think it was nothing, not when he winced each time he turned too fast.

"Sit down and let me whip these up." Kai pointed over his shoulder.

"Didn't you get shot too," Oz said but walked over to sit next to Alexa.

Kai ignored him, cracking two dozen eggs into a large bowl. She wondered if the men had brought them with when they'd come.

"We stopped and grabbed a few things before coming here." Oz rested his forearms on the granite, another grimace pulled at his features.

"You should go lay down or something." He didn't look like he was in a lot of pain, but being shot couldn't feel that great.

Oz's hand patted hers. "I'm gonna eat and then sit in that big ass living room and catch up on some movies. You can sit with me. What do you like to watch?"

Alexa wasn't sure how to answer that. Kai's back had stiffened, yet she didn't owe him any loyalty.

"I like comedy or action. No chick flicks or any Sparks' movies, thank you. Someone always dies and

I like to watch things that end with a happily ever after."

The big man at the stove grunted, but didn't say a word.

"Great, we should find something to our liking."

Coyle coughed something that sounded suspiciously like words. Alexa chose to ignore him.

They filled up on bacon and eggs with toast that Kai expertly fixed. She was amazed at how easily he navigated the kitchen.

"I'm going to relieve Sully," Coyle said after he finished three bacon sandwiches piled with eggs. The swiveling barstool scraped as he stood and his heavy footfalls echoed in the quiet room.

"Ignore Coyle. He's butt hurt I was shot while he was there. Man thinks he's superhuman and should've been able to stop the bullet or some shit." Oz shook his head.

Alexa thought they were all a little crazy, but kept her mouth shut.

Chapter Seven

Kai had never wanted to break his teammate's fingers like he wanted to Oz's. Watching him flirt with Alexa had him thinking of all the ways he'd trained to kill a man. He shook his head and turned away from the couple sitting at the island.

"I will clean up." Alexa's soft words startled him.

"Go watch a movie with Oz, I got this." He dismissed her, pouring the grease from the bacon into the trash can now that it had cooled.

"Listen, you guys cooked, I get to clean. Please. Let me do something."

He dared a glance down at her face, and saw the need for more, sure the same mirrored in his. "Fine, I'm going to check the monitors."

"I'll go with you," Oz said standing up with ease.

Kai didn't wait for him, walking to the room Rowan had set up for security purposes. Several monitors showed him the property from all the different views, making it easy for him to see where Coyle and Sully were talking.

"You got a thing for our girl or what?" Oz leaned against the wall.

His temper flared as he switched the monitor to a camera farther back, ignoring Oz's words.

"She's been through a lot and doesn't need to have any more grief in her young life, Cap." Oz walked further into the room.

Spinning around, Kai faced Oz. "What the hell does that mean?"

Oz shut the door. "What that means is, she doesn't look like the love em and leave em type. On the way here, I did a little research and found she isn't a player. She's been a product of the system since her parents left her, and then she aged out of the foster system. That tiny little bundle of female is not like what we are used to. What I'm saying is don't play with her, then drop her like last week's mission."

"Are you her daddy or her boyfriend warning me off," Kai growled. "This life. Our life, isn't meant for happily ever afters as she put it. We don't have time, nor should we put a woman in the place to sit at home and wait for us while we are out on a mission. Our families are bad enough, waiting for that possible call, or for someone to knock on their door telling them we were killed. The only thing I have to offer is a few weeks at best. I've never led a woman to believe anything more." Kai wished for more, and could see Alexa being that woman who he had waiting at home for him.

Oz shook his head. "That's bull and you know it. There are lots of SEALs who have wives, lovers and the like. What makes you so much worse?"

Kai looked back at the monitors. "What about you, Oz. I don't see you putting a ring on some ladies finger. None of the men on my team has a significant other. What's that say for us?" Movement caught his eye to the North of the property. He zoomed in and was sure he saw a figure.

"Oz, I need you to watch the cameras. I think we have company." Kai strode to the door.

"You going to wake Tay?"

Indecision warred within him, but if they did have someone out and about, and it turned out to be a hunter, Tay would need his rest.

"No, let him sleep. If I need backup I got Coyle and Sully. Don't let anyone in but us three or Rowan. Period. I don't care if they say Rowan sent them, or they are his brother from another mother. You ignore them. Tay has reset the codes so only our team has access to the house."

Kai went to the weapons closet and slung a rifle over his shoulder, made sure his weapons belt was tightened and slipped out the door on the South side. He kept to the trees and made his way back to where he thought he'd seen movement, looking for signs of a trespasser. Neither Coyle nor Sully would have come out so far into the woods, but if they'd heard anything they'd have come out to check. Kai looked for tracks, watching where he placed his feet to keep from making any noise. His clothing helped him blend into the foliage, and he wondered if he was on a wild goose chase when the first sign of an intruder was found.

The indent in the dry leaves clearly showed where a large person had stood for some time. Kai pressed his back up against the tree, looking toward the house, but without binoculars couldn't see anything. He glanced up and noticed scrapes up the trunk, and wanted to curse. The fucker had climbed a tree and watched the house for god knew how long.

Not trusting he was gone or working alone, Kai worked slowly in tracking the man. A good fifty feet back he found tracks of an off road vehicle that appeared to be a four wheeler or something similar. The man could have been a hunter, but it wasn't hunting season unless you were hunting a human.

He felt the grass and leaves where the vehicle had sat, checking to see if the tracks were cold or warm. The fact the trail was indeed still warm meant he'd missed the intruder by minutes at most, yet he'd not heard the sound of the motor. Wind whistling in the woods mocked him, making him wish for the eerie stories where all was silent except for the heavy breathing.

Making his way back toward the cabin, he circled back, checking for more signs. If the man wasn't alone, and more were up in a tree, they were in a shitload of trouble since the cabin was surrounded by hundreds of the big fuckers.

Coyle and Sully stepped out of the tree line on either side of the house at the same time as him, both wearing similar gear that helped them blend into the landscape. Their grim expressions didn't ease his own doubts. Using hand motions they all made their way to the home, entering as one. Kai took one long last look, before he closed the door, making sure the locks engaged.

"Tell me what you saw," he looked to Sully first.

Bright green eyes stared behind Kai.

Before he turned, Kai knew Alexa was there. His inner alarm had already told him she was aware of their presence, and instead of waiting for her to leave, or taking the conversation to the room Rowan had set up for security, he walked further into the kitchen. "Go ahead, Sully. She should hear what's going on."

"I saw markings on a few trees, like someone had climbed them recently. I backtracked to see if I could find the fucker, but there was no trace. Whoever it is was really good, or more than one."

Exactly what Kai thought.

"I noticed tracks on the ground. They'd tried to be careful, but I got an eye for detail. When I circled back and met up with Sully, the markings there were not made with the same weight. Meaning, we have more than one threat out there. I wish I could say it was a group of hunters, which in a sense is true, only they aren't hunting anything that runs on four legs. Of that I'm positive. The scrapes on the tree were far enough apart I could tell one of the men was around two hundred pounds, and the other around one-eighty. They were using special shoes that allowed them to climb, without causing too much damage to the tree, and by my guess, they were on a reconnaissance mission." Coyle's voice held no inflection.

"We should leave," Alexa said, her hands were balled into fists against her chest.

Kai shook his head. "It's too late for that, luv. We leave now, they could be waiting on the road, or set up traps that nothing short of a tank could survive. Our best bet is to see what they come at us with. This house is a veritable fortress, not to mention you got five SEALs here to protect you. If worst comes to worst, there is the safe room. You go in there and nobody can get in or out unless you let them." Kai's arm reached out, his fingers brushed down her cheek, the need to reassure her too much for him to resist that small caress.

"Hey," Tay cut in. "Y'all are being fatalist. This is a huge area that for the most part is empty. Maybe they are just hunters who got scared when they realized there were people staying in the cabin."

Oz's booming laugh cut across the room. "I got some ocean front property to sell you in Kansas for cheap."

Kai held his hand up. "We have to think there is a threat. Oz was shot at point blank by a friendly. I got a scrape by an unknown who shouldn't have been able to get into a secure building. We have another team's member who was injected by some drug that incapacitated him. Hell, for all we know that entire team is on the take. I want Alexa to keep to the interior rooms. I'm sorry, but no TV watching for you in the great room. Those floor to ceiling windows are a nightmare even though they are bulletproof."

"I'm fine, damn it." Oz pulled his shirt up, tugging off the white bandage covering his right upper chest.

Alexa's indrawn breath drew Kai's gaze. He'd seen a lot of bullet wounds and knew Oz's injury was nothing, but wasn't sure why she was freaking out over the sight of his friend.

"That was so close to your heart." She moved around the island. "Why would you put your life on the line for someone like me?"

Her hand touched Oz's chest tentatively as if she was afraid he'd knock her arm away.

"It's what we do. Besides, I'm alive. You know, failure is not an option."

Kai grinned as all five of the SEAL team said the last at the same time, making Alexa's eyes widen.

"You are all crazy. You don't know me. I could be some deranged woman...or deserving of..."

Oz cut off her words with his palm over her mouth. "Don't do that. We serve with honor and integrity on and off the battlefield, don't take that from us by belittling yourself. Your life, every life is worth saving, except asshats who are traitors to our country or theirs. I have no qualm about taking them out. Hoorah." The last was yelled.

"I hate being scared. Why can't I just have a normal life?"

Alexa looked around, but Kai noticed Oz shrugged and stepped away.

"Oz is right. We've put our lives on the line for people we've never met for our country. You are a woman who in my book is a good person. I'd be more than happy to stand in front of you as a shield." Tay smiled.

The fear reflected in the unusual eyes didn't sit well with Kai. "Okay, listen up team. We are stepping this up. I don't want us out in singles, it's a two man team from here on out. Nobody goes out alone. Got it? Sully and Coyle, you two partner up and do a perimeter check. Make sure if you see anything fresh, you report back. We have cells for a reason. They clearly know we are here, so I want to know what you know when you know it. Tay and I will take the next round."

"Bullshit," Oz growled. "I'm not a fucking liability. When is my turn? I'm not a babysitter, who's not good for anything else. No offense, Alexa." He turned and grimaced at the stricken look on her face.

"Oz, you are guarding the girl. That's the most important job."

"Great, then that's the perfect job for you." A muscle ticked in Oz's cheek.

The urge to punch the big redhead in the jaw was almost overpowering. "Fuck," he swore and spun on his heel.

"Why don't all of you go out, and I'll stay inside by myself. I mean I'm safe you said?" One dark brow raised in question.

Kai looked at his four SEAL team members and wanted to beat the shit out of each of them. The smirks on their faces let him know they were waiting to see how he'd handle the situation.

"Alexa, you are safe, and we mean to keep you that way. However, we are not leaving you alone. I'll take first watch inside. This is a large property. I want everyone checking on the thirty mark. Let's set our clocks." Each man raised their wrists, making sure their times were exact.

Sully and Coyle slipped out the back, while Oz and Tay eased out the front. Kai heard the alarms engage, yet he inspected each one to make sure the red light shone brightly, indicating they were working properly.

"Want to play a card game, or something," Alexa asked.

He stared down at the woman he wanted beyond endurance, and imagined a game of strip poker. "Do you know how to play poker?"

She smiled. "Yeah, but is this gonna cost money or clothes."

Damn! Just like that his body responded. "Baby, you are tugging a tiger's tail with words like that."

"You sorta left me hanging earlier. I think turnabout is only fair."

The little minx licked her lips, and giggled. Kai decided he didn't mind her teasing if it wiped away the fear she'd had for the last few hours.

****

Alexa couldn't believe the way she was acting or the things that were coming out of her mouth, yet she wasn't able to stop. Watching the play of emotions flash across Kai's face was a wonder in itself, and knowing she was the one to surprise him gave her a boost of confidence she'd lost somewhere along the way. She wasn't sure how long the other four men would be gone, but had decided he wasn't slipping away from her again.

Her big bad SEAL was about to see how far she was willing to go to get what she wanted.

"I don't know what you are thinking, but it's a bad idea, Alexa."

She shook her head. "Are you scared of little ole me?"

Kai backed up. "Let me go find some cards and I'll see how good you are at five card stud."

As he hurried down the hall, she barely kept from laughing. She only wished she had something sexy under her borrowed clothing.

A glance at the clock and she calculated they had approximately twenty-six minutes before the guys checked in for the first time. Surely they could get a few rounds of cards in, and hopefully most of their clothing off in that time.

"Here we go. A brand new deck. I hope Rowan wasn't keeping it for anything. It looks like a standard one to me." Kai shrugged, then sat at the small breakfast nook in the kitchen.

Watching his fingers expertly shuffle the cards, Alexa thought about earlier and how it felt when he'd been touching her. She looked up to see his eyes staring intently at her breasts, and knew he could see the outline of her nipples through the thin material.

"What game we playing?" Her voice cracked.

"You are playing with fire." He nodded toward the stack of cards.

Alexa shook her head, not wanting to separate them, actually wishing she could leap across the table and kiss the stubborn man. "Just deal, big boy."

One of Kai's eyebrows raised, but a hint of a grin kicked up his lips. By the time he realized she did in fact know how to play poker, he got serious.

"Okay, now let's play for real. Next hand, loser loses an article of clothing." She grinned at his indrawn breath. "Unless you're chicken that is."

"Baby, I'll have you know I am the best card shark out there."

From the feral look he gave, she had no doubt he meant it. However, he didn't live in a foster home with kids who had to live on street corners where their next meal depended on their ability to outfox others. When his phone chirped at the designated time, they'd both lost several pieces of clothing, but she'd had more to begin with.

She enjoyed looking at his muscular chest, but was shocked to see he had several faint scars, and what appeared to be a bullet wound above his camo pants belt, near his hip. Her lips ached to kiss and sooth all his old injuries, even knowing they no longer hurt.

"All is clear," he said laying the phone on the table.

Alexa glanced down at her bra and leggings. The only things she had left to lose were the thin scrap of lace on top and bottom, leggings and one sock. Kai had his camo pants and a pair of socks. She wondered if he went commando beneath, or if he still had the boxer briefs from earlier on.

"Wanna go all in, big guy?" Her hand was more than good with the straight flush, her highest card being a king. The chances of him having anything better were slim to none.

His dark eyes stared at her from across the small table, making the air still. "You show me yours, and I'll show you mine."

Shaking her head, Alexa swore her heart was going to pound out of her chest. Like a professional card dealer she fanned her cards out, excitement stirred in her belly.

****

Kai smiled. Her hand was good, but his was better. He couldn't wait to see her naked.

Laying his own cards on the table, he watched her eyes register what he held, smiling as she recognized he won.

"Read em and strip, baby." Kai sat back and folded his arms across his chest.

"But...how," she sputtered.

He looked at the deck then at her. "I guess the cards liked me better."

She smiled a smile that could only be described as devious, and he knew they were both winners. The strap of her bra came off one side at a time, and he had to clench his teeth to keep from reaching across the table to help. Her breasts kept the cups in place while she reached around to unclip the back, almost making them spill out. Kai was sure his zipper was going to leave a permanent indent in his dick. The only thing protecting him was the thin briefs, and even they felt too tight.

Like the prize it was, her bra was tossed to the middle, falling on top the cards. Sweat beaded on his brow at the sight of her pebbled nipples he couldn't wait to taste.

Without getting up she shimmied out of the leggings and then they along with the panties were added to the pile.

"Now what?" Alexa's voice was a mere rasp.

"That's not fair. I can't see anything above your ribs."

Alexa reached for the cards. "One more hand, and if I lose I'll stand up. If you lose, you take it all off and show me the goods."

He had a seconds thought that she might be hiding a couple aces, but then realized she had nowhere to put them. "Deal em."

The cards were placed down, she swallowed and licked her lips. Kai sincerely hoped he won, but if not it was no loss to show Alexa his body, riddled with scars and all.

"Let's turn one card over at a time. See the suspense sorta unfold," she said.

Damn, he was sure he fell a little in love with her right then.

Her first card was a jack of clubs, while his was a three of spades. By the time they were down to the final two cards, neither had anything, but her Jack was high. Kai was sure he was going to lose until he flipped over another three, but he didn't exhale until her last card flipped over and she had nothing but another random card.

"Looks like I'm the winner again." Kai couldn't help but smirk, pushing his chair back he stood up sucking in a breath at the absolute perfection of the vision in front of him. If Venus had come to Earth, surely she was gracing the kitchen.

"I still think you're a card shark." One hand raised to cover her breasts, then dropped.

It took him three steps to stand in front of her. He raised his arm, brushing a lock of hair away from her face. "Damn, you are so beautiful you take my breath away."

"I bet you say that to all the naked girls you see," she joked.

Kai pressed his thumb against her lips. "Don't. Don't diminish this gift. Yes, I've seen naked women, but none that compare to you. You're in a category all on your own."

Alexa's mouth opened, her tongue licked his thumb, making all his blood rush from his big head to his little head. "I want to make love to you in the worst way possible" He shook his head. "I don't mean in a bad way…just that I want to…"

She stopped him by placing her fingers over his mouth. "I know what you mean." Her fingers reached for his belt.

"Hold on a second." Kai looked around the kitchen and wished they had more time. More privacy.

"Are you changing your mind again?"

"Fuck no. It's just that I can't get completely naked with you as much as I'd like to feel you skin to skin. If something were to happen I can fight with my pants undone, but not with my junk hanging out. It takes me less than ten seconds to get dressed if my pants are around my ankles, a little more if I had to put my shoes and everything back on. Make sense?"

A glimmer of amusement lit her features. "I could just see you shooting at the bad guys while buck-assed nekkid. That would be comical."

Kai tickled her sides. "You saying my junk is laughable, woman."

Screeching, Alexa twisted against him. "I felt that thing, and that is no laughing matter."

Chapter Eight

A few months ago if anyone would've asked Alexa if she'd be laughing and joking when she was undressed with a man, she'd have said hell no. However standing in a stranger's kitchen with Kai she was doing just that, and it felt good. If she died tomorrow, then at least she'd have one good memory.

"Okay, no nakynaky for you. How you gonna do this super SEAL?" Alexa trailed her hands up his sculpted chest. The man really was hard all over.

Kai twisted his head to the side, then turned back toward her. "You up for a little adventure?"

"Hello, I'm standing here with no clothes on after a rousing game of strip poker. Pretty sure I just adventured all over this here house."

"Not yet you haven't but we will."

His words sounded like a promise, but Alexa wasn't going to let herself believe their interlude was anything more than a one off. Maybe more if they could sneak it in. She'd never wanted to sneak around as a teenager, mainly because she didn't want the foster people to think she was open for that type of thing. Now, she wanted Kai to know she was open for that and much more.

He lifted her up by the waist, making her gasp. She forgot he was so strong. When he placed her on the cold granite, her breath came out in a whoosh, which he immediately swallowed.

Expertly, Kai kissed like he did everything, with so much skill she had no choice but to follow where he led. Her tongue traced his, licking along the roof of his mouth, tasting the rich coffee they'd had while playing cards.

Alexa felt his hands pushing her knees apart and realized she'd squeezed them together. Her hands shook as she reached for his belt, the fastening coming undone quickly, and then she had the button and zip open. "Not commando then, huh?"

"That's only in books, sweets."

She inserted her thumbs into the sides of both his coverings, happy when he was finally exposed for her to see. "Damn, that is not only in books." Alexa looked up at Kai.

"I'm hoping that is a compliment?" He bent, sealing her mouth with his.

Whatever she'd planned to say was lost as his hands moved over her breasts, tweaking both at the same time. Alexa locked her ankles around his thighs drawing him in closer and felt the heat of his body against the center of her. Aware he could feel how wet she already was.

His mouth pulled back, trailing down her neck and nipped her shoulder, making her shiver in delight.

"Put your hands on the counter, luv." Kai gripped her wrist placing them where he wanted them.

Looking between them she saw the head of his cock standing proud, and wished they were in a bed where she could explore him too. Instead she did as instructed.

Kai's lips and tongue trailed along her collar to her right breast, latching on while he pinched the left one. She writhed against him, needing more.

"Patience," he murmured.

God, she hadn't known she'd spoken out loud.

He didn't let up on his assault with kisses, and licks, moving down her body until he was between her thighs. Alexa wanted to watch, but the first swipe of his tongue had her lifting against him. She dropped down onto her elbows, the cold counter vaguely registered in her brain.

She wasn't sure how he was able to manipulate her entire body, but no part of her was left untouched.

****

Kai stared up at Alexa, gauging her reaction to his touch. She was so tight he had to work slowly to get two fingers inside her. He latched onto the bundle of nerves at the top, making her entire frame spasm. Tiny little flutters had his dick envious of his hand.

"Oh, god, I'm so close," Alexa moaned.

"Give it to me. Let me see how beautifully you come." Kai added a third digit alongside the other two, her slight flinch was overrode as he sucked her clit into his mouth, and pumped in and out until he pushed her over the edge. The tiny flutters became a vice like grip. He waited for her to come down, then placed a kiss on her tummy.

Looking at her lying on the counter where they'd eaten breakfast, and now he'd just had the best dessert ever, Kai fit his dick against her opening, then remembered protection. He grabbed a square packet out of his wallet, then within seconds he was sheathed and at the apex between her thighs.

"You sure about this?" He needed to ask one more time. If she said no, he'd go to the bathroom and go blind from rubbing one out, but he'd do it.

"Yes. Oh, if you change your mind I will personally beat your ass."

With her hair fanned out, a rosy flush covering her body, Kai was sure she was the only person in the world who could truly harm him. Somehow, the tiny woman beneath him had taken a part of his heart. He pushed aside his thoughts and pressed forward, working inside until he was wedged as tightly as he could get.

Alexa lifted her legs, wrapping them around his hips. "Soldier, I think you need to move."

"I'm a SEAL, ma'am." Kai leaned forward, his arms hooking under her shoulders and began to move. He wanted to make it last, wanted to make love for hours, but his body had other plans. With each forward thrust he ground against her clit, rolling his hips, then pulled back and repeated.

The sound of their panting breaths filled the air, her short nails raked his back.

Kai held her, staring down at the wonder in her eyes as he made love to Alexa for the first time. He felt his impending orgasm, and needed her to come with him. He moved his right hand between them, and flicked over the swollen bud, and had her crying out, her heels dug into him.

"Come for me, Alexa."

"Right there. Keep doing that, Kai," she panted.

He was a good listener, and followed the signs of her body, rubbing in just the right pressure and the right speed until she came with a yell. His own body reacted to the constricting muscles, making him jerk forward, and cover her mouth to silence the scream he wanted to yell.

Kai's hips continued to gyrate long after he was spent. He pulled Alexa into a sitting position and held her against him. "That was perfect."

She laughed. "It was the best ever," she agreed.

They both stilled as the clock on the wall clicked indicating the hour. Kai slowly withdrew, pulling the spent condom off and disposed of it in the garbage. He straightened his clothes, and looked at his silent phone, expecting his team to have texted to let him know all was clear. Two minutes passed, and he knew something was wrong.

"Alexa get dressed, and get some shoes on, now." He shrugged into his shirt, checking his weapons belt.

Kai typed a message to both teams, but didn't expect a response. The code he entered would be meaningless to anyone but the five of them. If he got no response he knew his guys were in...he cut the thought off before he allowed it to go any further.

He heard Alexa running up the stairs while he went back to the room Rowan had set up for surveillance. After rewinding the cameras for the last half hour, he scanned each one, looking for his teammates. What he saw made his blood run cold.

Both teams were nowhere to be seen. He zoomed out, using the heat seeking cameras. Kai stopped at the sign of two signatures within a few miles of the cabin. Neither men could be his guys. He hoped like hell his boys had a plan, and knew they'd been found, or he was going to beat their asses.

"What's going on?" Alexa asked coming into the room.

He felt like a sitting duck as he searched more of the property, seeing more heat signatures, counting a total of eight.

Alexa's eyes locked onto the screens. "We're outnumbered, aren't we?"

Not wanting to lie to her, he nodded. Kai figured he had few choices. Send Alexa to the safe room and go out in a blaze of glory, or call in for some reinforcements. Of course he didn't know how long it would take Rowan, or what kind of man power he had. Man being the key word.

"I need to make a call, luv."

She wrung her hands. "What should I do? I hate feeling like a liability, and I won't be taken again. Promise me you won't let anyone take me. Kill me first, Kai. Promise."

Kai jerked Alexa onto his lap. "Listen to me. Nobody is going to kill you, least of all me. Damn it, you can't give up now." He watched tears form in her gorgeous eyes, hating the bastards who did this to her.

"I need to make a call. Hold tight." Kai grabbed his cell, speed dialing Rowan Shade.

"Shade here, what's going on? Please tell me you didn't blow my cabin up."

"Not yet, but it looks like I have some unwanted company and it's just me and my girl."

Rowan's indrawn breath was all Kai heard for a few seconds. "It'll take me a good fifteen minutes to get there. How many you got coming at you?"

Kai explained what he knew, and hoped Rowan got there in time to save Alexa.

"I'll be coming in hot, so is there any mods I need to know about?

The man was smart, so Kai explained about the change in security code.

"Of course Tay did, the fucker. Do we know if they're on our side, or..." he trailed off.

"Until I have confirmation one way or the other, I'm assuming it's you, me and who you bring. Trust no one but me and Alexa." The words tasted like ash coming out of his mouth.

"Hey, I get it, Cap. Right now you're sitting in a damn good place. Don't be Captain Fucking America. You're not bullet proof, so use the damn safe room with your girl. Yeah, I totally heard that by the way. I'm hopping in my rig now and got a half dozen guys with me. I think we can even the odds out."

Kai didn't like the reminder, but hung up before he said something he'd regret. "Rowan's on his way. We just need to hold down the fort for about fifteen minutes. I need to change the security entrance codes. Give me a second." Kai wasn't an expert like Shade or Tay, but he was no dummy. It took him a couple minutes, but he made the change, using the numbers he'd given Rowan. If in fact his team had gone rogue, they no longer could get access to the property. He knew they'd never voluntarily give up the info if they'd been captured.

"Hey, I know your guys. They wouldn't betray you or our country."

He wanted to believe that, but with her life in the balance, Kai wasn't willing to take that gamble.

"Want to help me watch the monitors?" Kai asked to distract Alexa.

"Do you want a drink while we wait?" Alexa got off his lap.

Kai swallowed and realized he was thirsty. "Yeah, a bottle of water sounds good. Thank you." He reached out and grabbed her hand. "You're being really brave, baby."

"That's because you can't see me shaking in my shoes. Trust me I am." She let go of his hand, turned and walked out the door.

****

Alexa stared around the kitchen, unable to believe just a short time ago she was having wild monkey sex with Kai on the counter. Now, she was scared out of her wits. Seeing the cards spread out on the table she quickly gathered them into a neat pile, then went to the fridge for their drinks.

A sound near the front of the house had her heart pounding. Holding the two bottles, she crept back toward the long hallway to Kai, only to come to a stop at the sight of Tay through the floor to ceiling windows. His bloody face pressed against the windows made her whimper. A man holding a gun pressed it against Tay's head, waved his hand at her. He was dressed all in black, from head to toe. Alexa was sure he looked like the cliché bad guy and a nervous giggle escaped.

One black gloved finger raised to the man's lips. Tay didn't appear to be awake, hanging limply in the other man's arms, and then his mouth moved against the glass. Alexa looked down the long hallway, thinking she should get Kai. Another body was pushed against the glass. Oz's red hair was plain to see, along with blood marring his face. The two men holding Kai's team didn't appear to care that she saw their faces, and she wondered if they planned to kill both men while she watched. A third stepped up, a white board in his hand. Written on it was a single sentence 'Come outside, and they live.'

She stood there frozen. Why did they want her? She was nobody.

The white board appeared again. 'For each minute that passes a bullet for them.'

Her eyes flew to Tay and Oz, both men shook their heads. She couldn't allow them to be shot because she stayed inside. Making a quick decision, she ran to the door, remembering the number Kai had given Rowan, she punched it in.

Alarms began blaring.

"So good of you to come out and play, Alexa."

The white board was dropped, and all hell broke loose. Tay and Oz were dropped.

She heard her name being yelled from inside, and the man who'd spoken her name, like he knew her, grabbed her by the back of the hair, yanking her to him. "It's taken us twenty-seven years to find you. Now, we have our pawn. Too bad you brought a little trouble with you." He sighed. "Oh well, nothing we can't handle."

Alexa screamed as he began firing into the open door, jerking on his hold. Her elbow went back, hitting him in the abdomen. His grunt satisfied her.

She rammed her head backward, but his grip kept her from connecting, and then something hard hit her in the side of the temple. Alexa smelled the scent of copper, her nose tingled, and then all went dark. She was sure she heard the sound of roaring, but her body hit the ground next to Tay's, and she let the darkness claim her.

****

Kai yelled Alexa's name as he heard the alarm beep. He'd changed the number sequence every five minutes like Rowan and he'd set up, knowing the other man would know the proper ones when he arrived. The scene he saw made him stop in mid-run. Tay and Oz both were pressed against the glass, blood smeared on the surface while the three men with them seemed to be talking. Alexa purposefully opened the secure doors, but why was his question.

As the apparent leader grabbed his woman roughly, then slams the gun in his hand against her head, he began firing. The return volley made him roll out of the way, barely escaping from another bullet wound. When he glanced around the wall, all three men and Alexa were gone. Kai eased out, keeping low in case they were still there. His heartbeat erratic, a new sensation he wasn't sure he liked. Usually on a mission he was able to keep calm and in control. Yet knowing Alexa was in the hands of the enemy had him on edge. The sound of vehicles roaring into the yard, made him rush toward the door and his fallen teammates. Kai recognized Rowan and several of his pack.

"Shit man. What the fuck happened?" Rowan cleared the distance, kneeling next to Tay's prone form.

Kai swiped his hand down his face searching the woods for any sign of Alexa or the men. "I've no damn clue, man. There were over a half dozen heat sigs some distance away, but none close enough to the property. I figured we were safe enough. I sent Alexa to get a drink, and then all of the sudden she was opening the door. Hell, if I hadn't reset the alarms, she might've slipped out without me knowing a thing," Kai cursed.

Oz's moan had him hurrying to his side. "What the hell happened, brother?"

"We were jumped by several. They just fell out of the trees, man." Oz coughed.

Tay and Oz both struggled to sit up.

"We need to get you to the hospital. Laikyn is on shift, and believe me she's the best of the best. Let's get you loaded," Rowan said waving at a few guys.

"Have you seen Sully or Coyle?" Fear ate at him. If Tay and Oz had been ambushed, he hated to think his other two friends were lying out in the woods somewhere, possibly dead.

"We lost contact after our last check in," Tay grunted.

Oz held his hand up. "Sorry, man."

"You apologize again and I'll beat your damn ass when you get out of the hospital."

Kai nodded at Rowan and his friends, watching as they lifted Tay and Oz and carried them to two waiting vehicles. "I need to find Alexa, Sully and Coyle."

"Let's do it." Rowan slapped his hands together.

The other man's blue eyes shone bright blue. Once a SEAL always a SEAL.

A chorus of 'Hoorah" rang out. The need for stealth truly forgotten until they hit the woods, and then Kai fanned out his fingers, and was impressed as Rowan and his men split up as if they spoke beforehand. He hated to admit it, but he missed working with the big southern bastard.

On silent feet they both moved through the woods. He let Rowan lead since the man owned the property and knew it like the back of his hand. Every few hundred feet they'd stop and Rowan would lift his head, looking around then they'd make an adjustment to their trajectory. Within ten minutes they came across a mound. Kai's icy calm threatened to crack as Rowan bent, jerking back what was actually a netting of some sort.

"Shit, we are not dealing with amateurs here, Swift."

Beneath the covering were the still forms of Coyle and Sully. Like a marionette, he moved forward, and pressed his fingers to Coyle's throat. The steady beat made him fall on his ass.

"Easy there. Sully's still alive as well. Looks like they've been tranqued, but by what I've no clue. We need to radio for help. This," he shook the netting. "It hid their presence. I'd say these guys knew what I had for surveillance and came prepared."

Rowan used his cell and called for his guys to bring in a quad, giving them the location of Coyle and Sully.

"Shit, we need to keep moving, but I don't want to leave them unprotected."

Rowan nodded, his head lifted and turned in the direction to the left. "They are not unprotected. Let's go."

Kai saw a man walking toward them and recognized him as one of the members of the Iron Wolves. With a nod, he and Rowan stood and began walking further into the woods. Since Rowan and his team had come in from the front the only logical way the other men could've escaped was out the back. With them using a camo that hid their heat signatures, Kai needed to rely on tracks. Or in this case, Rowan and his abilities.

"There, they camped here. Shit, look at this." Rowan walked around the circular opening. A clear path had been made recently into the river. "The damn water. I can't believe I didn't think to look here." I assumed my cameras would show you if they got close. I'm sorry, Kai."

Shaking his head, Kai paced back and forth. "They shouldn't have known where we were unless they tagged her. Fuck!" He looked up at the towering trees and wished to hell they could get a helo in the air. "Where does this river lead to on each end?"

Rowan explained it was more of a small outlet, and that only small boats could get in and out. Kai figured they'd need to have more than one boat for all the men who had been on the property, or they were still out there hiding in plain sight. "Shit, Ro, they may still be there under their fucking shields waiting to shoot us." Kai spun around.

Pointing at his nose, Rowan shook his head. "I'd know, and so would my guys. Some went that way, and a few went there. Your girl went on the river."

"How do you know?"

Again Rowan pointed at his nose, making Kai roll his eyes.

"There has to be a reason they want Alexa. We just need to find out why," Rowan said. "What do you know about her? I mean really know."

His mind went back to the intelligence they'd gotten on her, and thought about her paperwork of before she went into foster care, and swore something was off. "Shit! We need to find out what happened before her parents were killed."

Chapter Nine

Alexa woke with a pounding headache. Darkness surrounded her and at first she thought she was back at the compound. The hard mattress beneath her reminded her of the same one she'd been given there, but the voices she heard coming in sounded foreign.

She tried to move, quickly realizing she was tied down. Terror washed over her. Did they mean to rape her? Mutilate, before they killed her, then dump the body somewhere? "Oh god," she cried.

Heavy footfalls alerted her that she'd been too loud. Light filled the room, momentarily blinding her.

"Ah, you are awake, mon ami," a man with a French accent said.

Blinking she tried to see his face. "Who are you?"

"I'm a friend of your parents. A shame we had to meet under such...harsh circumstances. Are you thirsty?" He brushed a lock of hair off of Alexa's forehead, making her flinch.

"What are you talking about? My parents are dead."

His smile made her stomach flip. The term feral was exactly what he looked like in that moment. His dark hair and eyes, and square jaw made him one of the most appealing men she'd ever seen other than Kai, but she could see he was wholly evil.

"I assure you they are alive, and I plan to use you to get them to come out to play. It was a fortunate thing you getting attacked the way you did." He tapped his finger on his chin. "Aside from the fact you were almost killed. I mean that would have been a shame, but then again they may have come to your funeral, and then I would have found them. But, I'm rambling. Now that I have you, I will alert them and they will come out of their hidey hole, and I will finally get my revenge."

Alexa was dealing with a mad man. She'd been in foster care for as long as she could remember. She had no memory of her parents, and didn't know why this man thought they were in hiding. "I think you have the wrong person. I'm a nobody from Chicago.

Please just let me go and I promise I won't tell anybody." Yeah, like that was going to work, but a girl had to try.

He laughed. "Oh, Alexia, you are so beautiful. I believe you are even more so than your mother."

"See, my name is Alexa, not Alexia. Wrong person. It happens all the time." She winced as he grabbed her by the jaw.

"That is where you are wrong." He released her as quickly as he grabbed her. Standing he walked back to the open door. "Your parents were supposed to be my friends. We set up a network together, and then they fell in love and decided they wanted out. There is only one way out, and it's not a door."

"Wait," she protested. "I need to go to the bathroom."

The man looked at her prone form, then jerked his head. More footsteps and then a brute of a man came into the room. The zip ties were cut, pain lanced down her arms from being in the same position too long. She wondered how much time she'd been there and worried about Kai and his team.

"Oh god, did you kill the men back at the cabin?" She asked, rubbing her arms trying to ease the ache from shoulders down.

"Pascal, you should come see this."

Alexa registered the man's name being yelled from outside the small room. The small log cabin looked cozy from where she now sat, waiting for the feeling to return, but the man who'd cut her free didn't seem inclined to let her sit for long. The deadly looking knife he'd used to cut her free, got her up before she was ready with just a menacing wave of the blade.

On wobbly legs she stepped out of the room, the bright lights hurt her eyes. It took precious seconds to get her bearings, before she could make out what looked like another hunting cabin. Hope fluttered that she wasn't too far away from Kai and the others, then she remembered he hadn't answered her question about their health.

She wanted to ask again, yet feared what they'd do to her. She was such a loser. The man behind her gave a hard shove to her shoulder, making her stumble further into the room. Inside the small half bath there was a tiny window where she could see more trees, similar to what was outside Rowan Shade's place. Still she didn't let it mean she was close.

"Two minutes and then I'm coming in to get ya," the man snarled.

The last thing she wanted was him coming in while she was using the facility. Quickly she got up and flushed, washing her hands she stared at her reflection. She would have laughed if it wasn't so remarkably stupid. She'd survived how many times when she should've been dead, only to now be in the hands of a foreigner who thought she was a pawn in some game. A tear fell down her cheek before she wiped it away. Alexa knew she would be killed as soon as the one named Pascal realized he had the wrong woman. She wasn't this Alexia he thought she was. She was plain old boring Alexa.

She reached for the door at the same time as it opened. The gleam in the short, muscular man's eyes let her know he'd wished she was still indisposed.

"Let's go." He waved his hand.

Alexa sucked in her breath, squeezing past him without touching.

"Basile, bring Alexia here."

"Come." Basile's fingers dug into her arm.

Pascal sat at a small table. His head lifted as they approached. He really was attractive, if you discounted the evil.

He pointed at the computer in front of him. "See, I told you." Pascal turned the screen toward her. "You see those two figures. Those, my dear, are your parents." He sat back with a contented sigh.

"How do you know? I mean how do you know they'll come for...me?" She stared at the grainy image. The couple looked like two well-dressed older people. Not some international spies, or whatever he thought they were.

Pascal laughed. "Because, Alexia. Your parents were sent footage to a place I knew they checked. Footage of you tied up and unconscious. They can't deny their own flesh and blood. Just as they knew of your attack a few months back, and had set up your secure transfer. I of course set up your little diversion. None of us planned that little pit stop you made in between, which threw us all off, but it's been rectified. Had you not had that little mishap in Chicago, all three of you would have stayed off the radar, possibly your entire life." He shrugged his shoulders.

She stared at his arrogant face and wanted to claw his eyes out. The way he spoke of her past, like being beaten within an inch of her life, then stalked across a few states was nothing. Instead she stayed mute.

"Would you like a drink?" He kicked out a chair with his boot. "Sit."

Alexa hesitated, unsure what his agenda was.

"The boss says sit, you sit." Basile lifted her roughly, then dropped her like a sack of potatoes into the hard wooden chair, making her cry out with the pain.

"Basile doesn't like it when people are not quick with the compliance."

These men were not only well organized, they were crazy. Pascal snapped his fingers, making another man jump up and grab two bottles from the fridge.

"As you can see, they are sealed so you need not worry I've drugged you. If I wanted you dead, you'd be dead." His words held no inflection. Like killing someone was an everyday occurrence, which she assumed it was.

"What do you plan to do with me once you have the couple you think are my parents?" She was proud her voice came our steady, uncapping the water to hide the fact her lips were trembling.

"Alexander and Katalinia Smirnov are your parents, and I plan to kill them, and then you of course."

Alexa choked on the water. "I see."

"Yes, it is best to be honest. I could have given you false hope, but that is not the way I operate. You will live only as long as you are needed. Then," he flashed a grin that sent chills down her spine. "I will make sure it is quick and painless."

"Why can't you just let me go? I don't know those people, and you can disappear with nobody the wiser." Setting the bottle back on the table she leaned forward, hoping he would agree with her.

"You think I am a fool?" He stood abruptly.

Shaking her head, Alexa kept quiet.

"You were with SEALs, you little bitch. That means they could and would trace me. I bet you're sitting there now thinking you could help them and memorizing every detail. The dead don't tell tales. I haven't survived this long by being stupid enough to leave loose ends, and you'd be one. Don't mistake my kindness for ignorance."

"I promise, I won't tell a soul. If you let me go I'd swear I was blindfolded and unconscious the entire time," she pleaded.

Pascal bent down, his nose brushed the side of her face. "And when you were fucking that SEAL again, would you lie to his face?" His hand gripped her by the throat and lifted her off her feet. "Didn't know we'd seen that, huh? Technology is a beautiful thing, my dear."

Alexa felt the blood drain from her face, the air being cut off as he held her suspended up by the throat. She wrapped both hands around his arm, scratching at his cloth covered forearm to no avail. Dots covered her vision.

"I will not kill you, yet."

When he tossed her aside, her legs hit the chair, making her fall onto the floor. The corner of a table hit the side of her head near her eye. Alexa kept the yell of pain inside. She raised her hand to her face, feeling the wetness, she brought her hand in front of her. Blood. God, she was tired of all the blood and death.

Laying on the floor, not wanting to draw attention to herself she curled up into a ball and used her palm to put pressure on the wound. She was going to die soon. It didn't matter if she bled out now, or later.

"Can we play with her before we kill her, Pascal?"

She heard a few minutes later from a new voice.

A whimper escaped her closed lips. She would die fighting before she allowed any of them to touch her. Looking around she spied what looked like a hunting knife beneath the sofa. Moving in small increments, she stretched until finally her fingers latched onto the weapon. Lying on her side, she waited to see if Pascal agreed to let the men have her. Alexa planned to kill the first man to try it, and then she'd kill herself.

****

"We've got a trace on a satellite that was zeroed in on my property. Motherfucker was hacked into our government. This looks like it goes all the way up." Rowan punched in codes on one of his computers.

Kai didn't give two shits how far it went, he wanted to get Alexa back. "Can you trace it back to where it came from? I didn't see any helos going in or out, nor hear any, so I'm assuming they were on the ground." His phone beeped.

Looking down he recognized Coyle's number. "What the hell you doing calling me?"

"Sully and I are enroute back to you. What the *hell* were you thinking having us transported out? We were lying down on the job is all." Coyle's deep rumble sounded strained.

He shook his head. "You both need to stay where you are and make sure that shits out of your system. That is an order."

"Too late, Cap. We are about ten minutes out."

Kai raked his hand through his hair. "You are going to give me grey hair."

Coyle snorted. "Love you too. See you in nine."

Rowan turned in the chair. "He's on his way back I presume."

Nodding, he took a seat. "Find anything useful? I'm not kidding man, I can't..." Kai looked away.

"This woman means more to you than just an assignment?" Rowan's blue eyes assessed him.

Standing back up, Kai paced the room again. "I don't know how she did it, but she got under my skin. It's not gonna work. I mean as soon as this mission is over, I'll be on another, then another, while she goes on with her life. She deserves better than I can give her."

"Yeah, she does. I mean imagine her sitting at home and you off fighting for our country. Every woman deserves better than that, asshole."

"I could die any day, man," Kai snarled.

"So could I. So could she. Hell, she's in the hands of a crazy dude right now. She's been in the hands of some asshats how many times. Does that mean she's not worthy of love because she might have died, how many times now? Get your head out of your ass, Kai." Rowan spun back toward his monitors.

Rowan's words sunk in, but Kai couldn't let himself believe them. His life was not meant for the picket fence and bullshit like that. An incoming text kept him from responding. JoJo had been keeping him up-to-date on Blake. Luckily, the other man was already bitching to get out.

"Is that the team that had the traitor in it?" Rowan asked without turning.

Kai wasn't sure if the other man had eyes in the back of his head or what, but decided to answer him. "Yeah. He's going to be fine."

"Figured as much. How about the other ones. Any leads on them?"

"Tay was working on it. I'm sure you can see what he found." Kai tilted his head toward the computers.

Rowan sighed. "You're lucky I like Tay."

Yeah, both Rowan and Tay were geniuses when it came to electronics.

"Ah hah. Bingo. He made contact with a Hailey. I think we need to send a team to check on the girl. From the looks of it, she might be in trouble."

He didn't need another damsel in distress, but the woman was a SEAL. If Tay thought she was truly in trouble, he'd have said something. "What makes you think that?"

"Tay started digging and from what I can tell, she's in way over her head, and trying to get out. A man named Dex is the one who shot at you she says here," he pointed at the screen. "She and her partner Mad are tracking him, but again, she isn't sure if she can trust this Mad because he's best friends with Dex."

Fuck, what a god damn fucknut. "I only trust you and my team right now, Ro. If I call this in, I'm worried it'll go to someone who could alert whoever has Alexa. That same person could clearly be the one who hired Dex. This is huge, brother."

"Let's not forget about our friend Tyler. He's still out there as well."

Anger burned in his gut, but he didn't think the two cases were connected. However, he had to assume the worst at all times. "I don't think Alexa's latest kidnapping has anything to do with Tyler, but I do believe his escape from a federal prison was orchestrated by someone high up. We've got two separate entities who just happened upon us at the same time. Hoorah motherfucker."

"I'll send a couple of the Iron Wolves over to scout out the area. Believe me, they know how to be discreet."

Kai thought of the tattooed bikers, and the word discreet didn't come to mind. However, he did trust Rowan's opinion, and knew if he was willing to send a group of the guys out on a mission, then they were good enough for Kai as well.

"Thanks," Kai said.

Rowan's head lifted and then an image of a vehicle pulling into the front of the cabin came into view. "Your boys are back," Rowan said unnecessarily.

The pair getting out of the truck looked beyond pissed. Coyle and Sully climbed the steps, and waited. Kai shook his head before heading to the front door.

"You realize you're both stubborn sons of bitches, right?" He didn't wait for an answer, pulling first Coyle in for a back slap and hug, then doing the same to Sully. Although he was giving them grief, he was relieved they were relatively unharmed, unlike Tay and Oz who were still being treated for the injuries.

"Love you too, Cap," Sully said.

Coyle grunted as he brushed passed Kai, heading for the room Rowan was in.

"Tay and Oz are both in recovery and madder than a hornets nest that was dropped and then kicked," Sully muttered, following in Coyle's wake.

He looked at his phone and wondered why he hadn't been apprised of his teams' prognosis. "How did you find out about them?" Kai shut the door, resetting the alarm.

"Commander Lee set a guard at each of their rooms. Said he didn't trust anyone but ones he selected personally." Coyle looked up, his eyes alert.

Kai punched in the Commander's number, walking out of the room in case he became insubordinate.

"Lee here. Find anything, Swift?"

"Why wasn't I informed my guys made it out of surgery and were now under protection?" Kai couldn't keep the accusation out of his tone.

"Boy, you questioning my integrity?"

"Commander, at this point I'm questioning everything, and the lives of my men are my priority." He couldn't let the man's authority scare him.

"You're a good soldier. Don't push it though. I have put men I trust with my life on duty guarding both Couper and Rouland. I'm not leaving their protection up in the air, but I need your focus on the matter at hand. I give you my word on that. Now, go find the girl and the traitor, Swift."

The line went dead before he could ask more, making Kai curse.

He relayed what Lee said to Rowan, Coyle and Sully, watching the shock register on all three men's faces. He knew his own face showed the same. "I hate the unknown."

Sully snorted. "Dude, we go into the unknown all the damn time. That's our jobs."

"Check it out. I found a ping," Rowan announced.

Kai forgot his misgivings about Alexa and him. He'd cross that bridge when they came to it. "Whatcha got?"

After Rowan described the location where the satellite was picking up the pings, Kai was ready to mount a rescue. Only Rowan's hand on his arm stopped him from jumping up and doing just that. "Let's do this right. We've got four of us, up against who knows how many. Let me see if I can get satellite surveillance to see what they've got there."

Damn it! He knew Rowan was right, but thinking of what they could be doing to his Alexa...he stopped the train of thought.

Within a half hour, they knew more men were needed. They were SEALs, but four against twenty odds was a suicide mission. "Men, I know it's dangerous, but hey, that's what we do. If you want to stay back I understand." Kai looked at his team.

Coyle looked at him. "Let's roll out."

"Hold up. I have a few coming in. They'll be here in five."

While Rowan kept watch over the video feed, Kai and his guys armored up. They made sure each had on the thin Kevlar inspired long sleeved shirts. Once they were set to head out, Rowan seemed to know his guys were there as well, standing at the same time.

"Let's go. I've got a couple rigs that will make it through just about anything." Kai followed Rowan out, admiring the large vehicles lining the drive.

"Cap, can we order a couple of these?" Sully ran his hand over the hood of the shiny black four wheel drive in front.

"Hands off, pup." Kellen climbed out.

Sully flipped Kellen off, showing no fear.

Kai climbed in with Kellen and Rowan, leaving Sully and Coyle to catch a lift with one of the other guys. "These things are definitely not subtle," Kai murmured from the backseat.

"What we got coming in from the other side will be our ace in the hole." Kellen turned the wheel, the engine roaring as he accelerated.

Kai hoped like hell they weren't too late, and prayed Alexa didn't hate him for not keeping her safe. When he got his hands on her, he planned to make sure she was safe and unhurt, then after he was sure she was indeed okay, he planned to tie her to his side. Of course, tying her to his bed sounded a lot more pleasurable.

"Hey, mind out of the gutter," Kellen growled from the front, reminding him he wasn't alone, and the men with him were more than mere men.

Kai grunted and raised both his middle fingers in the air.

Chapter Ten

Alexa waited, her head throbbed, blood pooled from the wound. Still she waited for the moment one of the men decided to come to her. The knife safely tucked into her boot. Her only hope lay with them not tag teaming her. Lord, when did she start praying for the lesser of two evils?

"Fine! It's not as if she has to be clean for her parents to come collect her," Pascal laughed.

"I want her first." She recognized Basile's voice.

The sound of arguing ensued. "How about we do this diplomatically? Pick a number between one and ten. The one closest gets her first."

She wanted to snort, or shout, but kept quiet. The dickbags were seriously acting as if raping her was an everyday thing they did.

As each man shouted out his number she was unnerved to hear four different voices other than

Pascal and Basil. Her chances at coming out of the ordeal alive just went down exponentially, then she reminded herself she was a survivor.

One of the men whooped, like he'd won the lottery. Basile cursed fluently in what she supposed was French, but wasn't a hundred percent positive. A hand grabbing her roughly came as a surprise, she was focused on the conversations, and didn't hear him approaching.

"I'll make sure you're nice and prepared for the others," he grated, jerking Alexa to her feet by her hair, fresh blood oozed out of the cut into her eye, making it hard for her to see.

"Here, you may need to wipe off her face or cover it," Pascal joked.

Alexa wished she were closer to the asshole. She'd take her one shot and stab him in the heart.

A towel was thrown at her face, the rough fabric hurt, but she grabbed it before it hit the floor, using it to wipe away the blood. The man leading her away from the other five was huge, in a short fat man sort of way. She looked over her shoulder, trying to gauge the other five. Pascal and Basile along with the other three were all tall and buff. It figured the largest of the group would get his turn first.

He pushed her toward the full sized bed, slamming the door and turning the lock. Interesting! He didn't trust his comrades not to come in while he was having his fun.

She wondered if she could actually kill the man.

He pulled his black sweater off, revealing a large stomach, with a few scars showing he'd been in more than one battle.

"Strip, bitch." His heavily accented voice jarred her from the perusal of his body.

Alexa fell onto the side of the bed, shaking her head. "Please don't do this," she begged.

Laughing he took a step toward her. "Oh, we are going to do this. It's up to you if you are awake or asleep."

Two more steps and he was in front of her. Alexa nodded. "Fine." She slipped her top off, watching his eyes widen. "Can I take my shoes off? I can't get my pants off over them."

He licked his lips and stepped back.

She bent, reaching into the boot and gripped the knife in her right hand. She felt his breath on her back, his hand trailed along her spine. So close, she knew where she was going to aim, and that he was likely to squeal loud enough to bring the others barreling in.

With all her might she lifted the knife, and stabbed him between the legs, his heavy weight fell onto her, knocking them both to the floor. When he didn't make a sound, she worried, trying to get out from under him.

The handle of the blade was warm and wet. Alexa pushed and rolled until she was able to get free of him. He stared up at her, his mouth moving soundlessly. She grabbed the pillow from the bed and put it over his face, fearing he'd yell out. Grabbing his gun before she pulled the knife out. Looking down she noticed she'd cut into his thigh, missing his groin, but the amount of blood flowing out of him was huge. Wiping the blood from her hands on the bedding, she looked around the room. The window was her only way out, but more men patrolled the perimeter.

"What am I going to do," she whispered. It would only be minutes before the next guy was knocking on the door, wanting his turn. Sure she could shoot him, but she'd be dead by the time the third guy came through, if not the second.

She went to the corner of the room far away from the unmoving man and slid down the wall with his gun in one hand and the bloody knife in the other, uncaring she only wore her bra and pants. Her plan was to shoot as many men as she could, before turning the gun on herself. The song by an old eighties rock band came to mind, something about a blaze of glory, making her wish she had one more night with Kai.

A sob broke free. She used her shoulder to wipe it off. Blood from her cut dripped into her eye, making it hard for her to focus on the door, but the sound of raised voices had her tensing. Alexa raised her knees and rested her elbows on them, pointing the gun at the door, she waited.

****

They decided to barrel in and say screw it. Kellen's man had told them there was an urgency in one of the bedrooms with a woman that had Kai all in. The big XV Urban Assault plowed through several men with rifles in hand. Kellen didn't stop in the yard. Hell no. He rolled right up to the steps, and through the front door.

"Yippee-ki-yay, motherfucker," Kellen yelled.

Rowan tossed open his door, laying down a line of fire. "It's great having a crazy family."

Kai shook his head, rolling on the wide porch. Coyle and Sully ran up next to him, their guns at the ready. He appreciated the Iron Wolves more in that moment as they kept the others busy while he and his team entered the cabin. Two men lay on the floor, dead from gunshot wounds to the head.

Using his hand, he motioned for Coyle and Sully to go one way while he went the other. The cabin's layout was a one bedroom, open floor plan, with a mudroom in the back. He sucked in a breath as he eased toward the closed bedroom door, unsure what he'd find.

The door was locked, which didn't surprise him. No noise came from inside, but he knew that didn't mean it was empty. Kai lifted his gun, and shot the lock, then kicked the door open. A bullet came out the door followed by several more. The random shots made him think they weren't being done by a professional. "Alexa, it's me, Kai."

He waited a beat before risking his life by showing his face around the doorjamb. The first thing he saw was a half dressed man lying in a pool of blood with his face covered by a pillow. He winced when he noticed where the blood was coming from. Scanning the room, he finally found the object of his desires hunched in a corner. Her appearance had him covering the distance with more haste than caution even though she had a gun aimed in his direction.

"Baby, what happened," he murmured.

She sat in silence, unblinking. Kai worried she was in shock. Blood oozed from a wound near her eye, but he didn't think all the blood on her body was hers. He looked at the dead body, then back at her. Putting two and two together, he came up with the fact she'd killed a man with her bare hands. He wanted to pull her into his arms and hold her, but they weren't out of danger.

"Come on, luv. Let's get you out of here."

"I kill...I...him" She pointed to the body on the floor.

"I know, baby. You did real good. I'm so proud of you." He found her shirt on the bed and pulled it over her head. "Come on." He put his body between her and the dead man. Sully and Coyle stood in the entryway, taking in the scene.

"Looks like a few got away."

Alexa whimpered. "Which ones?"

Kai looked down at her. "Baby, we don't know." Again he was calling her endearments, but couldn't stop himself.

"Let me see who's here." She stepped away from him, staggering a bit.

He pulled her back into his arms. "Wait for me," he growled. Damn it, she had him acting like a caveman, and that wouldn't do.

"It's okay, they're not too bad." Sully led the way over to the downed men. Meaning they were clean kills.

She looked at the two men on the ground then buried her face in Kai's chest. "Neither of them are Basile or Pascal. Pascal was in charge, and Basile I think is his right hand man. There was one other man in here with them." Alexa shivered in his arms, her head once again buried against his chest.

Holy shit. The woman was surely going to be the death of him. The woman defied all odds in getting herself kidnapped, not once, but twice by madmen, and lived to tell about the experience. His body vibrated with the need to claim her, he wanted, needed, Alexa to understand she was important to him. He sighed and held her closer. Rowan was right about one thing, life did not promise you tomorrow, only the here and now. For as long as he could remember he'd never wanted to promise a woman he'd be there when they woke. His mouth opened, and then closed, unable to utter the words.

"Alright party people. Let's roll out in case there's some sort of device left here as a welcoming that I don't want. You feel me," Kellen stood near the busted up entrance, hands on his hips surveying the scene like he saw dead men every day.

Kai was glad for the interruption. "Here, let me carry you. You're swaying on your feet." The gash on her head was still seeping blood, and her color looked a little too pale.

"I don't feel too well." Alexa's eyes rolled to the back of her head.

"Shit, we need to get her to the hospital now."

Kellen shook his head. "Laikyn is at the club and we have resources there that are much faster."

"Do you trust her?"

Nodding, Kellen jumped into his vehicle and waited for the others to get in. "With my life along with my pack."

That was good enough for Kai. He massaged Alexa's back. Although she was out cold, her breathing was steady. Applying pressure to the wound he kept her from losing any more blood. He let his other hand do a quick exploration of her body, checking for injuries. Other than a few bruises and a knot on the back of her head, he didn't see anything. Damn it. He wished he'd been there sooner, wished he could have protected her from all of this.

"Hey, don't beat yourself up, man. Crazy men do crazy shit." Kellen spoke from the front with one hand draped over the wheel.

Kai wrapped his arms around her waist, drawing her into him so their chests were pressed against one another's. He could feel her heart beating, the steady thrum reassuring. Fuck. He had it so bad. Was this what love was? If so he wasn't sure he was ready for it. Surely there was a rewind, or pause button. His life wasn't made for the hearts and flowers sort that she deserved. No. Not just no, but hell no it wasn't. *Keep telling yourself that Swift.*

They pulled up to the Iron Wolves club, several big men stood outside watching as they passed through. Only Kellen's rig and the one carrying Coyle and Sully kept driving to the back. Kai looked out the rear window, then forward, a question in his gaze as he met Kellen's eyes in the mirror.

"My guys are gonna hit the bar, drink, and get laid. We're going to the clinic in the back. I've let Laikyn know we are coming. She should be ready when we get there."

Rowan hopped out and opened the door for Kai, his offer to take Alexa went unnoticed. The big man shook his head, then they followed Kellen to the steel door marked Clinic. A tall red haired woman stood in the doorway. Her beauty was astounding, yet when she looked at Kellen sadness clouded her features.

"Is this my patient?" She walked up to Kai, taking Alexa's vitals while he held her.

"Yeah." He walked into the surprisingly well equipped triage like space.

"Lay her down. Anyone who isn't going to assist, get out," she said pointing at the door.

Kellen growled.

"In here, I'm the boss, Mr. Styles." One red brow raised.

The alpha growled again, but stomped to the door. "Treat her with respect, and make sure no harm comes to her, or I'll kill all you."

After securing his woman to the indicated place, Kai stepped back. "From what I can tell she's got this nasty gash and a bump on her head." He stayed near the bed.

Laikyn looked at the other men in the room. "Do you want them to see her naked?"

With those words, everyone filed out, leaving Kai alone with the two women.

"I'm going to cut these clothes off of her, assuming most of this blood isn't hers." Laikyn grabbed a pair of scissors.

Kai helped her remove Alexa's boots and socks, then the pants. Relief hit him at the sight of the briefs she'd had on before she'd left Rowan's cabin still on. Surely if they'd had them off her, they wouldn't have been in one piece. The top was ruined, so he silently agreed to allow the doctor to cut it off, along with the bra. More bruises mottled her side, and Kai wished he could find all the men who'd been in the cabin and inflict pain on each of them. He made a mental note of the things he planned to do to the ones who'd escaped when he found them.

By the third bowl of water, Laikyn finally had Alexa cleaned up enough for them to see her injuries. The wound on her head was sewn up with precision that he was reassured wouldn't leave too much of a scar, but Kai didn't think his woman would care too much.

The sight of the needle going into the still unconscious Alexa didn't sit well with him. He noticed within minutes Alexa began to look better.

"Calm yourself. She didn't lose as much blood as you think. She's unconscious more from the exhaustion and knock to the head. I want to keep her here overnight. When she wakes, I'll call you." Laikyn waved her hand.

Tearing his eyes away from Alexa, Kai silently agreed. They needed to speak with the Commander and find out what, if anything, they'd gotten out of the cabin and its inhabitants.

"Here's my number." He scribbled his number on a piece of paper.

Kai caught sight of Kellen a few feet from the door, and with one last glance at Alexa he went toward the other man.

****

Alexa moaned in pain. Her head throbbed. Her side ached, and she was thirsty as all get out. A fresh wave of panic rushed through her veins as she struggled to figure out where she was. She tried to remember the last thing that happened. Kai coming in and rescuing her. *Where the heck am I?* She looked around the room that resembled a hospital room, but not one she'd ever seen before. Under the blanket she grimaced as she realized she was wearing only a thin gown and a pair of underwear. Unable to move her arm, Alexa jerked, then became aware it was due to the IV hooked to her. *Jesus, what the hell is going on?* Monitors beeped, and in the darkness her heart sped up. Did Kai drop her off at some obscure location and leave her?

"Ah, you're awake. How are you feeling? My name is Laikyn. And before you ask, yes, I'm a doctor."

As Alexa's panic began to fade and her eyes adjusted to the dim room, she stared at the tall red head. "Where am I?"

A stethoscope was pressed to her chest before she was answered.

"You're at the Iron Wolves Club. We have a triage center here. I guess you can say I'm the on call doc."

Through her peripheral vision, she watched the doctor moving about the small room, picking up a phone and typing in something. Figured she was texting her boyfriend or something, but seriously, all Alexa wanted to know was where Kai was.

Fear washed over her when Laikyn came back with a syringe. "I don't need any more meds or anything like that. I'm good really. Could you um, unhook me from this thingy so I can go?"

Laikyn laughed. "Aw, you are just so darn sweet. However, I fear I enjoy my life way too much to do that. And, I do believe you have a visitor."

Alexa was sure the doctor had been doing drugs. Maybe she'd been hooking herself up to some IV meds, but with the needle still too close for comfort she didn't feel it wise to say anything.

The door opened, and in walked Kai, melting away some of her fears. "You look much better, luv."

Laikyn snorted. "She's giving me fits, is what she is."

Kai looked at Alexa then the doctor. "What's this nonsense?"

In the middle of all the chaos and terror, she immediately settled. Kai did that for her. She wasn't sure if that was a good thing, or a really bad one. One thing was certain, he was here and she could breathe easier.

"I just told the doctor I was ready to go and didn't need any more meds." She winced as a sudden, piercing pain shot behind both eyes. The small light coming from the hallway became too much, but she didn't want to miss seeing Kai.

"Humor me, hmm? You were just beaten. Again. Kidnapped. Again. Seriously. I think we may need to invest in a giant bubble like in that eighties movie where that boy lived in a bubble. I could totally get behind that, only it would have to be big enough for two." He winked.

"And on that note, I'll give you two some privacy after she agrees to letting me give her this." Laikyn held up the needle.

"What's in it," Kai asked.

She explained it contained a sedative to help with the pain, and with the amount of pounding that had started up, Alexa was ready to agree.

Nodding she held her hand out for Kai. "Will you stay with me?"

He looked at Laikyn then nodded.

The needle was pressed into the IV, and then Laikyn was gone.

"I was scared when I woke and didn't know where I was," she admitted.

Chapter Eleven

Kai climbed into the bed next to Alexa. The club clearly knew most of the patients wouldn't want to spend the night alone, or their mates wouldn't want to leave their wounded alone. Either way, he was more than happy to take advantage of the oversized hospital bed.

She sighed against him. "Where did you go? Super-secret military stuff?"

Her words were beginning to slur, but he answered her. "I had to call in what happened and find out if they were able to trace the men who'd escaped. Tomorrow we'll talk more. Tonight, you rest, I won't leave you."

He was whipped. That is what the guys would call it. Wrapped around the little woman's finger like one of those Chinese finger toys he'd had as a boy. The thought of sticking things into tight spaces had him hard in all the wrong places, and he had to shift so he wasn't poking a sleeping Alexa in the back. Knowing she'd been attacked, again, made him truly want to take her far away from danger. A notion completely absurd for a SEAL, especially one who led a team into some of the worst parts of the world.

Kai took a breath and inhaled, hating the scent of the cleanser Laikyn had used. He preferred the peaches and cream scent that reminded him of Alexa.

The slight vibrating of his phone made him shift enough to where he could reach into his pocket. As he read the incoming text, Kai wasn't sure what the hell was going on. Two French hitmen, who were high up on the most wanted list were named Basile and Pascal. Until Alexa woke, they wouldn't be able to get a positive ID, but the back of his neck itched, telling him they were the same men who'd kidnapped her. The million dollar question, or possibly billion dollar question was why, and how it was all linked to Tyler. Kai's gut told him it all circled back, and somehow his woman was unknowingly involved.

A few quick taps on his device and he let his team know where he'd be if they needed him. When he got another text that Tay and Oz were awake and ready to get out of the hospital, he smiled in spite of the situation. His men didn't know what the meaning of downtime was.

He trusted Lee to keep them safe, but at first light he planned to head there himself. He needed to see Tay and Oz and assess the damage to them both. Rowan had said the video footage showed Alexa opening the door of her own freewill, but Kai knew there was more to it than that. He'd find out from her why she allowed herself to be taken, and then find out what happened in the cabin before they arrived.

Exhaustion hit him. With several men standing guard outside the thick metal building, Kai let himself fall into a light sleep wrapped around Alexa. Tomorrow would come soon enough. He figured he'd need all his wits about him when it came to dealing with the gorgeous thing who owned a huge chunk of his heart if not all, plus facing two fierce SEALs who no doubt wanted retribution.

Noise from the hall woke Kai, bringing him fully alert in seconds, his hand automatically going to the Sig Sauer on his hip.

"Whoa, I just came to check my patient," Laikyn said, arms raised.

Kai holstered the gun, shifting to get up.

"Kai," Alexa whispered.

He smoothed the hair back from her forehead. "Yes, luv?"

"You stayed." Astonishment sparked in her gorgeous eyes.

Uncaring they had company, he lowered his head and kissed her, brushing his lips over hers.

"Oh, god, I have morning breath I'm sure." She turned her head away, a rosy hue lighting her face.

Laikyn laughed. "I'd say you are feeling much better. How's your head?"

Alexa raised her hand, feeling the bandage. "How many stitches do I have?"

"Only four, and they're really close to the hair line. If I do say so myself, your scar won't be very visible, especially if you wear bangs, and even if you didn't it's a badge of honor. You're a fighter. If anyone looks at you sideways send them my way." Laikyn made some notes in her chart, her eyes meeting Kai's.

"Is there something you're not telling me?" Alexa looked from the doctor then to Kai.

"Whatever you have to say, you can tell her as well if it's about her health."

Nodding, Laikyn pulled out a glass tube. "While I was triaging you, I was informed you may have been tagged," she looked at Kai, when he nodded she continued. "We've dealt with something similar. In fact, exactly like this." She held the tube up. "It's virtually undetectable by metal detectors and the like. Similar to say, IUDs or surgical staples, however, after a couple of our people had this done to them, Kellen allowed me to order a device that can detect them. Yours was located at the base of your skull. I'm sorry but I made a small incision that required no sutures, but as it wasn't in long it was easy to get out." Laikyn reassured them.

Kai rolled off the bed to get a better look at what was in the tube. The small cylinder like thing inside didn't look as if it could do any harm, but he knew what damage something inserted into a body, no matter the size, could do. "Have you been able to track its origins?"

Shaking her head, Laikyn offered the glass vile. "No, although we do know the others were injected in the large muscles. Had you been suffering headaches? Vision loss? Things that were out of the normal for you?"

Alexa put her hand to her forehead. "I'd been having headaches, but I assumed it was from stress. I mean I've had a lot going on lately."

"Well I don't know if you have a doctor in the area, but I'm just moving back and would be glad to take you on as a patient. I don't really have an office yet, and haven't actually given notice, but I feel as if you should have someone familiar with your case. You don't have to say yes right away, just think about it. If not, I could give you a couple names of colleagues I know at the hospital close to here. I'm assuming you're planning on staying local?" Laikyn tapped her pen on the clipboard.

An uneasy feeling took up root in his gut. He didn't live in South Dakota. Heck, he lived out of a duffel bag most the time. If Alexa decided to stay, he'd gladly make a move to stay with her, at least when he was between missions. The last thought had him pulling back.

What kind of life could he offer her?

"Yes, that would be wonderful. I hadn't even thought of all those details. Can I get dressed? Holy crap. I don't have any clothes except...oh god, my clothes were ruined by that..." her eyes searched Kai's.

He closed the distance between them, and lifted her up, before settling back on the bed with her in his lap. "You did what you needed to survive." He stroked her back and let her cry into his neck. When Alexa finally let go, the damn of tears and shaking sobs seemed never ending. He looked over her head at Laikyn and watched the doctor shake her head, her lips mouthed 'It's normal', but he wasn't so sure.

Minutes, or hours later, she quieted. "Am I going to go to jail for murder?"

"Hell no, baby. I'm going to need to ask you some questions, but they can wait." They couldn't, but he'd make it to where they could.

Alexa straightened. "No, I need to tell you or your boss, or whoever what happened. Those men are crazy. They think I'm someone I'm not. They were using me to lure some couple here. They called me Alexia."

"Start from the beginning," Kai ordered.

He pulled his phone out and hit record, not wanting to miss a detail. From the sounds of it the men who'd had her were French, yet the names of the people they called her parents sounded Russian, or at least the man. When she finished he sent the recording to Rowan along with a text. "Did they say anything else?" he asked.

"He said they were aware of my attack and made arrangements for me to be sent here, only they stepped in. I met a woman named Marley who I thought was a woman's advocate, only now I don't know who she was. Maybe she was friends with this couple, or maybe they meant you guys. I don't know. I feel so confused." Alexa was shaking.

"Alexa calm down. Let's think this through." Kai tried to soothe her.

"When I was attacked by Danny, Marley came to me and offered me a way out. I got a burner phone and she offered me a place in South Dakota. What are the chances I'd then get abducted by some crazy woman who just happened to have ties to a government man gone rogue, and then meet up with you? I mean I'm all for coincidences, but come on."

Kai had to agree. Something else was going on, and he needed to find out what and who was behind all of this, or Alexa was never going to be safe.

"You met this Marley woman face to face?"

At her nod, he asked if she would be able to give a description. With facial recognition software, Rowan would be able to possibly get a hit on her if she was in the system.

"I want to go back to Chicago and be a normal twenty-eight year old woman. I want to wake up and find out this was all just a bad dream," she sobbed.

Her words were like a dart to his heart, and he had to shore up the strength to give her what she wanted. Life with him was far from normal, or predicable. "I know, baby. We'll figure this out and get you back to something resembling normal. I promise." Even if it was ripping his heart in two to say those words, he'd give it to her. She'd been through too much and deserved better.

He rubbed her back for a few more minutes, then got up, placing her back onto the bed. "Listen, I need to get with Rowan and see if he has found out anything new. I'm also going to see about getting a sketch artist who works with us and see if she can meet us at the hospital. I'd like to get that image of the woman named Marley into the database sooner rather than later."

"Okay. Can I take a shower, and maybe get someone to bring my bag from the cabin here?" Alexa plucked at the gown.

"No need. I can get you something from the club. I'm sure we have something in your size. I'll also bring a little kit with toothbrush and toothpaste and necessities like that. You can shower and wash your hair, just try not to get the bandage wet. I'll check before you leave to make sure the stitches are good to go. Any questions, or need anything else before I go in search of supplies?" Laikyn asked.

Alexa shook her head, drawing her knees up to her chest.

"I'll be back shortly. There are guards outside the door, but nobody should come in except me or the doctor." Kai kissed her forehead. "It's going to be fine. Trust me. I know it's hard because I promised to keep you safe and I've failed miserably, but I won't again."

She grabbed his hand. "It wasn't your fault. I went with them because they threatened to kill Tay and Oz. If I hadn't opened that door when I did, he was going to put a bullet in each of their heads. I couldn't stand there and let that happen."

Kai felt the wind go out of his lungs. He knew she'd gone out voluntarily, he just didn't know why. Hearing she'd done it to save his team members made him weak in the knees. He strode back to the bed, placing his arms on each side of her hips. With her knees in front of her body it was hard for him to get close enough, but he got in her face. "Woman, you are the most courageous, beautiful being in the world. I...my men, owe you a debt of gratitude. Thank you for saving their sorry asses. They are more than just my team, they're my brothers." Careful of her stitches and the small incision on the back of her neck, he weaved his fingers into her hair and kissed her long and hard. She may deserve better than him, but he poured all his heart into that kiss.

****

Alexa's eyes watered at the emotion welling in her heart as Kai kissed her. She'd never been kissed as if she meant something to someone. She didn't fool herself that he loved her, but he must truly care about her, or maybe it was his way of saying thank you for saving his friends. Yes. She decided it was the latter. When he pulled back she ducked her head, hiding her tears from him.

"Thank you Alexa Gordon. We owe you." Kai left before she could tell him she was the one who owed him. They'd saved her countless times.

"Men can be so obtuse." Laikyn walked in with her arms full of clothes, and a small bag.

She wiped the back of her hand across her face. "He was just being nice. I mean I got myself kidnapped while they were guarding me. I sorta offered myself up in exchange for two of his guys so he thinks he owes me."

Laikyn nodded. "Oh, yeah. Men always kiss me like I hung the moon when I save their sorry asses." Working silently she removed the IV and put a band-aid over the small wound.

Alexa pretended to agree, unfolding her legs. "Can I shower now? I feel fine. No headache or too much pain." She winced on the last words. In reality the side of her head ached like a bitch, but she didn't want any drugs. They made her woozy.

"I know you're fibbing about the pain, but I'll let it slide until after your shower. Once you're clean you'll feel a hundred percent better, then I will give you something that won't knock you out, but will take the edge off the pain. Come on, let's get you to the shower. There's a seat in there so you don't have to stand. I can get in there with you if you'd like. PS. I am sooo not into girls, so don't think it's a ploy to get you nekkid or anything. I am all hetero," Laikyn laughed.

She couldn't help but smile while the gorgeous red head helped her to the large bathroom that was nothing like a normal hospital one. "Well, if you were into me I'd have to break your heart as I'm also not into women, but if I was you'd be one I'd go for."

They both laughed while Laikyn showed her how to work the controls and placed a couple towels on the shelf. "Remember to try to keep the bandage dry. I'll be right outside if you need help, just holler."

Alexa looked at the clothing the doctor had procured for her. A pair of red boy short underwear, with the clubs logo on it that still had the tags on them were on top, with a black t-shirt sporting the same logo and a sports bra along with a pair of jeans.

She was pleasantly surprised to see they were all in her size, except the jeans may be a tad too tight, but they were clean, so she wouldn't be complaining.

The shower felt heavenly as the warm water pummeled her back until she turned and the spray hit on the bruises, reminding her she'd been through quite an ordeal. Her legs shook, making her glad there was a bench for her to sit on. She wanted to stay in the spray for hours, but made short work of lathering up the shampoo, being sure to keep away from the incision and then rinsing before conditioning. She used the razor to shave and felt as if she'd ran a couple miles.

Alexa didn't think she had the strength to shut the water off, let alone dry and dress herself. Standing, she turned the knob, then grabbed the towel and sat back down. Breathing heavily she patted her face dry, and after another ten or fifteen minutes, she was dressed with her hair on top her head in a towel.

Laikyn came in with a frown on her face. "You look exhausted. I should've come back in earlier, but I got a call. Here, let me help you back to the bed."

"It's fine. I'm just still kinda weak I guess."

"You need to eat. I ordered you some breakfast."

They walked out together to see a small table set up with two plates piled high with eggs, bacon, toast and an array of fresh fruit.

"Are more people joining us, cause that's a lot of food for just two people." Alexa moved to the table, inhaling the scents.

Smiling, Laikyn pulled out a chair and sat. "Girl, you ain't seen me eat. I could eat most people out of house and home. At my practice in Kansas City, my two partners used to complain that I ate more than the two of them, so I should pay for two instead of one. They were total porchdicks, but damn they were hot as fuck. Too bad I wasn't into threesomes," she sighed, filling her plate up.

Alexa nearly choked on the piece of bacon she'd taken a bite of. "What?"

Laikyn chewed on a grape. "You know what a ménage is, yes?"

"Of course." Alexa read books, actually loved to read stories about them. One of her favorite authors wrote a series about threesomes that made for some really hot fantasies.

"Well, the men I worked with were into that sort of thing, I entertained the idea for like a hot minute, but my heart wasn't in it. They really didn't take no for an answer very well. Have you ever had two men pursue you at once? I mean holy shite. I'd have one in front of me, one behind me, and they were hard all over." Laikyn fanned herself.

A growl sounded from the door leading out to the hallway.

Laikyn's eyes widened. "Hello, Kellen. Our patient is doing much better. Can you inform Mr. Swift she will be ready in about thirty minutes? I'm going to help her dry her hair after we finish eating."

"Oh, I'll tell Mr. Swift, and then you and I are going to have a nice, long conversation, Dr. O'Neil." Kellen stomped away.

"He sounded very angry."

Laikyn smiled. "That's his normal voice. Anyhoo, don't worry about him. Are you done?" Laikyn indicated Alexa's empty plate.

She looked at the half empty plates in front of them, and realized she and Laikyn had devoured most of the food. "Yikes, I keep eating like that and I'll never fit into any of my clothes."

"Girl, you have a figure most women would love. All hour glassy and shit, so hush your mush."

Alexa decided she really did like Laikyn, and for the first time she might have a female friend.

"Well being a glamazon like yourself would be awesome, not to mention I love your red hair."

Laikyn snorted. "Yeah, well being five foot nine sucks when you're a teen girl, and most boys are shorter than you."

"Do you have a boyfriend now," Alexa asked.

"No. I'm sorta in between places, and not wanting to settle down. I want what every girl wants. A man who can't live without you, and is willing to give up all other women for you. The one who is meant to be mine has denied me for years, and I'm done beating my head against a brick wall. I've decided to put my big girl panties on and settle for Mr. Right Now, instead of Mr. Right, if you know what I mean." Laikyn winked.

Not really sure what she meant, Alexa nodded.

"Let's get your hair dried before Kai gets back here. You don't want to look like something the cat dragged in, when your Mr. Right comes back." Laikyn stood and began clearing their breakfast dishes, taking the tray outside. She returned a few minutes later with a cart loaded with all the things from a portable salon.

"I borrowed one of the staffs stuff."

Great, so she was using some chick named Cinnamon or something like that's stripper gear. Beggars couldn't be choosers, and Alexa didn't judge a woman for taking off her clothes. She suspected the club was probably one of the better places to do it in. Alexa thought it best not to ask.

Chapter Twelve

Kai's mind was spinning. The intel they were getting back on the couple, who were supposedly Alexa's parents, were reported to be dead, and were indeed Russian. They'd gone off the radar shortly after an assassination attempt on them and their young child Alexia Smirnov, had gone wrong. Then reports of their bodies being found were given to multiple governments, case closed, until now.

"From what I'm piecing together, the Smirnov's were Russian officials who knew too much. Somehow they got out, but didn't get out. I don't know how they got separated from Alexa." Rowan shook his head.

Looking at the image of Katalinia, she was the striking image of Alexa. Kai didn't understand how parents could abandon their child to the foster system, unless they thought she'd get lost making it virtually impossible for the Russians to find her. Even then to give up a child was not something he could see doing. Not when they'd stayed together all this time. Or at least it appeared that way from the image they'd been able to procure with the facial recognition.

"Any leads as to where the Smirnov's are as of now?"

He hated the unknown. There was a shit storm going down, and it was being brought onto U.S. soil. With two factions, the French and Russians, add in the bastard who betrayed them, and Kai feared if Tyler was in cahoots with the men who'd held Alexa, he'd be throwing his career away when he killed the man without a fair trial.

"I should have more within the next couple hours. Believe me, these two are smart. If they entered the country, they aren't gonna come in looking like themselves." Sitting back with a sigh, Rowan crossed his arms over his abs. "You can't go off halfcocked, man. I know you want to, I'd do the same in your position for Lyric, but you can't. Think with your head, not your heart."

"I'm heading to the hospital to check on Tay and Oz. Can I get an escort and take your rig?" Kai ignored Rowan's words.

"You're a stubborn sonofabitch, you know that right?"

Flipping Rowan the bird, he waited.

"Of course you can use my truck. I'm going to see if Kellen is cool with sending a few guys for backup, and before you say shit, remember our boys are hard to kill, and you need it."

"See, you don't know shit. I was going to say thank you." Kai smirked. He wasn't taking Alexa's safety for granted ever again, nor did he want to leave her behind.

"Asshole," Rowan growled.

He left the space his ex-team member had claimed as his own, hurrying toward the clinic where he'd left Alexa.

His heart nearly stopped at the vision she made in a pair of tight denim jeans with strategic rips, and an even tighter T-shirt, that should be illegal for a woman who was built like his Alexa to wear. "Fuck me running." He ran the back of his hand across his mouth, sure he was drooling.

"Laikyn brought me these from the club. They're a little snug." She plucked at the top.

A little snug his foot. He wanted to rip the outfit off and bury his dick into her tight sheath. The outfit fit her like it was made just for her. He knew the men outside the club would all be salivating when they caught a glimpse of Alexa. Jealousy and the need to make sure they all understood she was his rode him. "Come here," he ordered.

Alexa crossed to him, allowing Kai to pull her into his body. He sealed his mouth over hers, taking possession while his hands gripped her ass in his palms. The fullness filled them. Her lush breasts pressed against his chest, the hard peaks of her nipples tempted him to lift the T-shirt and taste them, but time wasn't their friend. The next time he made love to Alexa, and there would be a next time, he wanted to do it in a bed where they had more than a few stolen moments.

"God, I want to say screw everything and make love to you," he said between kisses.

Her breath sawed in and out. "Me, too. You make me horny damn it, and I only have one pair of panties." She blinked up at him.

He liked that she teased him. "Let's go before I forget my good intentions." The large bed they shared the night before mocked him. "How are you feeling?" The bruising on the side of her face ate at him.

"A little sore, but Laikyn gave me some high dose ibuprofen. I told her I wouldn't take anything stronger. I hate being loopy."

Kai understood her need for control. Taking a step back, he kept hold of her hand and walked toward the door. "We're heading to the hospital to check on Tay and Oz, then we'll go back to Rowan's cabin. I don't think the men who came at us will think we'd use the same place again. With the tracker gone I'm hoping they won't have an upper hand."

"That's a lot of supposition and hoping." Her hand flexed in his.

"We have more backup this time. Ones who don't rely on sight and who know the lay of the land. Don't worry. I'm not letting you out of my sight for a minute."

"Really?" She looked up at him with a look of promise in her eyes.

He stopped next to the truck. "Not even for a second. Where you go I go. Where you sleep, I sleep. Feel me?"

She nodded, a blush covering her from every exposed inch he could see.

"Good. Now in you go." He lifted her easily, before climbing in next to her on the driver's side. He fastened her seat belt before doing up his own. Coyle and Sully climbed into the big king cab pickup with them without a word. Two vehicles filled with men lined up with blacked out windows. Kai had spoken with Rowan and agreed one would lead and one would take the rear. All three rigs looked alike, so anyone tailing wouldn't know which one held who.

"This is like the presidential thing, only not," Alexa joked.

Kai rested his palm on her thigh. "Hey, you are just as important to me." Truer words had never been uttered from him.

"Damn, I hate fucking losing," Sully groaned, handing Coyle a crisp twenty.

"What the hell you talking about?" Kai fixed them both with a stare in the rearview mirror.

Sully held the money in his hand. "Just a friendly wager between friends."

He was pretty sure he didn't want to know, nor did he want to embarrass Alexa, but planned to punch both men when he had a moment alone with them.

"Back to the business at hand, boys. When we get to the hospital, I want Alexa flanked on all sides. We don't know what the danger looks like, and they could already be there for all we know. She is not to leave our sides for a second. If I'm called away, then you two are not to allow her out of your sight. Period. I don't care who orders you otherwise. Feel me?" Kai met both men's gaze. Even if Commander Lee were to order them, they'd listen to Kai, taking a court martial in the process. Kai would do the same for them.

Hoorah echoed in the cabin of the truck.

"I don't want any of you getting hurt or in trouble for me." Alexa entwined their fingers.

He flipped his hand over, sealing their palms. "This is my mission, luv. You do what I say and no going against my orders or I'll tan that luscious ass red."

Her gasp made him smile.

****

Alexa couldn't believe the outrageous things Kai was saying. And in front of his fellow SEALs for that matter. She glanced a quick look over her shoulder, to see both men looking out the window on each side as if Kai hadn't just threatened to spank her.

"You can't threaten to spank me, Kai," she whispered.

"Just did." The infuriating man said without letting go of her hand.

She could see the corner of his mouth trying to hold back a grin. Lord, she was in love with the big bad SEAL. He was intent on keeping her safe, even if it meant throwing his own life on the line. No one had ever done that for her. Like she mattered. Kai Swift was her salvation, but she didn't want him to die because of her. She'd be his too.

"I don't like that look on your face, woman. You best not be plotting anything that will get your fine ass into danger. I may only have been joking about spanking you, but I'm not above locking you in an undisclosed location until this threat is eliminated." Kai's dark gaze slid toward her.

"Promise you won't do anything foolish?" She couldn't live if anything happened to him because of her. The world would be a sorry place if Kai wasn't in it. No one would even know if she left.

"I can do that. I never do anything foolishly."

Two simultaneous snorts came from the back.

"I don't think you two want me to respond to that. Now do you?" Kai pulled into the parking garage of the hospital.

"No, Cap. You are not a foolish man," Sully said with a straight face that Alexa didn't buy at all.

They entered the floor where Tay and Oz were being kept, shocked at the amount of military personnel with guns outside their door.

"Our Commander promised he'd keep them safe until they were able to get out." Kai showed the guards on duty his ID before they were allowed to enter the room.

Alexa's breath came out in a sob of relief when she spotted both men sitting up.

"Hey, don't you ever offer yourself up as hostage for our sorry hides again," Tay muttered.

Alexa let go of Kai's hand, rushing to the first bed where Tay was. "I couldn't let them shoot you in the head. How are you?" She reached a hesitant hand toward his bruised face.

Tay grabbed her hand, his grip strong. "A couple bruised ribs, some internal bleeding. Nothing major."

"Hey, what about me?" Oz's deep voice growled from the next bed. He looked just as bad with his dark red hair and usual tan face almost pale.

She placed a chaste kiss on Tay's cheek. "I'm glad you're going to be okay."

Hurrying over to Oz, she touched his whiskered cheek. "Poor thing. How bad is it?"

"I fear I won't be jumping out of planes anytime soon." He pointed at his leg.

"Is it broken?" Kai asked from the foot of the bed.

Oz glanced up. "Nah, just cracked. I'll be right as rain in a few weeks. You, young lady, should listen to Tay. We wouldn't have been able to live with ourselves if something had happened to you because of what you did for us."

"Well I guess we are even. You both are here because of me." She looked up at Kai, questioning whether he was going to tell them about the couple who was supposedly her parents. She still couldn't wrap her mind around that one.

Kai pulled her in for a hug, and explained in hushed tones how he was going to use hand motions to explain to his team there was more going on. It made sense he wasn't sure if the room was secure with doctors, nurses, and cleaning staff coming in and out. Tay and Oz nodded, letting them know they understood. Both men were ready to get out, but health wise they needed a few more days.

Motion at the door drew all their gazes. Coyle jerked in front of Kai and Alexa.

She recognized JoJo's voice in the hallway.

"Let him in," Kai said.

JoJo came in with a woman and another man. Alexa thought the woman looked familiar, but she couldn't place her.

"Kai, thanks for letting us in. I felt a little exposed out there." JoJo stood with his hands at his side.

"Who you got with you there, son?"

"My name is Mad, and this is Hailey, or Hales. We are aware you think we are traitors, but I can assure you we are not." Mad's hands flexed in agitation.

"Hailey. You worked at the office I do. Or did?" Alexa looked up at Kai.

The other woman shook her head. "I was there as part of your protection. My name is Hailey Ashley." She stood between JoJo and Mad.

Alexa envied the blonde woman for her obvious confidence. She was a little taller than average. Lean or more like muscular. In the outfit she was wearing it was hard to tell, but Alexa remembered seeing Hailey in a form fitting dress and wished she had the skinny figure to wear such a thing.

"I'm assuming Blake is doing well?" Kai kept his body in front of Alexa.

JoJo nodded. "Yeah, he came home yesterday."

"Listen, we ain't here to kill you or your team. None of us have death wishes. Dex is still missing, and that puts us all at risk. He knows all of our homes. Damn, man, he knows our families." Mad ran his hand over his bald head, his deep voice gone deeper.

"Lee spoken with the three of you?"

Mad snorted. "You mean interrogate, then yeah. We ain't lying. Dex tried to kill Blake. Hales and I trailed him, but he lost us in traffic. That fucker has help. Like major help is all I can surmise. I told Lee all this. Did he not convey it all to you?"

Kai raised his fist and everyone stopped speaking. Every word Mad spoke may be overheard by whoever was listening if they'd bugged the room. Alexa hated the need for all the precautions. Her life was one big ball of crazy. Yet, looking at Kai, she didn't think she was too upset since it also brought her him.

The three newcomers nodded.

"I'm assuming you're still at the apartment building where Alexa was to be staying?"

JoJo nodded. "We all have apartments there. Dex hasn't been back and all the security has been upgraded. Trust me, computers weren't his thing."

Kai tilted his head. "No, but they were others. Don't relax your guard."

"Never. Not after this." JoJo agreed.

Mad stepped forward. "Hales and I would like to help you."

"You'd help by guarding your team's back, and keeping me informed if Dex reaches out to you. More than likely when he outlives his usefulness, he'll be disposed of."

His harsh words made her heart clench. Luckily his arm reached out to steady her.

Hailey lifted a file, making Sully jump in front of her. A gasp left the blonde woman's mouth. "Easy there. I was going to give you a file on Dex. I compiled a list of his strengths and weaknesses. Things you might be able to use."

Alexa didn't think the other woman sounded frightened. More like she enjoyed being manhandled by the large man.

Sully took the folder, flipping through it before tucking it under his arm. "Thank you." He ran his knuckle down the middle of Hailey's chest. "You should get an upgrade on your Kevlar."

"Yeah, well, we aren't as high up as y'all." Hailey stepped away from Sully.

Undercurrents zipped between the two SEALs.

A knock sounded on the door, then Commander Lee walked in with a petite blonde woman next to him. "Holy shit, Jaqui Wallace. As I live and breathe. Come give me some sugar." Oz held out his arms.

"You always were a charmer, Oz." The woman walked with purpose over to Oz's bed, brushed her hand over his forehead, then kissed the tip of his nose. "Been jumping out of perfectly good airplanes lately?"

"What the hell brought you out here, Jaq?" Kai asked.

The blonde stood straight. "Well, seems you're a couple men short, and since I'm twice the man as most, I'm filling in."

Jealousy stirred in Alexa as she watched the gorgeous female stare at Kai with an unblinking blue gaze.

"Where's my hello, Ace?" Tay questioned from the other bed.

"Same place as my last goodbye." Jaqui muttered, but her gaze cut to Tay, flinching when she looked at him.

"With all due respect, Commander, I don't think it's wise to bring in another player right now," Kai said.

Commander Lee looked at the group. "Yeah, well with your computer specialist out of commission you need one. Jaqui just got back from the Middle East and was available. So now she's on your team until this is over. This is a high-profile case that needs people I trust on it."

Alexa looked from the commander to the woman. She guessed Jaqui to be around her own age, but wondered why he trusted her above all other SEALs. Kai sighed, but agreed. Alexa wanted to ask more, but in the hospital knew they wouldn't answer any more questions.

"I'm not out of commission, Commander," Tay gritted out between clenched teeth.

Commander Lee raised his brows. "Son, from where I'm standing, even the civilian here could probably take you. Rest and get better. I have no fear you'll both be back in fighting form in no time." Pivoting on his boot, the man left without another word.

"He's very intimidating." Alexa glanced around at the others.

Hailey laughed. "Ya think?"

Mad clapped his hands together. "Alright, we need to get. I'm sure you know how to get ahold of us. However, we have no way of reaching you if we find anything. Do you want to set something up, or what?"

"You find anything, type a message to each other. I'll see it," Jaqui said.

"Not another one," Mad groaned.

The blonde woman giggled. "Oh I assure you, I'm even better, or scarier than whoever you're thinking of, baby."

Tay growled. "Stop flirting with every damn man you come across."

Jaqui lifted her middle finger. "Sit and spin, Taylor Rouland."

"I got something you can sit and spin on."

"Been there. Done that. Got the skid marks from you leaving so fast. I don't need a repeat thank you very much." She smiled.

Alexa saw the hurt the woman didn't quite hide fast enough.

"Alright, we need to head out. Oz, you and Tay focus on healing and I'll keep you up-to-date on what's going on as much as I can. If you hear or see anything here let me know." Kai bumped knuckles with each man before he came back to Alexa's side.

She looked at both SEALs. Their swollen features hurt her, but she was glad they were both alive. "Thank you both for...everything." She went to Oz and hugged him, careful of his injuries, then did the same to Tay.

As they exited, she noticed Mad and JoJo flanked Hailey, while she and Jaqui were sandwiched between Kai and Sully. She wondered how they appeared to others they passed in the hallway.

"I bet they think we are the luckiest bitches in the world." Jaqui bumped her shoulder. "Call me Jaqui, not Ace even if the guys call me that. Okay?"

Alexa nodded. "I'm Alexa."

"I know. I read your file. Sorry about your shit storm of trouble. You're in really good hands. Now, for the most important detail. I've never slept with Kai. Not that he isn't drool worthy or anything."

"I can hear you, you know." Kai stabbed his finger on the down button of the elevator.

"Of course you can hear me. You're like two feet from us. And clearly you're not leaving Alexa's side anytime soon. I just wanted to make sure she didn't try to stab me with any daggers, real or fake."

Alexa decided then and there she was going to like Jaqui. Two women in one day who were truly nice. Heck, at the rate she was going she'd have two girlfriends. She who'd been virtually friendless. Fear of what could happen to them made her stop in her tracks.

"Don't borrow trouble, Alexa." Jaqui pulled her into the elevator.

Chapter Thirteen

The ride back to Rowan's cabin was made in silence, broken only by Jaqui's fingers tapping the keyboard of her computer. It reminded her of Tay and his penchant for always having his hands on a computer of some sort. Alexa wondered at the couple's relationship. If she was more adept at the whole girlfriends' thing, she'd ask more questions.

"Rowan's got men surrounding the cabin. I want all of us inside. Nobody in or out unless approved by me. Alexa is staying in the safe room now instead of one of the suites. I'll be staying with her as added protection. The only ones with the code will be she and I. Any questions?" Kai pulled up in front, shutting the truck off. The vehicle in front sat idle as did the one behind them.

"Is there food in there? I'm starving." Sully's stomach growled.

Kai shook his head. "Growing men need their food I guess." When he opened his door, the others seemed to take that as their cue, opening theirs as well. "All is clear. Come on, luv. Let's get you inside."

Alexa felt exhausted. She allowed Kai to pull her into his side, secretly glad he showed such caveman instincts. The front of the house had been cleaned. No sign of the blood marred the windows or porch. Nobody mentioned it so she kept her mouth shut. Inside looked the same, but she remembered vividly the sound of gunshots. Looking around she didn't see any holes, and wondered if Rowan had magic fairies come out, then laughed at the absurdity.

"What's that little giggle about," Kai questioned.

"It looks normal around here." She spun in a circle.

Kai placed his hands on his hips. "A few well-placed pics, some wood glue and things are like new. Believe me. Ro is a magician. This isn't our first rodeo, sweetheart. Come on, you look dead on your feet."

"Thanks. Just what a woman wants to hear," she said, taking his hand.

He looked over his shoulder. "Trust me. I still look at counters and think of strip poker. I'll never look at a deck of cards without getting hard and wanting to fuck you ever again. You are gorgeous, even though you look like you're ready to fall at my feet."

The rest of her heart fell in love with him in that moment. Alexa looked around to see if anyone had overheard his outrageous comment, but shouldn't have worried. Her SEAL was too smart and cautious to allow anyone into their personal business.

Once inside the safe room, he told her the code he'd had programmed in. The code was the hand he'd won the card game against her with. She had to enter the number three followed by zero, then the number three and repeat it again. Damn man had beat her with a pair of threes, but they were both winners in that game.

There was a good sized bed, nothing like the king one she'd had in the other room. She glanced at it and then at Kai, making a snap decision. "Make love to me, Kai."

"You're tired, and still sore."

She shook her head, then stopped at the pull to the stitches. "I'm not that tired. And I have faith you will be careful with me. We don't have any promises of tomorrow, only now. There's a quote that I've always loved. It goes something about *Yesterday is history. Tomorrow is a mystery. Today is the present. Treat it as the gift it is.* I don't want to regret not taking advantage of what I have been given. I've been given another day. Another day with you. None of us are promised another day, but we have now. We have what's right in front of us." She grabbed the front of the borrowed shirt, lifting it over her head.

Kai groaned. "Have mercy."

"They didn't have a bra that was pretty, only this little number." Alexa grabbed the elastic bottom and pulled it over, careful not to hit her stitches with the sports bra.

"Damn, I love your breasts. Hate that they're marked with these." He traced the mottled colors on her side.

"Ssh. Take your shirt off. I want to see you." Alexa kicked her shoes off, sat on the side of the bed and began removing her socks, watching Kai place his weapons on a chair next to the bed.

She licked her lips at the sight of his ripped abs, loving how they flexed as he bent to remove his combat boots and socks.

Standing, she unbuttoned the tight denim, shimming to work them over her hips. The red panties she left on, wanting to see his face when he read the words written on her ass.

"Nice briefs. Laikyn get those for you, too?"

Alexa nodded.

Kai swallowed. "She's got great taste in lingerie. I'll have to let Kellen know."

With a mischievous smile, Alexa did a slow turn, showing him her ass. The Iron Wolves logo, scrawled on the rear end, stating she was open for business had made her laugh, but now she wondered what Kai would think.

"The only business you are open for is me." He pulled her ass flush with his front.

"I certainly hope so." She wiggled against him.

His big hands palmed her breasts, tweaking her nipples while his head bent and kissed her full on the lips. Alexa closed her eyes, relishing in the feel of having Kai surround her.

One hand trailed down her stomach, easing under the edge of her underwear. "Damn. You're so wet."

"For you." She shivered at the feel of his teeth grazing her neck. The pleasure sweeping over her was beautiful in its all-consuming need. Kai lifted her, carrying her over to the bed, his lips continued to tease hers while he laid her down.

He lifted from her, the heat in his dark gaze ignited a fire in her belly, and then he was stripping himself bare. She hadn't seen him completely naked before, their quick tryst in the kitchen not nearly enough.

"Damn, you keep eating me up with your eyes, and I'm gonna pounce on you like a boy," he growled. "You have the most exquisite body. All soft curves. Makes me want to do dirty things with you."

A shudder of need, anticipation of what's to come worked its way through her. She wondered just how dirty he could get and if they had time to explore all those things.

He stood at the foot of the bed, completely naked. "Take those panties off for me. Slow and easy, luv," he ordered, working his shaft up and down.

Even before she realized she was complying, Alexa had worked the small red panties off and tossed them over the edge.

"Now spread those thighs for me. Show me how wet you are." His voice already so deep had gone gravelly, sending a shiver down her spine.

"You know I'm already wet, Kai. Don't make me wait, or I just might have to finish myself off without you." She trailed her own hand down the slight curve of her belly.

"Trust me baby. You want to wait for me to pleasure you, or I'll make you wait all damn night before I let you come," he said before taking her ankles in both his big palms, and pulling them apart.

Alexa whimpered, forcing herself to relax in his hold rather than fight him, knowing pleasure awaited her at his touch.

The bed shifted as he moved between her spread thighs on the mattress, his hands moving up her legs in a slow glide. He was killing her with his callused touch, and she wanted more. Gently, he parted her folds. A stream of warm air blew on her exposed flesh. "God, I can't seem to get enough of you," he crooned. His lips sipped, licked, drawing out her pleasure.

Alexa's nails bit into his shoulders, powerful muscles bunched under her hands as he took her with his mouth. His hands held her still when she arched up into him, feeling her orgasm rushing closer, she cried out. The feel of his lips suckling, then laving sent shards of sensation forking straight to her core.

"You like that?" He murmured against her flesh as she held his head to her.

When he captured her swollen nub between his teeth, and worked two fingers into her, she came undone. Shivers rocked her, muscles locked down and tremors of ecstasy rolled through her as she yelled out his name.

"Kai, I need you in me."

Kai brushed his lips up her stomach over her breasts, kissing one nipple then the other before claiming her lips. He reached over, keeping half his weight on Alexa while he grabbed a foil packet from the table next to the bed. He leaned back and smiled down while he made a show of rolling the condom on.

"Oh, you'll have me." His weight came over her, sheltering her, caging her in with both arms next to her head. "Put me inside you."

Reaching between their bodies, she guided the blunt tip of his erection to her opening, feeling it disappear inside her was almost enough to make her come again. Her inner muscles rippled around the latex covered flesh, working to accept him.

"Damn, baby, you feel so good, so tight. Perfect," he rasped as he pressed forward.

Her knees lifted, hugging his hips as he shifted. He was everywhere all at once, and she automatically tightened her legs and arms on him, making him groan against her neck.

"Keep that up and I won't last," he whispered. "My control is slipping as it is."

Kai pulled back almost completely out, then powered back in, pleasure washed over her in throbbing waves. She shifted against him. "More," she pleaded.

He gripped one knee and pulled it up higher, his hold tight, his breathing raspy. "You are asking for trouble." But he gave her more, moving harder and faster.

She moved her hips faster. Sensations of heat and wildness moved through her. Each hard push into her had her racing toward that place she'd only found with Kai. The rasp of his erection, rubbing against her delicate flesh, over sensitive nerve endings was her undoing.

"Yes! That's it. Milk my cock." He pulled back onto his knees, holding her legs as he shafted back and forth faster.

Alexa screamed in pleasure, his expression all the more carnal and arousing as he watched where they were connected. The feel of his hard flesh working in and out of her, his words turned her on as his thrusts increased.

Perspiration coated them both, sliding along their bodies and creating a friction against their slick flesh. She couldn't hold on. Didn't want to.

"Kai," she wailed, her inner muscles clenched, ripples of delight tightened around him. She held onto his shoulders letting the waves crash over her.

"Oh, God, I can't stop," he gritted out.

She didn't want him to.

They lay together for long minutes, catching their breaths. His weight a welcome presence over her. When he tried to lift off her, she held him with her strength, knowing he could have broken her hold at any moment.

Gathering her courage, she kissed his neck where he'd buried his face in the crook of hers. "Where do we go from here?"

Like pouring a bucket of water on a fire, he lifted up, allowing his body to separate from hers. "Let me get rid of this and then we'll talk."

****

Kai went into the small bathroom, disposing of the used condom and washing his hands. He stared at his reflection and thought of the woman in the other room. Damn. He loved her. A woman they didn't know who she truly was. He shook his head and went back out, finding a yawning Alexa barely awake.

He sat on the side of the bed. With the only other light from the bathroom, other than the small security lights illuminating the room, she looked like an ethereal being lying there. He wanted to climb in beside her and hold her while they both slept, but he knew there were things he needed to check on.

Kai bent his head, slanting his lips over hers, his tongue pressed between hers. Before he could allow hunger to spiral out of control, something that was always going to happen with this woman, he pulled back.

"You need some rest. I'm going to see what my team has found out. Don't open this door for anyone. If I want in, I know the code. Don't come out unless I come to get you. We are on lockdown here, Alexa. You need to take your safety as a top priority."

His need to keep her safe overrode everything else, and only seemed to grow with each minute in her presence. He saw the gleam of love he glimpsed in her amazing eyes when she looked at him, every soft sigh she made, and swore he'd make sure they had years to explore each other further.

She would be his destruction, but he'd be her salvation even if she didn't want him to be.

Lifting his head, he stared into her sleepy face, flushed with spent desire, he gave her one last kiss. "Get some sleep. I'll come back shortly."

She nodded, another yawn wracked her slight figure. He grabbed the comforter from the floor where it had been knocked off, and drew it over her. She made him all domesticated, and didn't that just make him scared shitless.

Hell yes it did.

He dressed, checking on Alexa one last time, then stepped out of the safe room.

"How's your girl?" Sully glanced up from a computer.

Kai walked to the fridge and grabbed a beer. He popped the cap and then faced his friend. "She's resting."

Sully's lips tugged up into a grin. "She's a tough one." He nodded at Kai. Taking the hint, Kai turned back to the fridge and grabbed a bottle for Sully.

"No thanks, I try not to drink on a mission," Jaqui said.

Coyle stood behind Jaqui watching as she pulled footage up with the facial recognition software. His glowering expression made him look savage. He was furious and Kai didn't know why. Moving around to see what they were looking at, he was shocked at the images flashing over the screen.

"Oh, they're good, but my program is better." Jaqui smiled.

"Are those her supposed parents?" Kai stared at the well-dressed couple at LaGuardia airport. The fact they were able to get into America proved they had some great contacts, or ironclad identifications. Since nine eleven, security had become tighter for international travel.

"Can you enlarge on the woman's face?"

Jaqui nodded, making the image of the female larger. "Damn, how do you know that's Katalinia? She looks nothing like Alexa." Kai tilted his head to get a better look.

Another image popped up of the woman going into the ladies room. They watched for over ten minutes while the man waited for his companion to come out. The lady who walked up to him, looked nothing like the one who went in.

"Holy shit. Prosthetics?" Kai asked.

"That would be my guess," Jaqui agreed. They learned all kinds of tricks when going undercover, but his team had never employed the use of such things.

"So who ticked you off, Coyle?" Kai asked, watching the couple making their way to the baggage claim. The expensive luggage with the LV logo stood out like a beacon.

"Look at the way they move. Them are trained individuals we are watching. Why the hell would they abandon their child to the system like that? Hell, look at their clothes and luggage," Coyle's grated, disgust evident.

He was a child of poverty. His own mother had no clue who his father was. By the time he'd been ten he'd been in and out of trouble more than he could count. His mother finally left him in juvenile hall until he was eighteen where he decided to join the Navy. He was one of eight, and even now had no connection to the siblings he didn't get to grow up with.

"They probably thought they were doing her a favor." Kai shrugged, thinking about the little Alexa owned.

"Yeah, let's just drop our child and go about the world and be rich playboys or what the fuck ever," Coyle said.

Jaqui tapped the computer a few times. "Alright, let's focus. I have them in New York this morning. From what I can tell they rented a car. I was able to tap into the GPS of their rental. Here is where it gets tricky. They drove down the coast, and you guessed it, hopped a plane to good ole South Dakota. Problem is I now have to watch video of every passenger who got on their flight, and match it with every passenger who got off. Tricky little buggers probably switched it up during the flight, but I won't know for certain until I watch." She sat back with a sigh.

"Well, that's just great. Mommy and daddy are coming home," Coyle snarled.

Kai placed his hand on Coyle's shoulder. "Dude, you need to chill. These people are not mom and pop to anyone. We don't know if they are friend or foe, only that they are supposedly Alexa's parents. For all we know they are part of the terrorist organization we took out a couple years ago. The same one that Tyler was working with." Kai breathed out.

He hated the hurt his friend still showed glimpses of. His mother gave up on her oldest child, leaving him in juvie for the last eight years of his youth. The dark eyes and smiling man hid scars that Kai was sure no child should have faced.

"Whatever. They are dicks." Short and succinct was Coyle.

Rueful amusement filled his eyes at the other man's words. "I agree, but let's not forget, even dicks get..."

Jaqui stopped him with a hard glare. "If you even think of saying something stupid I will bean you on the head with the closest thing possible, which would be a shame, cause I'm mighty fond of this baby." She hugged her computer.

Holding up his hands, Kai thought better of voicing his statement. "Have we checked out what's for dinner?"

"I'll make spaghetti. I saw the makings for it in the pantry, if you don't mind store bought sauce. There's spices that can be added, and you'll never know it's not homemade," Coyle promised.

"Sounds good. I can't cook to save my life. Microwaves and I are best friends. Or the take out menu."

While Coyle made do with what they had, Jaqui continued her search. Kai went to the room Rowan had set up for security. If the men who'd taken Alexa last time were using the same blocking material as before, they'd be in for a treat with the Iron Wolves roaming the grounds. His phone vibrated on his belt. At the sign of no caller ID, he immediately plugged it into the system.

"Swift here."

Silence greeted him. Long seconds passed, then a series of beeps. "Ah, you have a blocking on your phone. That is good."

Kai didn't recognize the voice, nor the accent. "I'm assuming you have a reason for calling and it isn't for small talk. Who is this and what do you want?"

"You have something I want, and I have something you need. I think we can make a trade that will be beneficial for the both of us. No?"

He kept his tone level. "First off, you didn't answer my question. Who are you? What do you have that I'd want?"

A few clicks on the computer alerted Jaqui and Rowan to the call, but he knew they wouldn't be able to trace it back to its source. However, he could make out sounds in the background, which meant they may be able to identify where they were.

"I thought you were smarter than that, SEAL," he tsked. "You don't need to know who I am to know what I have. How would you like to know where Tyler is?"

Not willing to give this terrorist anything Kai kept silent.

"You need proof I understand. How about I send you a little picture of the man you thought was on your side. A recent picture of him closer than you thought?" Will that work to convince you to make a trade with me?" Smug challenge lit his voice.

"What do you mean, closer than I thought?" Kai's head jerked in the direction of the door, seeing Sully standing there with his finger on his lips.

"I'll send you proof and then call you back. Stop trying to track me, SEAL. It's useless."

Kai stared at the phone. Without thinking twice he took the battery out before looking at Sully. "What are the chances he can track me through my cell?"

Sully shook his head. "How the hell did he get your number in the first place would be a good question." Sully took his phone out and removed his battery. They went into the kitchen, explained what went down and had Coyle along with Jaqui's cell phone and batteries separated.

"This is not good, brother." Coyle stopped stirring the sauce. "What did he say he wanted?"

"I think we all know what he wants," Kai grunted. "Over my dead body will he get his hands on Alexa."

"Good to know. I'd cut your nuts off if you even thought of using her as bait. Now, you need to go in and put your battery back in and see what he sends you. If he has the technology and was tracking you, he done knows where we are. You were on the line with him long enough for him to get a lock on you, unless the owner of this place has some sort of energy field blocking satellite frequency that I don't know about. My theory is he was fishing. He's hoping you are willing to trade a tit for tat." Jaqui's voice hardened.

"We all want Tyler, man." Sully sat down with a heavy sigh.

"We'll get him," Kai agreed.

Chapter Fourteen

Alexa's heart shattered. They vowed to protect her, but at the first opportunity to get what they wanted, she was dispensable. She shoved her fear down, and moved back toward the safe room, looking around wildly for something, anything to protect herself with.

If they gave her back to Pascal, or Basile, she knew she would die. Panic threatened to overwhelm her, making her stomach roll. The heavenly scent of Italian spices from moments before sending her into the bathroom, losing what little she had in her stomach until dry heaves wracked her.

"Aw, sweetheart, here," Kai murmured holding her hair.

She wanted to swat his hand away, but didn't have the energy. On weak legs she stood, staring into his liquid brown eyes. They were eagle sharp and fierce. Alexa couldn't look at him a moment longer.

The small bathroom too intimate. Having him help her while she tossed her cookies, too much. She needed a moment. A second to breathe. Her throat was raw. Betrayal burned in her gut.

"I need to brush my teeth." Truth. He'd know if she was lying.

Her lungs were having trouble working, as was her heart, the fast racing beat made her breathless. Pain still resonated through every fiber of her being. What did she expect? Him to vow to love her forever?

"Come out when you're done. Coyle's made some spaghetti." His hand brushed her back.

She wanted to weep for the loss of what might have been. What should have been. Waiting until she knew he was gone, she turned the water on and let the tears fall, wracking sobs silently shook her.

Her lips parted on a gasp as warm callused hands pulled her into a hard chest. "What's wrong, luv?"

She shook her head. How could he hold her like she was precious, and plan to give her to monsters? "I think it's finally catching up with me."

Kai leaned back. "That's understandable. When this is all over, you and I'll go out for a nice, normal dinner and movie date."

Alexa frowned. "You want to date me?"

He stared down at her, his arms tightened. "Do you think I sleep with every woman I rescue on a mission?"

Her gaze flickered away. "I don't know."

One of his arms came up, making her look at him. "No, I don't make it a habit of sleeping with women on a mission. Now, that's not to say I'm celibate during one, just that I've never wanted to make love to one like I do you. With you I broke all the rules. With you, all the rules went out the door except keeping you safe above all others."

She snorted, making him frown at her. "Why did you make that noise?"

"Let me go. I can't think with you so close." Alexa wiggled to be free.

"Not on your life, baby. Explain," he ordered.

Fine. The chances of her getting away were minimal at best. She wouldn't make it easy for them to hand her over to madmen. "I heard you," she stated.

"Heard what?" he questioned, his brows creasing.

"I heard you talking about trading me for the traitor you all want so bad. Well fine. If you do it, I will fight you every step of the way." Her voice cracked.

"Alexa, you didn't hear the entire conversation, baby," he said softly. "If you had, you wouldn't have been in here making yourself sick. I'd never allow anyone to touch one more hair on your head while there is breath in my body. Don't you know I'm in love with you?"

"You can't love me. I'm unlovable," she whispered, hope rising in her.

The naked truth was there on his face. "Oh yes, but I can and do, Alexa Gordon. I'm going to start by showing you just how much." He backed her up to the bed, stripping his shirt off when her knees hit the edge.

"Sex doesn't equal love, Kai." Breathlessly she took her own top off, loving the sight of his tanned chest.

"You love me too, don't you, Alexa?" His hands stopped at the button on his camo pants.

She nodded.

"Say it. Tell me you love me, and that you know I love you." Her hands shook, the need to touch him made her clumsy.

He stood before her gloriously naked. "Undress for me," he growled.

Her shorts and panties came off easily. "You are so beautiful." And he was. Her lips parted on a gasp as Kai pinched one nipple then the other.

"I love how responsive you are. Look at these sweet little berries," he said lowering his head, suckling one tight bud into the wetness of his mouth, and then transferring the attention to the next hard point.

Alexa knew she should protest, but it felt so good to be touched by this man. To hear him say he loved her, melted all her reserves. His mouth and tongue was so good, and wicked working her flesh. She wanted to do the same to him. If he continued on the same path, she would be a boneless mass of goo, and he'd be deep inside her.

She could feel her body preparing for him, the evidence coating her thighs.

"I want to blow your mind like you do mine." Alexa ran her nails down his chest.

"You do," he croaked, stroking his thumbs over her sensitive nipples.

Alexa's breath caught at the action, sizzling need raced through her from there to her core.

"Oh, you like that don't you?" he whispered.

She nodded, unable to say anything for the electric sensation his touch created.

"I want to know everything you like. Everything that makes you moan," he whispered, lips feathering down her neck as he spoke.

If she allowed him to continue she would never get to be the one in control. She scratched her nails across the flat disk of his nipples. His hand lifted from her breast, threaded through her hair and tilted her head back. His gaze, one of hunger, and if he were to be believed, love.

Licking her lips, his tongue swept inside, drawing against hers, making her cry out.

When Kai lifted his head away, she tried to pull him back to her, greedy for more. She parted her lips and bent, licking across his chest. Powerful muscles rolled, flexed beneath her kisses. As she moved lower, using her nails, testing the firmness of his skin, she tasted his flesh.

Kai's ass hit the bed, and then a pillow was on the floor before her knees could land on the hard wood. The erotic act had moisture seeping from them both.

She looked up, gauging his expression. Pure, unadulterated need looked down at her, an echo of what she felt.

Swiping her tongue over her lips, she gripped his shaft in her palms, leaning forward she took the engorged head of his cock into her mouth. Utterly fascinated at the way he tasted, she moved her hand up and down the satin-over-iron flesh. She parted her lips and took the swollen head inside, filling her mouth with him and his salty, all male taste she could easily become addicted to.

"Damn, that's it," he groaned, making her mouth tighten on the hard head. "Like that, Alexa. Harder."

She used her hands to work the shaft, sucking him down as far as she dared, working in counterpoint to her fingers. She lashed at the underside, rolling her tongue against the sweet spot, and was rewarded with his heavy groan. His hands gripping her hair pulled harder, his hips flexed forward, a sure sign he was losing control.

"Hell fire, you're gonna make me come."

She drew harder on his flesh, wanting to make him lose his cool, becoming lost in her own pleasure. She wanted to taste him. The heavy throbbing vein running down the length jerked in her mouth, his cock head flexed, his strokes became shorter.

"Baby, you better stop unless you want me coming down your throat, and as much as I want...damn, I really love your mouth," he groaned, pulling on her hair. "I want to be inside you when I come," he growled.

The wide crest throbbed under her tongue. She knew he was close. Working him with her mouth, she licked a slow path back down, and then up. She wanted to please him. To be pleased by him.

Firm hands gripped her, lifting her from her kneeling position and then rolling with her onto the bed. "You, are a bad bad girl." Wicked eyes, the color of melted chocolate they almost made your mouth water, grinned down at her.

A grin tugged at her lips. "I'm not into spanking, but I could be persuaded for a little payback." She wiggled against the throbbing length of him.

Kai chuckled. "You are so perfect for me."

Alexa was at the point of begging him to enter her.

He lowered his head, blocking everything but him from her view, capturing her mouth in a heated kiss. A shift of his body, and then he was where she needed him. Their bodies moved in perfect accord, hers straining to meet the downward thrust of his, arms wrapping around his shoulders.

Arching her back, she couldn't stop the agonizingly sweet pleasure of having him over her, in her. Her muscles tightened, locking onto him. White light flashed as waves of ecstasy shuddered through her. Her body jerked, and she cried out his name.

"Oh, yeah, squeeze me." His thrusts sped up, withdrawing and coming back inside, driving her higher again.

His pistoning strokes seared her with more pleasure, a never ending stream determined to destroy her with ecstasy. Driving her toward another precipice, this one higher than the last.

"Move with me, luv. Just like that." His hand moved between them zeroing in on the little bundle of nerves at the top of her mound, flicking his finger around and around until she splintered into a million little pieces.

Above her, Kai yelled her name, the sweet sound came out hoarse. She could feel his release jetting inside her as he continued to pump, and she collapsed boneless, utterly spent.

Long moments passed while they caught their breath.

"Love you, Alexa. Never doubt that. Anything else, you can question me on, but not my feelings or loyalty for you. I will never allow harm to come to you while there is breath in my body."

Her heart stopped and started with his words. "I'm sorry I doubted you. I love you, too. I'm tired of running. Of being scared...and just everything. Except you. You're the only good thing that's ever happened to me. I need to pinch myself to make sure I'm awake and not dreaming."

He lifted off her. "Let's go shower. Coyle's spaghetti will taste better reheated."

She looked down. "You didn't wear a condom?"

"I'm playing for keeps. I wanted to prove to you this isn't a ploy, or some bullshit game. A man only makes love to the woman he wants forever without one." Naked honesty met her stare.

"I'm on the shot."

He shrugged massive shoulders. "Come on. Let's go before they begin pounding on the door." Kai held his hand out, knowing she'd follow him anywhere.

"You realize that shower is not very big, right?" She stood, a whisper of air between them.

"Well, I guess we'll be real close," he murmured wickedly.

****

Kai left Alexa to finish drying her hair. He couldn't believe she thought he would give her up in exchange for Tyler. He walked into the security room, coming to a halt at the sight that met his eyes.

"Hello, Rowan. Find anything interesting?" Kai leaned against the wall, the smell of spices had his stomach growling.

Pointing at the phones, Rowan looked up. "You got a picture text from an unknown number with our friend Tyler looking way too healthy for my tastes."

"Did the others fill you in on what he," Kai nodded at the phone, "wanted in exchange?"

Rowan snorted. "Yeah, like any man worth his salt would give up his woman for a man, even one the likes of that piece of trash."

"What's the plan?" Kai asked, knowing Rowan had one.

Electric blue eyes blinked up at him. "A little yippee-ki-yay motherfuckers sounds about right."

"Damn, you been watching too many Die Hard movies." Rowan always did like to blow shit up. Kai clapped his hands together, the need to do something and do it now rushed through him.

The back of his neck tickled, not the itch that let him know danger was near, but that Alexa was. He turned to see her standing in the hall. He held his hand out.

"We're gonna warm up some leftovers," he announced.

"How do you know there are any left? Haven't you heard how much growing boys eat?" Rowan patted his flat belly.

Kai flipped him the finger. "There better be."

Laughing, Rowan turned back to the bank of computers. "I'm sure Jaqui put some aside."

He knew Alexa was aware of the undercurrents flowing between them. The full truth was heavy in the air. They weren't guests in a cabin, but they could pretend for a few. In a dark room he could make her forget for a short time.

In the kitchen they found two plates already prepared and waiting for them inside the large fridge. Alexa placed napkins and silverware on the granite counter, a smile playing about her lips. He caught her eye, the thought of the last time they'd both eaten in the space written on her face clear. "Damn, I won't be able to walk if you keep looking at me like that."

She winked. "That makes two of us."

They ate in companionable silence, while he wondered when the next strike would be. He knew there would be, it was just a matter of when, not if.

"Heads up. We have some new intel that you might want to see." Rowan's booming voice interrupted his musing.

"You go ahead. I'll clean up then watch a movie if that's okay? I promise I won't open the doors for anything." She held her hand up as if she was swearing an oath.

Rowan came into the room. "I hadn't thought of installing blinds or curtains. That was a bad on my part. While y'all were busy, me and the boys did a little improv with the decorating." Rowan's grin said he knew just what they'd been busy doing.

Alexa's face turned a nice shade of red, but she nodded. "I'm assuming since you are a guy and all, you have cable?"

Laughing, Rowan nodded. "Oh, yeah. Can't have a home without that. Help yourself."

Kai got up, but couldn't stop himself from stealing a kiss before following Rowan. He knew Coyle and Sully were also in the Great Room. More than likely they were already watching something, or reading on one of their many devices. He wondered where Jaqui had gotten off to, but figured she was off resting, or on her computer. She and Tay made a perfect pair if the two would quit bitching to and about each other long enough.

Jaqui sat in one of the chairs, her computer had images flashing across the screen at lightning speed. "What's going on?" Kai looked for the other members of their team.

"Shut the door, Swift," Rowan instructed.

His neck itched.

"Alright." He shut the door, then leaned against the steel frame. "What gives?"

"The Smirnov's are here. Like within striking distance of here," Jaqui pointed to the screen. "And so are our little friends." She pointed out what appeared to be nothing more than blobs on the computer.

"How did you come to that conclusion?" Rowan moved forward.

She snorted, clicking the mouse with her right hand. The images that came up amazed him. "If you know what to look for and where to look, you can find anything, if you have the proper equipment." She looked up. "Thank you United States Gov." Jaqui made it sound like a prayer.

Rowan pointed at the couple on the opposite side of the property before pointing to the larger group. "Do they know that they are here as well?"

Rowan rocked back in the chair. "I'd think they arranged it."

Kai ran his hand across the back of his neck. "Why? I don't understand. If Alexa is their child, then why did they give her up? Why now come back into the picture?"

"Could be they thought it was safer to do so at the time. From what Jaqui has found, the Smirnov's were high level Russian officials who pissed off the wrong people. They came to America seeking amnesty and from what we found were given it, until they betrayed someone, or someone felt they did. Around that time Alexa must've been a young child, and they decided leaving her here as an orphan was better than taking her on the run with them." Rowan shrugged his shoulders, looking to Jaqui to confirm his words.

"Yeah, a young girl in the foster system is much better off. Why was she never adopted?" He wondered at that since first meeting her.

Jaqui looked up. "She wouldn't speak for the first two years in care. They thought she was deaf and mute."

He wanted to go out and hold Alexa close and ask what had happened to make her pretend she was that way. His heart ached for the young girl who'd lost everything.

"Now, they what? Plan to come back and be all parenty?" he growled.

Rowan laughed. "Who the fuck knows. I'm assuming they feel guilty, or hell maybe they truly believed she was safe all these years. It wasn't until she was attacked and hospitalized that she was entered in the system again. She literally flew under the radar all these years. Her attack was quite brutal, and she needed blood, which is rare, and it hit off all kinds of markers in the FBI and CIA, which then set about the triggers we are now dealing with. Her parents clearly had a system in place that would let them know if someone was looking into them, and vice versa, the syndicate who nabbed your girl the other day."

Kai's eyes narrowed at the name. "So we are dealing with the fucking mafia or some shit now?"

Jaqui nodded. "Yeah, her parents weren't the squeaky clean Mr. and Mrs. Robinson type."

Which totally explained the LV luggage and high end clothing they both sported, not to mention the ability to disappear and not be found. Still, how could they leave their only child in poverty?

"If she'd stayed with them, she wouldn't be the woman she is today. Remember that, my friend." Rowan turned back to monitor the images.

"Is this real time, or is there a lag between them?" He needed to keep his head in the game.

"I've got guys in the field that none of them will know are there until it's way too late," Rowan assured him.

He put his hand on the door. "I need to tell her what we've found. I can't let her go on without knowing all the details of her past." He let out a deep gush of air.

Sympathy flashed in the blue eyes across from him. Jaqui's shoulders stiffened, but she kept quiet.

Kai left the two, entering the large room where Alexa sat curled up in an overstuffed chair watching a documentary with Coyle and Sully. Her eyes lit up as he walked in, and he hated to be the one to dim that glow. He held out his hand. "Come with me. There's been some new information."

She swallowed. "Okay. Thanks for letting me watch this with you guys. Now I know I never want to be *Naked and Alone*, especially for television purposes, even if it means dropping the pesky thirty pounds fashion says I should."

"Girl, you are perfect just like that. All hips and curves like a woman should be. Those skinny women on them magazines," he shook his head. "They look good, if you like that sort. Me, I like to have a little cushion beneath me. If that one tells you any different, you come to me and I'll treat you right." Sully winked, pointing at Kai.

Kai pulled Alexa to him. "Get your own woman. This one is taken, and yes, she is exactly how I want her. Mine." He kissed her in front of both men.

"Get a room," Sully groaned.

Breaking away from Alexa's lips, he made a smacking noise, sure to annoy the other two. "Sounds like a solid plan."

He didn't wait to hear what they said, leading Alexa back to the safe room.

"Okay, let me have it," she said pulling her hand free from his.

Without pausing he explained what Rowan told him, watching her body begin to shake. He stepped forward, intending to pull her into his arms.

"No, I can handle this. I need to handle this." She ran her hands up and down her arms.

"You're not alone, Alexa."

She shook her head. "I don't remember not talking. I mean…it's a blur those first few years. I was so young. My first memory was starting school. I was older than the other kids in kindergarten. They called me names, said I was stupid and that's why I was too old to play their games. From that point on I didn't even try," she hiccupped on a sob.

Kai didn't allow her to pull away from him. If he could go back in time, he'd beat all those snot nosed kids up who hurt her.

"I see that look in your eye, and I love you for it." Laying her head on his chest, she sighed. "I haven't thought of those years in forever. When I aged out of foster care I was only a sophomore. I sorta gave up on high school and got my GED. It was easier to attend those classes with people my age, than be eighteen and a sophomore."

"I thought you went to senior prom?"

She gave a bitter laugh. "His senior prom. I mean I was old enough to be a senior, but technically I wasn't."

He was starting to understand her a little more. "You realize you're like an onion, don't you?"

She lifted her head, squinting up at him. "I'm going to give you the benefit of the doubt and wait for your reasoning."

He kissed her nose. "With each layer you reveal, I appreciate you even more. You're not a simple woman who is defined by a single thing, but a complexity of layers. All these things have sculpted and molded you into the fighter you are today. Much like an onion. You peel back a layer at a time, and by the time you get to the middle, you may be weeping, but by damn, it's the best onion you'll taste. And we both know how much I love tasting you."

Chapter Fifteen

Alexa couldn't stem the tears flowing from her eyes. Kai's words melted her heart and any misgivings she may have had. This man reduced her to a puddle of goo, and put her back together with his words. He may think he was not good with words, but the man was a master at them.

"That is the nicest thing anyone has ever said to me."

"Stick with me, kid, I can do better than calling you an onion. Next week I'll work on flowers," he joked.

Three sharp buzz sounds interrupted them. "We better answer that, huh?"

Kai's head nodded, but regret shadowed his features. "Duty is a bitch sometimes."

She stepped back, hating to lose his warmth. "Should I stay in here, or can I go with you?"

He grabbed her hand. "Let's see what's going on and make decisions accordingly."

The monitor next to the door showed Jaqui standing outside, a worried frown on her face. Kai raised his hand. "What's up Jaq?"

"We've got movement and they're both heading this way. Fast."

"Shit!" Kai turned to look at her. "I need you to stay in here. Remember what I told you. Nobody but you or I in or out. Got me?"

Alexa nodded. "Got it. Kai, I need a weapon. I'm a sitting duck in here if for some reason they do get in."

He shook his head, then stopped. He pulled the gun out of his holster. "You know how to shoot one of these?"

"I was learning at the compound. I may not be able to shoot the pin off the side of a barn, but I can shoot the head off someone within ten feet."

"Good enough." He showed her where the safety was, then gave her a hard kiss. "Listen, I trust everyone in the cabin with my life. I trust nobody but me with yours. Do you understand what I'm saying? You shoot first and ask questions later. Nobody is to come in here but me. If someone has access, it's because they've broken in, and that is not good. Don't come out unless I come get you or you're given this code." He put his lips next to her ear and whispered words almost too low for her to hear. Her face heated at the explicit words. "Trust me, I wouldn't say that to anyone unless it was dire circumstances. Love you." He kissed her one last time, then slipped out the door, securing it as he went. She watched on the monitor as he and Jaqui headed toward the security room.

She chewed on her thumb nail as she waited, sat on the bed, and waited some more. Waiting was not her strong point, and the not knowing was making her insane.

At the door, she went back to the monitor hoping to get a glimpse of someone walking by. The fact the room kept any sound from reaching her, was deafening in its silence. Sully's big frame came into view with more weapons strapped on than she'd ever seen. She backed away, her hand against her chest.

****

Kai realized two things real quick. The fight was being brought to them was the first. The second was he wasn't sure if they would all come out alive.

"Rowan, you need to leave before the shit goes down. You've got a mate to think about." Kai stared him in the eyes.

Nodding Rowan stood. "I'll be of much more help outside. Here, if you need me talk. I'll do the same. Just press it once and it's on." He handed Kai a tiny ear device, inserting one in his own and began loading up with weapons. Grabbing his snipers rifle out of the case with reverence.

"Are you listening to me? We don't know what they are bringing to your front door. I don't want to be responsible for your death."

Electric blue eyes glared down at him. "You're not my captain, Kai. This is my land they are coming on. My pack is out there watching your back. I won't run with my tail between my legs, and I sure as shit don't plan to die today. Lyric made me promise to come home safe. Plus, she promised to kiss all my boo-boos. That woman is damn good at taking care of me. I might even let myself get a cut or two just so she can fuss. Now, get the hell out of my way before I give you a bruise you'll need to take care of."

Exasperation warred with relief. "Fine, but don't get killed. I'd hate to face her." He shuddered for effect.

"Yeah, me too. She'd skin both of us alive." Rowan slipped past them and up the stairs toward the balcony off the room he and Lyric slept in.

"Maybe you should go in with your woman," Coyle stood with an automatic in his hands, ready for battle.

"I want each of us to take a door. Where is Jaqui?" He looked toward the great room. The damn huge windows were covered, and bullet proof, but he still hated the memory of his team members' bloody bodies being pressed against them.

"She's in the kitchen taking point by the garage. The only other two doors are the front and the one off the master suite upstairs." Kai headed for the steps. Sully was taking over in the security room.

The alarm glowed red and no sign of Rowan could be seen. Kai missed the man on his team, but knew he was happy where he was. He spun as he heard a whisper of sound, seeing Sully standing with his hands up in the doorway. "You forgot your phone. A text came in from the man who has Tyler."

Looking at the message his body vibrated with rage. A smiling Tyler sat in the front of a vehicle in what appeared to be the surrounding woods. Was he the other man's captive, or part of his team? "Damn, is he working with them, or are they using him for leverage?"

"From the looks of it, he's their comrade. But, if we are to believe the text, he's willing to give him up if we give them Alexa." Sully shook his head. "Stupid bastards. Tyler will slit their throats if he has an inkling they're planning to double cross him. Or, it's all part of their devious plan. God, I can see them twisting their little mustache and rubbing their hands together. So cliché."

"It matters naught, since they ain't getting her," Kai growled.

Sully took a step back. "No shit, Sherlock. I'm thinking they don't realize her parents are here. Which could work in our favor. I say we get to them before they run into the asshats who took Alexa."

Kai was in total agreement. He tapped his ear and relayed the info to Rowan, hoping one of his guys were close to the Smirnov's and could intercept them. The minutes it took to get a response felt like hours.

"It's a go. Now, get your ass back down there and let me know when they have them."

Sully saluted smartly, turning on his boots and leaving as silently as he came. Kai shook his head and went back to watching his post. The need to see Alexa burned in his gut. After reassuring himself nobody could get in without their detection, he bounded down the stairs. Coyle raised his brows, a question in the dark stare.

"Need to fill Alexa in on what's happening. Keep an ear out for upstairs."

Coyle nodded, but he could see a bit of censure in his stance.

Before he made it down the hall, an explosion echoed outside. Kai pulled up short, he looked back to where he'd left Alexa and toward the front of the house. "Don't go outside, Coyle. This place is like a fortress Rowan said."

"I know how to do my job, Cap."

"Damn it I know you do." Frustrated with himself, and the fact the woman in the middle of the house was making him question everything he was trained.

"Go, check your woman, then get your head in the game. The explosion was a good mile out. I'm thinking it was a diversion."

He quickened his steps, entering the room to find Alexa in the corner like he'd found her a few days ago, only now she wasn't covered in blood.

The moment she realized it was him, she lowered the gun, then stood. "Is it over?"

"No. I just wanted to check on you."

Her lips trembled. Kai hated to see fear on her face. "I need to go back out there and be there for my team."

Alexa sucked her bottom lip into her mouth. "I understand. I'll be fine."

She was lying to him. But, he let her get away with it because he needed to stay focused. "I'll be back when it's over. Not too much longer now. Stay safe."

A hollow laugh escaped her throat. "You're the one out there loaded for bear, and you tell me to stay safe. I'm tucked inside like some princess. I think I'll be fine."

He pulled her to him and covered her lips with his, the guns in their hands forgotten. After a moment, he let them both up for air. "You better be fine." He wished he had another ear device for Alexa, one like he had so they could communicate if she needed him. "I'll be right outside. You know the rules." He tapped her on the ass, loving the mock growl she gave.

The slight buzz in his ear had him pausing on his way up the landing. "We got the parents. Two of my guys are bringing them in the back. Do you want to allow them to meet your woman?"

Kai thought of the heartache she'd suffered, and decided he didn't want them to do more damage to her until he'd had time to "talk" with them. "No. Where can we stash them until the others are neutralized?"

"Shit! Incoming. Get the parents to the room off the garage. It looks like a normal pantry, but it's a second safe room."

"What's going on?"

Kai headed toward the kitchen where Jaqui was keeping guard. "Head up to the second level and watch the balcony doors. We have company coming in this way."

She raised one brow. "You need backup?"

He shook his head. "Got it. Go," he ordered.

The silence thru the device was not comforting. Going out through the garage he watched through the monitors, thinking Rowan was a paranoid bastard.

The large SUV roaring up didn't give him the warm and fuzzies. All four doors opened at once. Had he not already met Kellen and some of Rowan's new friends, he may have shot first and asked questions last. As it were, he wasn't sure if he should open the doors to the five extremely large men sporting more tattoos than a tattoo shop.

"Open the fucking door, dickweed. Rowan said to tell you giddy up. Whatever the hell that means." A huge man with a mohawk said.

"I'm thinking that's a Brokeback Mountain reference, and we should totally tell Lyric about that freaky shit." Kai glared at the man with more muscles than brains who spoke last.

Jerking the door open, he glared up at the men. "Shut the fuck up, assholes. There ain't no Brokeback shit, except maybe your face if you fuck with me. Where is the package?"

Mohawk dude looked around. "Does he think we're drug dealers?"

"Oh, for fucksake, bring the parents inside before I shoot your asses," Rowan growled.

Kai stared at the men who he swore were escapees from a mental institute as they parted while the last three surrounded a well-dressed couple. He recognized them from their profiles Jaqui had gathered on them, and hated them on sight.

"I thought you weren't coming in, Ro."

"Changed my mind," Rowan grunted. Inside the pantry, he flipped a panel, and then they were inside a small interrogation type room.

The fact the room was equipped with comfy looking lounge chairs along with a fridge and microwave station, didn't mitigate the fact there was a table set up with chairs and a light above it. Okay, so Kai might be the only one who was thinking of it as an interrogation room. He planned to use it as such.

Rowan spun and held his palms up. "Give me your hands," he ordered the Smirnov's.

The woman paled at the deep tenor Rowan's voice went to, but the man stood taller. Each held their arms up and allowed him to apply the zip ties to each one. The nylon covering would keep the flesh from getting torn, but they were effective in keeping their prisoners from doing much, unless they were trained. Rowan didn't stop there. He grabbed hold and led them to the table, where he then fastened rope through each of the middle of their ties, and stretched it across and hooked it to the wall. "Have a seat. I've given you enough room to do that. Now, tell my friend here what he wants to know."

The guy with the mohawk pushed chairs behind them, and then proceeded to zip tie their legs to the chairs.

"You said we would not be harmed," Mr. Smirnov said, anger tinging his words.

"I keep my word. I said you will not be harmed if you are truthful, and help us get the ones who tried to get Alexa. I assumed you were on board with that." Rowan sat across from them, his hands folded.

Kai sat next to Rowan. "Who are they and what do they want with Alexa?"

Tears formed in Alexa's mothers eyes. "They want us. We thought we could keep her safe and ourselves safe by disappearing and separating. Now, they know and we had to come." Her accent was almost impossible to place.

Being a good judge of character, Kai knew there was more to it than that. These people didn't come out of some undying love for their daughter he didn't think, or at least that wasn't the only reason.

"Okay, that may be part of the reason. What else. They'll be here in about ten minutes with a man I'm willing to trade you both for. He's a traitor to the United States. Trust me, I'll hand you both over without blinking unless you tell me the entire truth in exchange for him."

The woman blinked back her tears, and the man sat up straighter. Anger tightening both their features.

"You wouldn't dare," Alexa's father spat.

Not agreeing or disagreeing they sat in stony silence. The only sound the breathing of the six of them in the room. With the two tattooed men standing guard at the door, Kai wanted them to answer so he could be done with them and hunt down the others.

"Fine. You want the whole truth and nothing but the truth?"

Kai nodded.

"I was supposed to give Alexia to Pascal when she was a child. He wanted her in exchange for keeping our secrets. I couldn't let that monster have my baby. She was too precious. We came to America and were able to hide for a couple months, but he always found us. We had to separate. If you left a child at the hospital, they will take them with no questions asked. Alexia was very smart for a child of four. We told her not to talk to anyone, and that we would be back for her. Only, we had to separate as well. I just found Alexander two years ago." Katalinia wiped tears from her eyes.

"Why would he want a child? Could he not have one of his own?"

Alexander barked out a laugh. "Are you that naïve? He is a sick twisted bastard that is why. He saw her and wanted her as his." He pounded his hand on his chest. "We owed lots of money to some of his contacts, and he paid them for us. We did odd jobs for him, and thought we were in good standing. I had no clue his price was much higher. Our own flesh and blood for his pleasure," he spat the last out.

A gasp near the door had them all turning. "That's why he didn't want me in the cabin. He prefers children."

"Alexia?" Katalinia murmured.

Kai stood so fast his chair flew out from behind him. "Where the fuck is Coyle and Sully? How did you get past them?"

Her eyes flew behind her. "Coyle is by the front door and I assume Sully is in the security room. I looked in the camera and didn't see anyone or hear anything until I got close to the kitchen. Then I heard those three men arguing about who was riding shotgun."

"I hope you plan to make them both do some major retraining, Cap."

Oh, there was going to be hell to pay when this was over.

"You are so beautiful," Alexander said, trying to stand.

"Is that necessary?" She asked.

Kai crossed the room. "Sweetheart, I need you to go back to the other room until we can neutralize the situation. We don't have all the facts and yes, that is necessary," he growled as she tried to go past him.

"Those are my parents, Kai. I want to meet them."

Damn it all to hell. "You stay by my side, and don't touch them."

She gave him a look he was coming to call her eat shit and die one, but he wouldn't allow her to disobey him.

Seating her between him and Rowan, the rope stretched between them, she glared at it then him and Rowan.

"Don't even think it."

"It's fine, mon petite." Her father's fingers reached out.

Instinctively Alexa's own did the same, but she put her fists on her lap.

"I hate to break up the family reunion, but we got company coming in," Rowan pointed at his ear.

Kai looked at his friend, wondering why he hadn't heard anything, and then noticed the two men at the door standing straighter. The laughing men gone. They even seemed larger.

"Shit! Go, I'll stay in here with the Smirnov's and Alexa," Kai glared at the couple.

"This man you mentioned trading us for. If he is with Pascal, he is either a very dangerous man, or he's a dead man walking."

Alexa's audible intake of breath at her father's words made Kai clench his back teeth.

"Nobody is trading anybody to Pascal." Alexa didn't look at him, her hands reached across the table and gripped both her parents.

"Of course not, luv," he reassured her.

"Inside here you will not be able to hear anything going on outside, and once I close the door, the only one who can open it is me." Rowan went to Kai, gripping his hand. He tapped a sequence of numbers, giving Kai the code to get out.

Kai nodded.

"Go with them, Kai. I'll be fine here. Leave scary dudes with us." Alexa looked up at him.

Indecision warred in him.

"Go. You know if those two behemoths can't keep me safe, I'm screwed."

"They'll guard her with their lives," Rowan agreed.

"Don't let them out of those restraints. And you," Kai pointed at Alexa. "You can sit across from them, talk to them, but don't under any circumstances release them until I get back."

"Yes, sir." She kissed him, uncaring who saw.

Before he did anything stupid, like throw her over his shoulder, Kai followed Rowan out the door. The other three men who'd come in with him stood at attention when they came out.

"Do you know what way they're coming and how many are with them?"

After a minute, Rowan held up his hand and the three men slid out the door to the side. "There are about ten with them, but we have over a dozen surrounding their vehicle on all sides. I don't think Tyler is with them though."

"Son of a bitch."

"So we keep them alive. I don't want them riding up in here shooting the shit out of my place again. My guys are going to stop them a half a mile up the road and take them down, then bring them in. Don't worry, it'll be clean."

It sounded strange to have Rowan refer to others as his guys.

"I'm going to go see if Sully has a lock on Tyler. The fucker can't get away again."

Sully stood at the entryway. "Just got an anonymous email. Tyler says better luck next time, and to watch our backs."

Jaqui came in with her laptop in hand. "Smug bastard. I've got him. He's in the cabin that you found Alexa last time. My guess is he thinks it's a good place to lay low for a while."

Kai looked at her. "You sure he's there?"

She nodded. "I was able to trace the email back to that location."

"I'll send a couple trackers out there. Let's focus on one set of crazy at a time."

Kai stood by the door to the garage, anticipation for the men who'd hurt his woman made his trigger finger itch. Rowan's hand on his arm kept him from racing out at the sound of the V8 engine entering the drive. "We need to be sure it's not a trap with Tyler first. Then, don't you think Commander Lee would want these guys?"

He hated when Rowan got all reasonable on him. Slinging the automatic behind him, he waited for the go ahead from the man beside him, even though it ate at him.

"All's clear. Let's go. There are only two of them. I guess one didn't make it."

"You such a big man, you had to send out a party to capture me. I will make trade. I know where Tyler is hiding. You give me girl." The large man fought against the man holding him.

"What's your name?" Kai strode toward them.

"Never you mind my name. I give you Jase Tyler. He's the man you've been searching for. You have about two hours before he disappears again."

"I get it you are not in charge. Cuff him and put him in the holding cell." Kai dismissed the mouthy man.

The other man remained silent staring at Kai like a bug.

"Should I bring out a little girl in a frilly dress? Would that get you talking, or just excited?" Anger flared in his eyes.

"You have the Smirnov's?" he roared, pulling away from the man holding him with surprising strength and rushing Kai.

The attack came as a surprise, but he held his ground as the man tried to tackle him. Bringing his arms up, he hammered them down onto the man he believed was Pascal's back two times. When the arms shackling his waist released him, Kai forced the man to stand up, nailing him in the face with his fist, and then his stomach. Each time he thought to stop, he pictured Alexa and her bruised face and body, and another blow was rained down. He didn't feel the hits the other man delivered, too focused on beating the life out of him.

As the heavy weight fell onto him, Kai stepped back and let him fall onto the stone ground, his leg lifted to give a hard kick. Only Rowan's hand pulling him back stopped him.

"You are going to pay for this." Pascal coughed.

Kai laughed. "Where you're going you will pay even more. You'll be Big Bubba's bitch."

He turned, aiming his anger at the mouthy man. The sound of metal scraping against concrete had him spinning, he grabbed the gun from his back and shot Pascal in the head. The gun falling useless from the man's fingers as he lay in a pool of blood.

"Dayum, boy's faster than you Ro," one of the men with Rowan slapped Kai on the back.

"You gonna tell me about Tyler, or you want to meet the same fate as him." Kai pointed at Pascal.

Basile raised his palms, then flipped them over giving them the bird.

"Always the hard way with these ones. Want me to take him in and work him over?" Rowan asked, cracking his knuckles.

Kai spared the dead man a last look. "Let's do it. Has your guy reported in about the other?"

"We're fast, but not that fast."

Back inside, they tied the last man up, and then Kai looked to Rowan. "Where are the other guys that were with them?"

"My guys have them secured a distance from here. Don't worry. No fatalities. Yet," he growled.

Another ten minutes passed, and then they heard word that Tyler was at the cabin. Rowan's guys were sure they could take him, but Kai didn't want them to go in alone. Knowing Tyler he'd set up traps or explosions that would kill them all.

"I'm calling Commander Lee. I'm gonna need a cleanup on isle four." Kai looked around the mess of Rowan's yard through the open door.

Rowan's men were instructed to watch and follow him if he left. Just as Tyler was pulling out of the garage, the entire house blew up. The men watching reported the man behind the wheel of the vehicle looked up as if he knew they were out there, and then shock crossed his features as the house exploded first, then the garage which rocked the vehicle.

"Well, holy shitnshynoma. Thank you jeezus that wasn't at my place," Rowan said as he watched the way the men were loaded up in military Humvees.

"At least you can go home without a scratch on you and your wife won't be pissed at me." Kai looked over at Alexa who was hugging her parents.

"You see, I was looking forward to a little tender loving care. Want to punch me?" Rowan raised his chin and pointed at his face.

"Hell no. I met your woman. She'd kick my ass."

Rowan smiled with a look of love. "I'm a lucky bastard."

"Go on home, and send the government a bill."

They both snorted.

"You gonna put a ring on that?"

God, he broke out in a sweat thinking about it.

"Get out of here, you old man."

Chapter Sixteen

Alexa watched the scene play out in front of her. Her parents were not wanted by any government, and although they did enter the country illegally, nobody was saying anything at the moment. She looked over her shoulder at Kai, wincing at his bruised knuckles and the blood on his once clean uniform.

She knew without being told that someone had died today, but until she had a moment alone with Kai, she wouldn't ask. She trusted him to tell her what he could. With all the military personnel circling about, her worry was more about being separated from Alexander and Katalinia. She couldn't call them mom and dad yet. Maybe never.

"Your young man is very handsome," Katalinia whispered.

"He's pretty great." She agreed.

Alexander sniffed. "I don't know that he is good enough for our baby."

Rolling her eyes at that, she looked at the two people who gave her away for her own good. They had a lot to catch up on. Her life sucked, and from what they'd said theirs was no picnic, always running and scared. Up till two years ago they were not together either. However, they had money, and that was something she never had. What she knew for a fact was money didn't buy you love, and although they wanted to give her everything they could now, she'd rather get to know them.

"We will stay here in America to get to know you better. If you will allow it?"

The tears in eyes so like her own had Alexa reaching out to Katalinia. "I'd really like that."

"Then it is settled. You will live with us."

Laughing, Alexa shook her head. "No, but we will take it one step at a time."

When her parents were asked to come in for questioning, Kai assured her they were not in any trouble. Alexander asked for a phone, and had an attorney on the line within moments. She was shocked that they were able to make connections, but shouldn't have been.

"Now, we must go and meet with our friend. Your friend, Mr. Shade said he would give us a lift into town where our friend is meeting us."

"How is he getting here so fast?" Alexa asked.

"Always have a plan B and C, child." Her mother tsked.

"See, I'm not the only one who does this." Rowan brought his arm around Katalinia's shoulder. "I always tell them. Have a plan B and C."

As the vehicle carrying her parents away drove off she was left with Kai and his team. Darkness had fallen some time ago, yet she didn't feel tired.

"Who's hungry," Coyle asked.

Three days later...

Tay stared at them from his hospital bed. Alexa was happy to see both men looking much better. The swelling had gone down, and the bruising not as vivid.

"Why is Jaqui with you? You replacing me, Cap?" Tay sat up on the side of the bed.

Kai looked between Tay and Jaqui. "Hell no. No offense, Jaq. Tay, you're Phantom Force. What the hell's crawled up your ass?"

"None taken. I'll just wait outside," Jaqui muttered.

"Oh, sure. Make me the bad guy," Tay growled.

Jaqui turned, her laptop bag slapping her leg. "I am not making you anything. You're an asshole. Period."

Tay laughed. "Pretty sure that's not what you called me last time we were together. God. Baby. A few other names, but asshole ain't one of them."

"I call all the men I fuck those names. That way I don't call out the wrong name during sex. I'd hate to hurt you men's poor little egos, especially at a delicate time like that. Sorry, did that just come out of my mouth." She covered her mouth. "My bad."

"You're a fucking bitch." He got up faster than Alexa would've thought possible.

"No, you are, Taylor Rouland. I'm the one who waited in that hotel room for two days. Two fucking days during my leave cause you promised you'd return. It's no big deal," she breathed. "It's been a year and I'm over it. Just don't expect me to be that same naïve little girl who believes everything that comes out of your mouth. I filled in for you. I don't want you or your place on your team." She looked over at Kai and the others. "It was great working with you. I'm shipping out tomorrow. Take care, Alexa."

"What do you mean shipping out?" Tay growled.

Blonde hair braided down her back, hitting her ass swung around. "I'm active duty soldier. I only filled in until my squad was called up. We leave for Afghanistan tomorrow. Hoorah, boys."

Alexa watched the petite SEAL leave with her back straight, but she saw the tears ready to fall.

"She's too damn soft to go into a war zone. What the hell, man?" Tay asked.

"That woman is far from soft," Commander Lee said. "She's one of the best communications experts in the Navy. Why do you think I leant her to you when Rouland here got injured?"

"Find out who was helping Tyler?" Kai steered the conversation away from Tay and Jaqui. There was a storm brewing with them, and he didn't want or need in the middle of it.

"It's being handled. You boys get on home, and be ready when you're needed."

Alexa hid behind Kai, but she knew the Commander was aware of her presence.

"Come on. I'm taking the next week to devote to Alexa. You guys take it easy, and don't call me."

Alexa pinched his side. "Kayan Swift. Don't say such outrageous things."

"Hey, I'm just being polite. If they call while I'm having sexy time with you, I'll be all mean and shit."

The four men in the room laughed, but nodded.

She tossed up her hands. "Fine. Let's go have sexy time. I think you have a lot to make up for."

Kai bent and tossed her over his shoulder. "See you in a week, and not a day sooner." Alexa smacked his ass. "Alright, you can come over in a couple days. I'll call you and set it up. We're using Rowan's cabin, so there'll be room. But," he pointed at his team. "Only after I call you."

"You're not going to carry me through the hospital over your shoulder, are you?" Alexa asked.

He slapped her on her behind, making her giggle at the little tap. "Woman, I thought this was romantic? It was even in a movie about a military man and stuff."

Alexa started laughing. "That was so not how it happened. But I love you anyway."

He pulled her into his arms, cradling her to his chest. "Not as much as I love you, Alexa. God created you for me, you know that right? Had you not been born, my life wouldn't be nearly as bright as it is with you in it."

"Aw, isn't that the sweetest thing in the world?" A nurse whispered.

"See, I told you it was romantic." Kai strode through the halls of the hospital in his military fatigues holding Alexa, and she didn't want to be anywhere else. Well, in bed with him, but that was coming. She smiled.

"You're thinking about getting naked with me aren't you," he whispered at the elevator.

"Always."

"Damn, I'm a lucky SEAL."

"You're my salvation is what you are."

His head bent, and all words were silenced as they kissed and missed the elevator as it opened and shut.

The End

Lyric's Accidental Mate
Iron Wolves MC book 1
Chapter One
Elle Boon

Lyric Carmichael eyed the trio of giggling women on the dance floor, then looked at her best friend Syn Styles. "Tell me again why we hang out with them three?"

"Should I count them off, or do you just want the number one reason?" Syn sipped on her margarita, laughter sparkling in her blue eyes.

They both knew the main reason they came in a group was their big brothers would never let them come to a nightclub alone, but they also loved the three women. Renee shimmied her ass in a tight red leather skirt against the groin of a random dude, making him grab her around the waist. Lyric watched the couple for a few seconds, making sure her friend hadn't gotten into a situation she couldn't get out of.

Only when Renee tossed her long brown hair back, laughing, and the grabby dude eased off, did Lyric turn back to Syn.

"Maybe we should rescue them?" Lyric pointed her beer bottle toward Magee and Jozlyn, who were the center of attention of what looked like a frat party.

Syn looked at her like she'd grown two heads. Renee—better known as Nene—Magee, and Jozlyn were great friends, but they definitely didn't need anyone to rescue them. They'd come to party wearing tiny bits of fabric, while Lyric had on a pair of comfy jeans similar to Syn's that fit like they'd been made for them. Strategic rips kept both just this side of decent. While Syn wore a tight V-necked T-shirt, Lyric wore a tank top with a lace back. Since they'd driven their motorcycles, she and Syn had worn boots, unlike their friends, who were sporting heels that screamed *fuck me*.

"Excuse me, but I like my freedom. Could you imagine the look on Kellen's face if he saw me try to walk out of the house dressed like that?"

She thought of Syn's brother Kellen and the look of horror he'd have, if he saw his baby sister dressed

357

in a miniskirt short enough to show her ass and a crop-top barely covering her voluptuous breasts. Kellen wasn't only the head of the Iron Wolves MC, but he was also their alpha. What he said was law, and nobody, not even Syn, crossed him. Her own brother, Xander—better known as Xan—was his second-in-command, and was just as scary if not scarier. Both stood at over six feet two inches tall, but that's where the similarities ended. Kellen was black haired and blue eyed. He and Syn looked very much alike in their coloring and tall stature, while Xan had blond hair and brown eyes.

"I think we'd have to go into the witness protection plan if we tried it." Lyric laughed.

Raising her glass, Syn clinked her drink with Lyric's. "True that," she agreed.

Lyric got up from the table. "Let's dance, girl."

"Bottoms up, baby." Syn downed the rest of her drink before standing. Their shifter metabolism kept them from getting drunk, but they enjoyed the slight buzz they got from the alcohol, even if it was only short-lived.

They ignored the college guys who called out from several tables as they passed on their way to the dance floor. Lyric was tempted to flip a few of them the bird, or toss a couple backward but restrained herself. "Seriously, do they think yelling hey baby, come sit on my face, will get them laid?" Lyric asked, scooting between the tight tables.

"I'm thinking the answer is yes," Syn tossed over her shoulder.

The DJ played a mix of country, hip-hop, and rock. The song that came on was for a popular line dance that had half the people on the floor sitting down, including Renee, Magee, and Jozlyn. Syn shrugged her shoulders and got in line. Lyric smiled as their three friends flipped their middle fingers from one of the tables, even though she couldn't hear what was said over the music. She got lost in the dance steps, enjoying the beat and movements.

Several songs later, all five of the girls were on the dance floor. Lyric loved letting loose; she loved feeling the loud bass vibrating all the way up, from her toes to her head. She rolled her body with the music, imagining what it would be like if she was with a lover, and thought of the amazing orgasms it would cause. Of course, living with her older brother, she'd not had the chance to experience anything of the sort with anyone, other than her trusty vibrator.

"What's put that frown on your face?" Renee asked.

She bit her lip, but a nervous giggle escaped. "I think it's time for me to get my own place."

Jozlyn and Magee stopped dancing, their eyes looking ready to pop out of their heads. Only Syn seemed to understand her need for independence, since she had just recently been given a cabin by her older brother. It was still on his property, but not in his home. Kellen was giving his sister a little breathing room, unlike Xan, who Lyric swore still thought she was in grade school.

"Xan will never allow that," Jozlyn and Magee said at the same time.

Syn growled at both younger girls. "And when did either of you become so in the know when it came to the second of the MC?"

Oh shit! Lyric recognized the anger blazing in her best friend's blue eyes and was shocked to see it aimed at their friends. If she didn't know any better, she'd think Syn was jealous. Which was absurd, since they each thought of both Kellen and Xan as brothers.

Renee stuck her finger in her ear and shook it. "Excuse me, but did you just growl at us?"

Before a fight could erupt, Lyric stepped between them. "I gotta pee. You need to go with me." She jerked on Syn's arm. By the time they wound their way through the throng of gyrating people and into the bathroom, Syn seemed to get herself under control.

"What the fuck was that all about?" Lyric jerked her thumb toward the closed door and the club beyond.

A deep sigh left Syn in a gush as she leaned against the counter. "I have no clue. There's this wild feeling inside me that seems to be growing lately. I feel like I'm going to snap, and if I'm not careful, I'm liable to bite someone's head off. Ya know?" She placed her palm over her heart, tears swimming in her eyes.

Lyric did the only thing she knew how to do and wrapped her arms around her best friend. "I understand, truly I do. Maybe that's what I'm feeling, too."

"You should move in with me." Syn pulled away, wiping her tears away with the back of her hand.

Laughing, Lyric shook her head. "You think Xan would let me?"

"If it's safe enough for me, then why not you?"

The logic wasn't lost on her; however, she wasn't sure her brother would see it the same way. "When do you move in?"

"Next week. Well, I guess it's more like nine days, but who's counting."

"You owe the Bitches an apology." They were all referred to as the Bitches by their friends; each one had a nickname that ended with Bitch.

"Fuck me running, I know. I was such a beotch." Syn's voice sounded chagrined.

Lyric walked back toward the last enclosure, she really did need to go to the bathroom. She shut the stall door and let the silence stretch.

"You know, you could've disagreed with me," Syn groused.

"We pinky swore when we were kids we'd never lie to each other." Lyric laughed when her friend kicked the door on her way out, calling her a name as she went.

Straightening her blinged-out belt, Lyric stared at her reflection. People always assumed she colored her blonde hair—having dark brown eyes and tan skin it didn't seem natural—until they met her brother, Xan. He shared her coloring. Even in wolf form, they were blonde wolves, a rarity in the wolf world. Syn and Kellen were both black as night with the bluest eyes. Alpha eyes. Although, Xan had the same brown eyes in his human form, when he shifted to his wolf, his eyes also turned a beautiful shade of blue, while hers shifted to amber. Had he wanted to be alpha, Lyric had no doubt he could've been, but Xan was happy being second. Their parents had been best friends with Kellen and Syn's, who'd all been killed ten years earlier.

She shuddered and pushed the memories away, grateful her brother, along with Kellen, had been there to protect her. Xan, all of twenty-five at the time, had been left to raise his fifteen year old sister. Now at twenty-four years old, Lyric felt like the world was passing her by. She'd gotten her degree at the local college instead of going away. Texas was a huge state, but with the club being so tight-knit, and shifters even more so, she'd wanted to stay with her pack. Now she wished she'd at least gone off to one a couple of hours away.

The MC built custom bikes on one side of the shop and was the local mechanics on the other. She and Syn ran the office, while she did more of the creative side of the business.

She planned out what she'd say to her brother about moving in with Syn, and before losing her nerve, pulled her phone out of her back pocket. Knowing him, he'd be with his flavor of the week and not see it till the morning, but at least it would give him a few hours to simmer down before she had to face him, since she was staying overnight at Nene's. Once she hit send, she turned her phone off, and put it back in her pocket.

Butterflies danced in her stomach as she walked out into the dark hallway.

When she got bumped from behind for the third time, she finally turned around and met the steely gaze of a truly mean-looking wolf. She had smelled him and a few of his pack when they came in earlier but hadn't thought anything of it.

"Excuse me, darling. Can I have this dance?"

She saw the way he looked her up and down, stopping at her chest and continuing down to her boots and then back up. "Sorry, I was just going to get a drink." She pasted on a fake smile, trying to step away from him.

His quick-as-a-snake reflexes caught her bare arm, squeezing hard enough to bruise. "Now, that's just rude. I watched you shaking your ass for the last half hour. I think you can dance just one more."

Looking around the crowded dance floor for Syn, Lyric knew she was no match for the wolf, even in his human form. "You are so fucked if you don't let me go. Do you know whose territory you're in?" Although she wasn't strong enough to take him on, any wolf with an ounce of smarts knew better than to come into another's territory and threaten their members. She was technically property of the Iron Wolves; therefore he'd just stepped over the line. If she could get Syn's attention and a little help from her friends, he'd move along, and all would be well. Or she hoped he would.

He leaned in close. "Your little friends ain't gonna help you, bitch."

Lyric tried to pull away from him, coming up against another solid form behind her. "What is wrong with you? Do you know who my brother is? Do you know who the Iron Wolves are? If you let me go now, there will be no harm, no foul. I'll pretend like you don't exist. But, if you keep fucking with me, I will bring the wrath of my pack on all your asses." The last wasn't an empty threat. Her brother Xan would kill any man, or wolf, for putting his hands on her without permission, some even if they had her permission.

"Do you hear her? She's gonna call her big brother." He sneered.

At some point during her struggle with the large man, they had maneuvered her closer to a side hall. If they got her outside, she had two choices. Let her wolf out and fight, or run. Either way, she had little chance of escape. Pack law stated you couldn't show yourself to humans, and the bar was filled with way too many for her to shift inside. She opened her mouth to scream for Syn, or anyone to help her, but one of the men slapped his hand over her lips before she could make a sound.

She counted three men with the leader, but the smells from the bar made it hard to be sure. Lyric pretended to be docile, allowing them to maneuver her outside, while she planned what she'd do as soon as the door opened. She'd only have one chance, and that was a slim one.

The lights from the parking lot speared into her face as someone opened the door before they could drag her outside. "Excuse me, boys, looks like you got a problem there," a man said in a deep rumble.

"Mind your business, punk," the leader growled.

Lyric felt the hair on the nape of her neck stand on end. The man standing by the door was tall and muscular, but was one hundred percent human. She wanted to ask him to help, but changed her mind at the simultaneous growls surrounding her. Although the newcomer was every bit as big as her brother and Kellen, in a fight against a group of wolves, he'd be massacred.

The man held the door open like a gentlemen, nodding as they passed. Lyric had to tilt her head way back to look up at him. The arms holding her captive didn't allow her to do any more than get a quick glimpse of black eyes. She tried to memorize his features, breathing deep to take his scent in before she was shoved outside and the door was shut behind them.

"Beck, I don't think this is the best place for us to take care of business."

She stumbled when the man named Beck released her, shoving the one who'd just spoken against the wall. "Are you questioning my leadership, Raul?"

Claws erupted from Raul's fingers. "Get the fuck off me, Beck. I'm pointing out the fact we should just take the bitch back to the hotel and have some fun with her."

"I agree with jackass, for once. Let's just simmer down. We can take the chew toy and play with her for a while."

Beck released Raul. "Kristof, go get the van and take Raul with you while Dean and I get acquainted with our toy. Call Marcus and have him get word to her brother. I want him to sweat knowing his baby sister is with us, and there's nothing he can do." He turned his cold gaze back to Lyric, licking his lips. "I was just going to kill you and leave you for Xan to find, but plans have changed."

"Over my dead fucking body, asshole," Lyric snarled, unsheathing her claws.

The door to the bar opened and slammed shut. "I don't think the lady wants to go with you."

"Be a smart man and go back inside where it's safe. I won't give you another chance." Beck turned his back on Lyric.

Seeing her opportunity, Lyric nailed Dean in the nuts with her knee and swiped him across the throat with her claws. The wound would be deep enough to immobilize him, but not kill, she hoped. She wasn't sure how long before Raul and the other would be returning with the van, but since the parking lot wasn't huge, she assumed minutes at the most.

Beck turned at the sound of Dean's gasp. "You stupid cunt." The animalistic growl he emitted scared her worse than the thought of what her brother would say if she exposed what they were to humans.

"I've already called 911. I suggest you pick your buddy up and go." The man from the hallway started walking toward them, cell phone in hand, bringing Beck's attention back to him.

"Run," Lyric yelled.

The sound of an approaching vehicle had Lyric sprinting away from the downed wolf and the open drive, putting her closer to Beck. An enraged werewolf was unpredictable, but she couldn't allow him to hurt a human. Xan and Kellen had made sure she and Syn had trained with their best fighters, and while she knew she didn't have the strength to take on a group of shifters, she prayed she was able to hold her own against one.

Beck had his back to her, but she could see he, too, had done a partial shift and was facing the gorgeous human. The thought of him harming the man was not something she was willing to allow. Using his distraction, she went low and took out his feet with a swift kick. Man, and wolf, tended to underestimate her because she was small and acted docile. Beck was no exception.

"Aw, fuck," the human rumbled.

At the same time she felt the air stir. Their window of opportunity had passed, and the other wolves had returned.

"Go back inside and find Syn Styles. Have the DJ call for her. Tell her what's happened. Go. Now."

Lyric rocked on the balls of her feet, pushing him toward the door with her back to his front.

He snorted. "Sure thing, gorgeous. Just as soon as unicorns fly by."

His big hand came around her, trying to switch their positions. Lyric wanted to snuggle into him. She also wanted to shove him through the door and into safety. As Beck got back to his feet, and the others helped the downed wolf to the van, she thought they were going to leave.

Beck sprang at them with all the speed and strength of a full-grown werewolf on a rampage. She placed herself in front of the human, knowing she could regenerate faster than he could. His hand came around her, trying again to place her behind him. She watched in horror as Beck brought his paw up, claws extended, and hit her with the full force of his strength on the side of her head. Lyric flew across the pavement, head slamming into the concrete wall, making stars appear before her eyes. She wasn't sure what she'd expected, but it wasn't to see her guy ready to take on a shifter. *Whoa, slow your roll.* She didn't even know his name. The hit to her head must have done something to her brain.

Seeing the other two men coming back from their vehicle, Lyric picked herself up. Her main goal was to help the man and hope they got out alive.

Surely, Syn was looking for her by now? The last thought gave her pause. Her best friend would never have allowed her to be gone for so long unless something had happened to her, too. She let more of her wolf out, hearing seams rip and not caring she was ruining a favorite pair of jeans.

* * * *

Rowan swore when the beautiful woman was thrown against the building. Fear for her safety had sent him outside to check on her; seeing her being manhandled by the obnoxious man who needed a shower, sealed the deal.

He'd come to the bar to get a drink or two and get laid. Looked like he was going to get in a fight, and need more than a few bottles of alcohol to erase the images of what he was seeing. Nine, maybe ten-inch nails extended out of the man's fingers, and the last time he'd checked humans didn't have that much hair let alone fur, and the guy didn't have either on his body earlier. In all his training, the wars he'd fought, not a single foe compared to what he was facing.

"What the fuck are you?" Rowan asked, thinking he should've brought his gun from his truck.

Three men advanced on him, looking more like something out of *American Werewolf in London*.

"You should've stayed inside like a good boy," the half-man growled.

Rowan felt the woman step up beside him, easing his fear that she was hurt from being tossed aside. Like all good country boys, he pulled the knife he had strapped to his side. The blade was longer than their claws, which he hoped was enough of an equalizer. She squeezed his free hand, sporting her own set of extra-long nails. Although she was on his side, he hoped.

"Since the lady doesn't want to go with y'all, why don't we skip the pissing contest and forget all about this?" Rowan released her hand, watching the body language of the three man-beasts. They were not experienced fighters, which gave him an advantage.

"There's no reasoning with them. You should've run when I told you to."

He didn't take his eyes off the men as they fanned out in a semi-circle. "Darlin', there wasn't a snowball's chance in hell I was gonna leave you out here to fight off these...whatever they are."

The sound of gravel shifting beneath the man to his right's feet, had Rowan kicking his steel-toed boot into his knee, followed by a roundhouse kick to the head. When he looked down into the face of the man, no longer was there any indication he was human. Gone was the shape of a human face, replaced with the muzzle of what appeared to be one of his worst nightmares. Without hesitation, he grabbed the thing by the hair and cut his throat from ear to ear.

"You will pay for that." One of the beasts' garbled words cut across the night. Before he could hop off the dead creature, he was hit so hard in the side, Rowan was sure a rib or two was cracked.

In his line of work with the military, he'd suffered a lot worse damage and had learned to suppress the pain. His training served him well as he rolled, keeping a firm hold on his serrated knife. Out of the corner of his eye, he watched the woman fighting with amazing skill.

He landed with a thud on his back, momentarily stunned. The large animal on top, snapping at his neck. Rowan grunted in pain from the weight on his ribs, knowing he needed to get the upper hand quickly or he'd be a dead man. What were wolves' weaknesses? Never had he thought he'd need a silver bullet, or wondered if that was a myth or truth. Either way, he was going to die if he didn't get out from under the snapping jaws.

Using all his strength, he heaved, bucking until he finally knocked the wolfman off. Claws slashing his chest as they fought. The burn, like acid eating his skin, made it hard to focus.

Rowan waved his knife hand. "Come on, pussy, is that all you got?"

An enraged howl, and then the animal came at him with more force than cunning.

Rowan sidestepped, slashing upward with his knife, slicing through fabric and tissue. He turned, giving a hard kick to the beast while he was doubled over. Erasing the distance between them, he snapped his neck.

A roar shook the ground. Rowan spun to face the leader, watching in horror as he tossed the woman aside. With a quick assessment, he saw her chest rise and fall.

"I understand it's hard to get laid when you look like you were dropped from the ugly tree, and hit every branch on the way down, but really, there has to be someone out there for you," Rowan taunted him, needing him to come closer, away from the woman. All of the men had partially shifted into part wolf, part man, a seriously grotesque combination.

The beast growled and lumbered on his jacked-up legs. If he made it out of this alive, Rowan was sure he'd be needing therapy for months, maybe years to come.

His side no longer burned, but had started to turn to more of a *kill me now* ache, the likes of which he'd never experienced. He'd been held prisoner for over three months in a foreign land, had been tortured for days on end, and had never wanted to die. Those days and nights were nothing compared to what was going through his system right now, but he fought the pain back. One more to dispatch then he could fall down.

He switched the knife to his left hand, using his right to shield the injured ribs, keeping his eye on his opponent. Basing his decision on the way he hadn't reacted to Rowan's words, except to growl and come closer, Rowan moved forward. A mistake, he realized a moment later, when he was within leaping distance and found himself with a two hundred-plus pound enraged beast on his chest. His knife flew from his hand. All the air left his lungs in a big whoosh, and then the large, gaping mouth that could easily enclose his entire skull, was heading straight for his throat. Rowan reached up with both hands, trying to stop the inevitable, but against the supernatural strength, he knew it was useless.

Not willing to give up and turn his neck for the thing, he stabbed his thumbs into the beast's eyes. Howling, the beast shook him off, but blood ran from the now empty right socket, making Rowan happy he'd at least caused it some damage.

The last thing he saw was razor sharp teeth coming straight for his face. As he grappled with the leader's head, he turned and felt the hot breath on his neck and then pain so immense he yelled out. Black dots swirled in his vision, and then the heavy weight was knocked off him. Rowan tried to get up, but his body wasn't listening to his mind. The sound of fighting brought him out of the daze and or darkness trying to swallow him. He saw the woman holding his knife, her back to him in a fighter's crouch, protecting him. From her posture, he could tell she was ready to kill. His nature wouldn't allow him to lie there and let a woman fight his battles. With the last of his strength, he rolled to his knees. The fight seemed to have gone on for hours, when it could only have been minutes. The sound of a car coming down the gravel drive had all three of them looking in the direction of the noise.

"Your days are numbered, bitch." The leader scooped his two fallen buddies up in a fireman's hold and tossed them into the still running vehicle, speeding away in a spray of gravel.

"We gotta get you outta here." His angel knelt next to him, her cool hand brushing his hair back. Rowan thought he would just lie back and let the darkness envelop him, but she had other plans. "Come on, big guy, I'm going to need you to help me. You're way too heavy for me to carry."

Grunting was his only acknowledgement. What didn't she understand about him wanting to lie down and rest?

"Lava is running through my veins, darlin'. Find my phone and call 911. Find out why they didn't send a car out when I called. That's the only thing that's gonna help me." His voice sounded raspy to his own ears, and lacked conviction. He knew he was dying from the injuries he'd sustained and wondered how she was going to explain to the authorities what had happened.

"Shit, you've been bitten. Fuck, fuck, shit." She leaned forward and sniffed his neck, ripping his flannel and T-shirt down the front.

On the verge of dying, Rowan was amazed to feel his dick harden when the woman licked at his wound, easing the pain. In the next instant, he nearly shot off the ground when her teeth sank into his already wounded shoulder. Instead of more pain, ecstasy rolled through him.

Rowan grabbed the woman around the waist, uncaring about his injuries, making her straddle his thighs. The last time he'd dry humped a female was in junior high with a girl three years his senior. Like then, the girl on top of him panted and climaxed right along with him. Only difference was then, he could get up and get a towel to clean himself. Rowan wasn't sure he could move, let alone get up. Clearly, his dick hadn't gotten the message they were in danger, the way it still pressed against his zipper.

"You two need to get a room for crying out loud." A man's laughing voice jerked him out of his musings.

"Don't move. Wait until he goes inside so he can't see the blood on you."

Rowan didn't want to tell her he didn't think he could move even if he'd tried, so gave a brief nod and stared into her beautiful brown eyes. Her golden-blonde hair fanned them like a curtain, shielding them from others. He wondered what she'd look like spread out naked on his bed and had an answering jerk from his cock. Damn, the thing had never perked up quite so fast before.

Jett's Wild Wolf
Mystic Wolves 3
Prologue

Taryn Cole felt the first skitter of fear slither down her spine as Keith pinned her with his black eyes. The man who claimed her as his daughter, or as one of his possessions, gave her one of his death stares. Others in the great room either dropped to their knees, or showed him their throats, but she did neither, barely resisting the urge.

"Where have you been, little girl?" Keith's voice grated like nails against concrete.

She'd learned at a very young age not to allow him to see how he affected her. A deep inhale helped steady her nerves. "My truck broke down." As long as she stayed close to the truth, Keith wouldn't scent a lie. Another thing she'd learned at his knee, fists, and claws.

Keith cleared the ten or so feet separating them in one leap, startling a gasp out of her. "Don't lie to me you little bitch. I know there was more to it than that. You were in the woods up in Mystic again. Which one of those bastards were you sniffing after?"

His face had contorted into his half-beast. A cross between wolf and whatever he could be. Even Taryn had no clue what all he was, but he was mean.

Her head tilted toward the two wolves standing off to the side. "I followed those two, yes." Again, half truths.

His chest expanded with his deep inhale. She was sure he'd give her some mundane chore, or take away her privileges like a child. At twenty-five years old, being treated like a five year old on a weekly basis was nothing new.

As his large arm raised with its muscles and veins covered by fur, she didn't flinch as he ran the back of his knuckles down her cheek. "Your skin is so smooth, and soft. Unblemished from time and age. Do you know how lucky you are to have my genes coursing through your veins?"

She swallowed. "Yes, alpha." Nobody could accuse her of being a stupid wolf. Her eyes stayed below his chin, yet she never gave him the respect due his status.

"When will you learn your place?" His voice didn't raise. One claw scraped down, lifting her chin to meet his eyes.

The hate and loathing staring back at her made her gut clench. Whether it was directed at her or the Mystic Wolves didn't matter. Alpha Keith was angry, or suspicious.

Her voice came out a croak. "I don't have a place. I'm the lowest member of your pack, below even that."

The blow that knocked her across the room shocked her, then the pain hit, blood filling her mouth. Before she could get to her feet, he was on her, his hand gripping her by the throat and lifting her up, dangling her feet off the ground.

The scary beast in front of her drew his arm back, the shifted paw of the wolf was larger than a full grown bear, and he flashed his black claws like they were knives. They reminded Taryn of the movie *Nightmare On Elm Street*, when the killer would taunt his victims before he'd slice the razor sharp talons, gutting them. Some days she wondered if he'd actually kill her. Had silently prayed for death on more than one occasion.

He laughed. "Oh, you are truly smart. Too smart maybe."

A rake of those too sharp claws swiped across her cheek, burning her flesh like liquid acid pouring down on her. Silently she screamed, knowing he fed off the pain and anguish of others. Oh, he loved to see his handy work, too. She watched satisfaction flare in his unholy black orbs at the blood running down her face, ruining one of her favorite shirts.

Still, she dangled a good three feet off the ground. His grip on her shirt never loosening while he held her at his height of over six feet four, give or take, in human form, but in his beast mode he was closer to seven.

His next blow broke several ribs, a gasp escaping before she could control it.

"Ah, let's see how much more you can stand. Hmm?" Keith asked, dropping her from his grasp.

Taryn tried to protect her head, knowing it was the most important part of her body. Everything else would heal itself within hours with no outward sign of damage. However, a head injury could take days.

The sound of the pack cheering Keith on became background noise as he continued to kick and hit her. She tried to curl into a ball, focusing all her energy on keeping her head from taking any of his abuse. Every now and again he'd give a grunt, but even that was for show. By the time he was finished, Taryn couldn't count the number of broken bones in her body on both hands.

Excruciating pain radiated out of every pore of her being. Both eyes had swollen to slits from the kicks to her face. Whatever had angered him, Keith had decided she was going to be his punching bag tonight. Not an uncommon occurrence, but this was one of the worst beatings she'd suffered in years. This time she didn't have a mother figure willing to crawl over and help her back to their rooms.

"Someone help the whelp up before I kill her this time. It's not her day to die, yet." He growled, sounding more beast than man.

She wanted to tell whoever came to drag her up to leave her alone, but the gentle touch and sweet scents of her friends washed over her. They hadn't been in the space when Taryn had been summoned by Keith, otherwise her friends would've tried to intervene. They'd have been hurt even worse than her, only their injuries wouldn't have healed as fast, nor as completely.

Joni and Sky eased their arms under her, their wolf strength gave them the ability to lift her with ease. When they reached the sparse room she called her own, they lay her on the full sized bed. A moan finally escaping her busted lips. "Could you get me a glass of water, please?" Was that her voice? She hoped they understood the garbled mess.

Her friend Sky rushed to the small room, not bothering to turn the light on. The cup shook in the other girl's hand. "You look so bad, Ryn."

It hurt to swallow, let alone to reassure her friends she'd be okay. They didn't know how fast she would heal. Heck, she wasn't sure how quickly it would take this time. "Need, time, ladies."

"We are staying with you, so shut the hell up. I brought wine," Joni whispered.

Too tired and hurting to argue, Taryn took another drink of water. Lying on her bed, knowing she was ruining the beautiful bedding, she wanted to cry. A weakness Keith would love to see. Already bones were realigning, bruised organs healing. The last parts of her to heal would be the outer package, which could take days. Days of agony where she would feel each bone and cartilage reform, refill with fresh blood and tissue. Her mind shut down as her last thought was of the alluring wolf Jett Tremaine. Goddess, but he was a fine specimen she'd love to do dirty things to.

The next time she woke it didn't feel like she'd been run over by a Mack Truck, and then backed over again. Lifting her eyelids, she risked a glance down her body, expecting to see blood crusted over every inch of her.

"Thank you jeezus. I didn't think you'd ever wake the fuck up. I swear you scared like ten years off my life," Joni said, coming to stand beside her, a glass in her hand.

It took Taryn a couple seconds to get her voice to work, and then she was able to speak. "How long was I out?"

"Three mother fucking days," Sky growled.

Taryn tried to sit up at the announcement, but the world spun a little. "What? I didn't wake at all?"

"I almost hauled your ass in to the hospital. One more day and you were going." Joni held the drink out, the anxiety she'd obviously felt clear in her tone. "Drink this, and then you need to eat, and no you didn't wake."

Gulping the orange juice down her parched throat, Taryn was glad her friends had stayed with her.

"How do you feel?" Sky asked.

The thought of moving her body didn't appeal in the least, but Taryn was no pussy. She stretched her legs out, expecting a little pain. When none came she tested her arms, again no pain.

"We took turns watching you, making sure none of the assholes decided to come in and take advantage of you. The second day we decided to wash you up a bit. I couldn't stand to look at the blood on you a moment longer, but we didn't want to jar you too much. Do you think you're up for a bath?" Sky was the mothering sort. Someday she'd make a great mate, just not to one of the jackholes in their pack.

A bath sounded divine, but her rooms didn't boast that extravagance, only a small stand up shower cubicle. Not that she wasn't completely healed, her friends just didn't know that. Both Sky and Joni had better accommodations than she had due to their parents being higher up in Keith's hierarchy. Their alpha would still slit their throats if he felt like it, but he needed them since they provided money to their pack. Sky's parents were lawyers, a needed attribute in their world, while Joni's were the technical geeks who kept Keith up on the latest gadgets. They were like the step sisters in the fairytale, while she was Cinderella. The thought made her giggle. She had no prince charming who would ride in to save her. One day her time would come, when Keith decided she wasn't worth keeping alive and end her. Until then she would enjoy what life she had, and lying around in bloody clothes, stinking to high heaven wasn't on the agenda.

She wished she could hang out with them like regular girls. Go out and have drinks. Dance at the clubs and meet guys. Their world wasn't normal. Sky and Joni's parents would never allow their girls to go anywhere with Keith's thing. Their fear for what he'd do to them if something happened to her, or their hate for her because of what she was made it impossible. Taryn accepted the fact she had no pack outside of her rooms. Joni and Sky loved her as much as they could, would even go against their parents if her life was at stake, which they'd obviously done to stay with her. But she'd never put them in danger. Again. They couldn't handle the beatings she could from Keith. Seeing their pain was worse than feeling her own.

No, Taryn would rather be friendless than have to witness Sky or Joni's tears, or hear the sound of their bones being broken.

About Elle Boon

Elle Boon lives in Middle-Merica as she likes to say...with her husband, two kids, and a black lab who is more like a small pony. She'd never planned to be a writer, but when life threw her a curve, she swerved with it, since she's athletically challenged. She's known for saying "Bless Your Heart" and dropping lots of F-bombs, but she loves where this new journey has taken her.

She writes what she loves to read, and that is romance, whether it's erotic or paranormal, as long as there is a happily ever after. Her biggest hope is that after readers have read one of her stories, they fall in love with her characters as much as she did. She loves creating new worlds and has more stories just waiting to be written. Elle believes in happily ever afters, and can guarantee you will always get one with her stories.

Connect with Elle online, she loves to hear from you:

www.elleboon.com

https://www.facebook.com/elle.boon

https://www.facebook.com/pages/Elle-Boon-Author/1429718517289545

https://twitter.com/ElleBoon1

https://www.facebook.com/groups/1405756769719931/

https://www.facebook.com/groups/wewroteyourbookboyfriends/

https://www.goodreads.com/author/show/8120085.Elle_Boon

Author's Note

I'm often asked by wonderful readers how they could help get the word out about the book they enjoyed. There are many ways to help out your favorite author, but one of the best is by leaving an honest review. Another great way is spread the word by recommending the books you love, because stories are meant to be shared. Thank you so very much for reading this book and supporting all authors. If you'd like to find out more about Elle's books, visit her website, or follow her on FaceBook, Twitter and other social media sites.

Love you so hard…Elle Boon

Other Books by Elle Boon
Erotic Ménage
Ravens of War
Selena's Men
Two For Tamara
Jaklyn's Saviors
Kira's Warriors

Shifters Romance
Mystic Wolves
Accidentally Wolf
His Perfect Wolf
Jett's Wild Wolf
Bronx's Wicked Wolf, Coming 2016

Paranormal Romance
SmokeJumpers
FireStarter
Berserker's Rage
A SmokeJumpers Christmas
Mind Bender, Coming 2016

MC Shifters Erotic
Iron Wolves MC
Lyric's Accidental Mate
Xan's Feisty Mate
Kellen's Tempting Mate
Bodhi's Synful Mate, Coming 2016

Contemporary Romance
Miami Nights
Miami Inferno
Miami Blaze, Coming 2016

Phantom Force
Delta Salvation
Delta Recon, Coming 2016

Anthology
Dark Embrace, Coming Fall 2016

DISCARD

 CPSIA information can be obtained
at www.ICGtesting.com
Printed in the USA
LVHW080510311018
595357LV00010BA/666/P